CHARMS & DEMONS

THE DARK FILES

BOOK TWO

KIM RICHARDSON

FABLEPRINT

This book is a work of fiction. Any references to historical events, real people, or real locales are used fictitiously. Other names, characters, places, and incidents are the product of the author's imagination, and any resemblance to actual events or locales or persons, living or dead, is entirely coincidental.

FablePrint

Charms & Demons, The Dark Files, Book Two

Summary: When a series of unexplained witch murders plague New York City,
it's up to Samantha to uncover the culprits and hunt them down with some
good ol' fashion magic.

ISBN-13: 9781678474997
[1. Supernatural—Fiction. 2. Demonology—Fiction. 3. Magic—Fiction].

CHARMS & DEMONS

THE DARK FILES

BOOK TWO

CHAPTER

1

A scream split the night air.

I scuffed to a halt, the hairs on the back of my neck rising.

The voice was female, young, and human, with a sound of such utter fear and insane terror that it made my stomach churn and my gut shake.

I was out on my routine patrol of the city, keeping tabs on any unruly demon sightings and standing ready to vanquish any stinking bastard that stepped through the Veil and crossed into our world to make meals of unsuspecting humans. Contracted by the dark witch court, it was my job to keep watch on any supernatural baddie that was up to no good. The pay wasn't great, but it was enough to get by.

It had been a quiet night until now.

I didn't have the luxury of time to decide on a course of action. When I didn't move quickly, people got killed. I'd been too slow with Julia, the girl whose parents had hired me to find her, and now she was dead. Killed by a Greater demon, no less.

Shit. I wasn't a great sprinter nor did I have the physique of a seasoned athlete, but I dashed toward the scream, pushing my legs as fast as they would go, with a spell forming in my head. My hatred for demons wrestled with my fear, fueling me with adrenaline and an extra burst of speed.

I despised them. I hated them to the very depth of my soul. And I was going to fry their asses.

The scream came from the direction of East 14th Street around the corner of 1st Avenue. I raced toward the dark alley squished between Moe's Vegetarian Lounge and The Pizza Shop, away from the light—always away from the light. To a demon, light was like sticking its finger in the flames of a fire. It burned them immediately.

Why did I always find myself in dark, dirty alleys with the demon of the hour? Because that's how exciting my life was. Yay for me.

I ran across East 14th Street just as another scream cut through the air. Cars whined into motion, tires squealed, and loud shouts were hurled from drivers as I maneuvered between them, the pounding of my heart loud over the revving engines.

"Watch it!" cried a voice.

"Idiot!"

"Crazy bitch!" shouted a driver from a gray SUV as its engine sputtered and caught, its wheels spinning on the pavement.

Smiling, I flipped him the bird and kept running.

Humans. Such an angry race.

Breathing hard, I leaped onto the sidewalk, zigzagged through a couple of humans in their mid-thirties and rushed toward the alley. If the humans had heard the scream, I saw no indication. Papers and plastic bags rattled and scraped over the streets in a sudden breeze, and the leaves in the trees rustled and sighed in the wind.

I reached the entrance to the alley, slipped through an opening in the chain-link fence, and darted between several empty cardboard boxes and metal garbage bins. The air smelled of beer, piss, and rot—the aroma of a night out on the town. Excellent.

I blinked as darkness hit me, and I slowed to a walk. The alley was cloaked in darkness like a giant drape had blocked all the light from the street and neighboring buildings.

There was only one explanation for that—magic. Demonic magic.

My breath came faster as I felt something wrong, unnatural. An uneasy feeling ran over me, cold prickling along the nape of my neck and up my spine. I stood there for a minute, frowning while contemplating whether I should pull out my chalk. But if I couldn't see, I couldn't draw a summing circle either, so conjuring a demon from the Ars Goetia was out.

Damn it. Blinking, I strained to see through the darkness, but it was like standing in a closet with the lights out. I could make out shapes, but that's where my vision ended.

Shit.

Pulse spiking, I swept my eyes around, trying to pin down the source of the magic and the screaming human. I stepped forward with my hands splayed at my sides and a spell on the tip of my tongue.

The air was hot and stuffy, and I realized the wind had suddenly stopped. Now just pure, brittle and crystalline silence and darkness surrounded me.

Then I heard a struggling sound accompanied by a few frightened grunts before the screaming started again. Closer this time.

And then I was moving again. I acted without thinking, but I couldn't help it. My instincts pulled me in the direction of that poor human. I had to reach her. I had to save her.

I sprinted into the alley as fast as I could through the darkness and toward the source of the sound, but I still couldn't see anything. Only darkness stretched ahead of me as though I could go on for hours and not see a single thing. Possibly I was even trapped in this magical abyss.

Screw it. I had no choice.

"Hello?" I called as I halted and listened. "Hello, can you hear me? Where are you?"

A figure appeared through the darkness, short and plump, the silhouette of a small male or perhaps even a small female. It remained hunched before me, about twenty feet away, but I couldn't make out the face or tell if it was human or demon.

The silhouette just stood there, giving me nothing. *Great.*

I tapped into the power of my sigil rings and held it with my will. "Hello?" I ventured. Yes, that sounded lame, but I needed to hear it speak before I started shooting off my magic. A dead human would look pretty bad on my record. A fried one, burnt to a nice, blackened and toasty crisp, was even worse.

And still the silhouette still didn't move.

I let out a breath. "Listen, I don't have all night. If you could just—"

An invisible force hit me. I never saw it coming, and I certainly never *felt* it coming either.

It struck me with the force of a linebacker on steroids. Despite my prepared spell, I didn't even have time to deflect it. Instead, it felt like a giant had slugged me with one of his massive hands head-on, driving me straight back.

I flew several feet through the air, hit the pavement with my back, and then clipped my head. My breath exploded out of my lungs as I scraped another ten feet along the alley floor.

Ouch. What the hell was that?

I tried to muster a breath, but my lungs didn't seem able to manage it yet. I blinked in the darkness as white stars swirled around in my vision. A sliver of panic slipped through me as the idea of facing another Greater demon formed in my mind. Damn it.

After all that had happened with Vargal, you'd think I'd have been more prepared.

Finally, I managed to take a gulp of air, panting as my lungs formed.

"Son of a bitch," I wheezed as I rolled to my feet. The world tilted, and I did my best not to fall flat on my face. Because *that* would look totally amateurish. And *I* was a professional.

Granted, that demon had some serious magical skill. Ten to one, I'd even go so far as to say he was more powerful than me. Yeah. I was having a great night.

Still, I wasn't about to let some degenerate demon kill me. Not while I still drew breath and had a human to save.

With my jaw gritted, I tapped into my sigil rings again, drawing power from them. Energy coursed through me, filling my veins with the staggering feeling of strength and magic.

My eyes narrowed, and my fingers splayed as I gestured. "Come on, you bastard!" I cried, trying to see through the darkness, but my eyes would never settle on anything solid. "Where are you? Afraid of a little witch?" I waited, adrenaline spiking through my veins as I listened for a single scrape of a foot on the pavement so I could blast him.

A wind rose around me, and then the darkness lifted.

Light spilled into the alley from the moon and the nearby streetlamps, bathing the narrow alley in hues of silvers and blues. Shapes became focused until I could see clearly.

Two things hit me at once. One, the demon was gone. And two, a body lay on the ground not ten feet from me.

Shit. I ran to the bundle. She was lying on her side. Female from her sheer size and the width of her shoulders under the thin black jacket she was wearing—at least what was left of her.

My lips parted as I ran my eyes over the body. Because, yes, it was a body. No one could be alive and look like that.

The skin over her face, hands, and neck was dried, as though all the blood and liquid from her body had been drained. Her teeth were too large, and barely a hint of a nose was left. Just two holes sat where the nostrils used to be amid skin stretched over a skull. There was no way to determine her age. It was as though I was looking at the dried face of a thousand-year-old mummy.

What the hell? The only demons I knew that could suck a human into a dried mummy were a succubus and its male counterpart, an incubus. And yet, from what I knew, it would take days or even months to ingest a human's life force and all of its liquids to end up looking like a dried prune.

Plus incubi and succubae didn't have the skills to conjure up a cloak of darkness. Their magical skills ended with just regular glamours and tricks of the minds. Easy stuff. They had nothing this complex and powerful in their repertoire. This didn't make sense.

Nausea bubbled up. Shit. This was bad.

"Damn it," I said. "I don't need this right now." I knelt next to her, grabbed her shoulder and gently turned her over.

Narrow scoops of flesh were missing from the side of her neck at the jugular.

I felt the blood leave my face and settle around my clavicles.

Holy hell. A demon hadn't done this. A vampire had.

Vampires were civilized, educated, and had mastered the art of passing for humans so well that even I could mistake them for a human every now and then. Plus they normally didn't go around killing humans—not for thousands of years at least. We had laws for this kind of thing. Humans were off the menu for vampires. If human blood was offered voluntarily, that was socially acceptable. But if you were caught killing a human, it was a stake in the heart for you.

Over the years, I'd heard the stories of vampires gone rogue on killing sprees. It was inevitable. All societies and races, human and half-breed, had their share of crazies.

Now it looked like I had a rogue vampire on my hands. And he or she was killing innocents in my city.

My stomach churned as I rolled my eyes over the dead human. Something wasn't right. It would take a normal vampire days to drain all the blood from its victim. Unless the vampire was old. Ancient.

Powerful. And if that were true, I had a bigger problem on my hands than a simple rogue vamp.

I had an ancient vampire with powerful magic.

"Oh my God!" screamed a female voice behind me, making me jerk.

Heart pounding, I whirled around and looked into the faces of four humans. This night was just getting better and better.

"What did you do?" exclaimed the same voice, belonging to a dark-skinned woman in her thirties. She waltzed right up to me in her tight red dress. As she stared at the body, her large eyes widened by the second, and her mouth opened in silent "o." I'd seen that expression before on so many humans and on so many occasions—the expression of disbelief, horror, and the usual "This can't be real." Yup, I'd seen them all.

A man with tanned skin and glasses came up next to her and pushed her out of the way to get a better view. He stared for a moment. Then blinked. A sound escaped his throat as he spun around, sending chunks of his vomit in wide arcs all over the pavement.

Lovely.

I stood up slowly, my mind swirling with spells and hexes, but I readied a memory charm instead. To hit four humans with a memory charm wasn't impossible, but it would take some expert coaxing to keep them still while I did it.

The other two humans, a woman in a black wrap dress and a man in a dark suit, kept their distance—obviously the smarter ones.

"She's a terrorist," said the man in the suit, his face twisting in anger.

Okay, I take it back. Not so smart.

"This is some kind of bio weapon," said the same man, pointing a shaking hand at me. "Like anthrax or something. It's not natural. It's engineered." He covered his mouth and stepped back, grabbing his date with him.

Okay, so I *did* look guilty, and this situation *really* looked bad as I knelt next to the body. Though without a magical explanation, human forensics would show that the body had been drained completely. It would have taken some kind of lab or medical equipment to do it, and a person in an alley alone wouldn't have been able to pump all the liquids out of a body.

"It's not anthrax," I said, my voice calm as I gauged the distance between me and the closest human who was still vomiting. Hit him when he's bent over, and all that. "Anthrax doesn't drain you of your bodily fluids. It attacks your lungs."

"And how do you know that?" accused the same man. "You sound like you know all about this."

Great. This was certainly going nowhere fast. "Google it if you don't believe me." I sighed. "But I didn't do this to her. I found her like this." Totally true. But the accusations that rippled over their faces and reflected in their eyes said otherwise.

"You killed her, you fucking psycho," said the same man in the suit, though from a safer distance from me and my supposed victim.

"I didn't," I said as I took a step forward toward the man who had stopped vomiting. His face was pale and looked like he might resume spewing chunks at any moment. Damn. Humans were so overly dramatic and so quick to judge. "You have to believe me. I heard a scream and I came to investigate. I only wanted to help her." I could tell I was just wasting my breath. I was already guilty in their eyes.

The man in the suit's face was screwed up. He shifted from foot to foot, looking like he was contemplating either bolting or hitting me with a hard object—perhaps hitting me and then bolting. "Then why aren't you calling 9-1-1?" His face went hard with accusation. "Where's your phone?"

Touché. Time to work the memory charm.

The woman in the red dress gasped. "Look, she's wearing gloves," she exclaimed, pointing at my hands, and I stilled. "She's got gloves! Gloves!" she shrilled. "It's anthrax! She's going to use it on us!"

Ah. Hell.

"You're not going to get away with this. You killed her!" cried the woman in the red dress, just as her friend pulled out her cell phone, pointed it at me and started taking pictures. I ducked my head just as her date pulled out his cell phone and dialed three numbers.

Yup. That was my cue to leave.

I turned and ran.

They didn't follow. Screw the memory charm. It was too late for that. And I wasn't about to stick around and wait for the cops. That wouldn't go so well—for the cops.

The last thing I needed was the attention of the New York City police on my case, especially when I had a rogue, ancient vampire skilled with magic loose in the city.

Yeah, this had turned out to be a hell of a night.

But something inside me said this was just the beginning.

CHAPTER

2

I stood before the bathroom mirror, naked, my eyes traveling down my arms where most of the scars were. The skin was marred in various shades of beige and red and pink. My palms were the worst—thick with scar tissue.

I let out a sigh and stuck my fingers in the Gypsy No. 5 Skin So Soft Healing Balm and scooped out a large gob.

"Please work." I rubbed the green-colored ointment on my arms and then my hands. My nose wrinkled at the smell of mushrooms, earth, and vinegar. If it had smelled like roses, I would have had my doubts. The worse it smelled, the better the ointment. That's when you knew it was going to work. Or so I hoped.

First, my skin pricked and tingled where I'd administered the ointment, and then it cooled like I was applying Vicks VapoRub. Ah-ha. It *is* working.

I looked at myself in the mirror again. Nothing. Well, nothing yet. The bottle said to expect results in two to three days. I had to give it time. My Aunt Evanora, the wisest and most powerful dark witch in the entire North American continent, told me the ointment wouldn't work. She'd said my scars were too deep, too thick, that the damage done to the tissue was irreversible. Nothing would smooth out my skin ever again.

And yet even the wisest people in the world could be wrong sometimes.

I had to keep hoping. I wasn't ready to give up. I wanted to rid myself of more than just the unsightly burn marks. The memories that came with them needed to go as well—specifically, my dear ol' dad.

The scars were a constant reminder of what had happened to me when I was eight years old. My father had tossed me into a fire like I was a piece of driftwood.

I hated the bastard. Whenever I looked at my arms and hands, his face would flash in my mind's eye. He was dead to me, and I wanted to stop him from creeping into my thoughts.

I stood facing the mirror for a long time, wondering if Logan could see past the scars. I didn't know why I was wasting my time thinking about him or the kiss we shared a week ago. It wasn't like I'd ever see him again. He was an angel-born after all—a mortal blessed with angelic essence in his veins—whereas I was a dark witch with demon essence flowing inside me. The angel-born and dark witches were like oil and water to each other. We just didn't mix. No matter how much you stirred, we always split apart. Some things just weren't meant to go together.

As a dark witch, I shouldn't even be bothered by scars. Most of us had plenty. As a general rule in our practices, it was customary to lose limbs, teeth, and parts of your soul when you borrowed magic from demons. It was just how things worked around here. My ex-boyfriend lost two pinky fingers when he tried to trick a mid-demon into giving him its powers. I always thought he was a dumbass. If I'd been the demon, I would have taken his head.

Still, I just couldn't get Logan's kiss out of my mind. It had been a damn good kiss—the kind that sent my knees wobbling like an idiot. Yeah. It was *that* good.

Why hadn't he stepped away? Why did he keep kissing me? Maybe he just wanted to know what it felt like to kiss a dark witch. Wouldn't be the first time. A male faerie had stolen a kiss from me when I was thirteen. I made sure he had no more mouth to kiss anyone after that.

After an insanely ridiculous amount of time in the bathroom, I pulled on a clean pair of jeans, a long-sleeved black T-shirt, and finally, my black leather fingerless gloves. I let my wet hair hang down my back as I pulled open the door and headed for the staircase. The thought of chicken tandoori and

15

creamy butter chicken had me salivating as I walked down the stairs.

"Is the Indian food here yet?" I called when I reached the kitchen. "I'm starving."

My grandfather stood by the kitchen island, a navy-blue bathrobe hanging on his shoulders. At six feet tall with a head full of thick white hair past his ears and white bushy eyebrows, he was ninety-two but didn't look past seventy.

"Here. Taste this," said my grandfather as he handed me a glass of clear, light blue liquid, his eyes alight with joy. "It's my newest batch. Finished boiling it in my cauldron just this afternoon," he added, smiling proudly. The fair skin around his eyes and mouth crinkled in seams and fine wrinkles.

"So, that's what the smell was." I reached out and took the glass. "What am I drinking? Gordon's Broomshine? Or is this something else?" I tipped the glass to my nose and made a face, eyes watering. "Smells like rubbing alcohol."

"That's because it is," came a voice. A flutter of wings rose in the air to my right, and a large raven landed on the granite counter next to me, his feathers gleaming under the kitchen lights like black silk. "You sure you want to drink that? It might be better served to wash the toilets."

My grandfather glared at the raven with his lips pressed into a tight line. "What do you know of refined gin-making skills, demon? Of the craft and hours of endless and meticulous preparation?" He pressed his hands on his hips. "I'll tell you. Absolutely nothing." He looked at me, his blue eyes expectant. "Go on, Samantha. Have a taste, and let your palate dance with the delights of the grain spirits and natural botanicals."

"More like *magical* botanicals," grumbled Poe as he ruffled his feathers.

I had to agree with my familiar on that. I knew gin wasn't made the same way as wine. The process was somewhat faster. Still, there was no way my grandad had brewed a new batch in a few hours without some magical help. If I took a sip, I'd be subjecting myself to whatever magic he'd used to speed up the process. And knowing my grandad, this stuff had more magic than it did liquid.

I narrowed my eyes. "I thought gin's supposed to be a clear liquid. Why is it blue?"

My grandfather's eyes widened. "Blueberries. You like blueberries, don't you?"

I thought about it. I did like blueberries. I liked them in my cereal or in a pie with ice cream. Never in a magically induced alcoholic beverage.

I swished the contents in the glass, eyeing the liquid. "And you've tried it already?"

Poe laughed softly, and I bit my tongue to keep myself from laughing.

"Cauldron be damned. It's not poison!" exclaimed my grandfather as he grabbed the bottle on the counter next to him, poured himself a glass, and chucked the entire contents in one shot.

He smacked his lips. "There." He wheezed, his face turning a slightly darker shade. "See? It's not poison." He coughed, and coughed some more. "Nothing to it." His gaze fixed on mine, eyes watering. "Better do it in one go," he advised.

"Right." I put the glass on the counter. "I think I'll wait for the food."

Poe snorted—because birds can actually snort—and I looked at him. A large diamond ring was wrapped around his leg like a metal leg band, winking in the light.

I leaned closer. I didn't know much about diamond rings, but I did know the larger the stone, the larger the price tag. And this one happened to be the size of a large pea.

"Poe. Where did you get that ring?" Cauldron help me if the raven started to steal from the local jewelry stores.

The raven looked away and crossed his legs, hiding his ring foot with his left as though that would keep me from seeing the huge rock. It didn't.

"Poe?" I demanded, and I placed my hands on the counter next to his right foot. "If you've been lifting rings from the local jewelry stores... I think I might have to pluck all your feathers." The nerve of that bird. I had enough problems without having a warrant out on his ass. Familiars weren't exempt from thieving or other lawbreaking gambits. Plus witches were responsible for them. If your familiar broke the Coven Law, he or she would be labeled as an Un-familiar, and they'd either be returned to the Netherworld or be destroyed, depending on the degree of the crime and the circumstances surrounding the situation.

I didn't want either of those options. I loved Poe, but he was more than capable of driving me insane.

"Give me the ring, Poe, or I'm gonna whip your ass."

The bird tutted. "And you kissed Logan with that mouth?"

Heat rushed to my face. My eyes settled on my grandfather. He was slushing his gin around in his mouth like mouthwash and didn't seem to have heard the raven.

I'd had enough. "Give it." I reached out toward the ring with my right hand—

In a blur of black feathers, Poe lashed out, and his beak sliced into the soft flesh of my finger.

"Ow!" I cried, yanking my hand back. A nasty red welt stood where Poe had bitten me, and blood seeped through a small cut. He'd broken the skin. "I'm bleeding," I hissed at the bird. "You made me bleed! Are you crazy?"

The raven glared at me, eyes bright with anger. "You know better than to surprise a Malphas demon. You came at me. I acted on instinct. It's not my fault your hand got stuck in my beak."

"Like it won't be my fault if you accidently fall into my boiling cauldron." I clenched my jaw. "You know damn well I was just going for that ring."

The bird shrugged. "I'm not Colin, the boy psychic. I don't read minds."

19

A laugh escaped my grandfather, and I glowered at him.

"Don't give me that look, girl," he said as he refilled his glass with his cauldron-brewed gin. "You chose a raven for your familiar when you had your pick of cats. Everyone knows ravens are too wild and too unpredictable to make compatible familiars. Even a rat would have been a better choice."

"I wanted a familiar to pick me. Not the other way around." It had sounded right at the time, but now I wasn't so sure anymore.

I moved toward the wicker basket next to the fridge and pulled out a pen. I drew the anti-pain sigil on my finger, just below the cut. "Sine dolore," I breathed just as I finished drawing the sigil.

A tingle spread over my hand to my fingertips. After a few seconds, the throbbing in my finger subsided. It wasn't a huge cut, but he had broken the skin. My own familiar had made me bleed.

I was going to kill him.

I let out a labored breath, straining to keep my anger from seeping through my pores. "Poe," I said, trying to keep the anger from my voice. I waited for the raven to turn his black eyes on me. "Do you want to be branded as an Un-familiar? Is that what you want? Because if you don't stop stealing, that's exactly what's going to happen, and I won't be able to do anything about it."

"You're getting all worked up for nothing," said the raven as he walked over to the center of the island to the wooden fruit bowl. He jumped up and clasped his claws around the rim of the bowl as he peered inside.

I pressed my hands on my hips. "It's not nothing if you're stealing diamond rings."

A puff of annoyance sounded from Poe, and then he picked out a peach from the fruit bowl, jumped back down on the counter and began to tear it apart.

"You really disappoint me sometimes," I said, thinking perhaps my grandfather was right. I should have picked the old, one-eyed, orange tabby as my familiar instead of a stubborn raven.

The large black bird looked up at me, juices trickling down his beak as he swallowed a large chunk of peach. "Did you tell your grandfather about the kiss?"

The little shit. I am going to kill that damn bird.

My grandfather set his glass on the counter and raised his brows at me. "Kiss?" he asked, wiping his mouth with the back of his hand. "What kiss? Did you get kissed, Samantha?"

How old am I? Twelve? I glared at Poe. "There's a nice boiling cauldron upstairs with your name on it, Poe. Care to take a dip?"

The raven chuckled, cementing my anger.

Ticked, my lips parted. "I swear—"

Something gray and white shot through the open kitchen window.

My heart slammed against my chest, a spell forming on my lips, as the thing skidded to a stop on the island. It wasn't a thing. It was a pigeon.

21

Poe let out a cough of laughter. "Well, I'll be damned. A freakin' messenger pigeon. Hallelujah. The mortal world is saved."

"Bite me, crow," shot the pigeon as he puffed out his chest proudly. He was a beautiful bird with gray and white feathers and a bit of purple on his wide chest. He was large for a pigeon, but he was still half the size of Poe.

The raven walked up to the pigeon slowly in a show of size and strength. "I would, but I wouldn't want to soil my beak with the taste of pigeon servitude."

"Servitude?" laughed the pigeon as he raised his brows indignantly. "Looks to me as if you're the slave here. A witch's slave. Whereas I have a job. A real job, which consists of getting paid, three weeks off a year plus benefits and a retirement plan. I have my independence, which is more than what you have." He eyed Poe. "You're nothing but a witch's pet. A familiar. Bound to do what they demand. So tell me now, crow," the pigeon mocked, "who you calling a slave?"

Poe made a strange sound in his throat. "What do you want, duck?" His words came out a tad higher than usual, and guilt tugged in my chest. I didn't want to think of Poe as my slave, but familiars were bound to us witches and were expected to follow our instructions.

The pigeon straightened. "A message from the dark witch court."

My grandfather came around the counter. "Who's the message for, Tank?"

"For Samantha Beaumont," replied the pigeon as he turned to look at me. The bird stuck out its leg, revealing a rolled-up piece of parchment clasped to it.

I stiffened, staring at the parchment. This wasn't my first messenger pigeon. The pigeons were common in Mystic Quarter—the witches' version of emails, just a little dirtier.

This had to do with the vampire attack last night. I was sure of it. The timing was right. After the human police conducted their primary investigation, the scene and the particular way the victim was killed would have alerted the paranormal community. Hence the pigeon.

And I was the idiot who'd forgotten to inform the court. Great.

I reached out and grabbed the piece of parchment from Tank's leg. I looked up at the sound of wings, and my chest contracted at the sight of Poe flying out the kitchen window. Damn. He didn't even wait to hear what the message said. Guilt swam up anew.

I took a breath, smoothed out the parchment, and began to read.

Dear Ms. Samantha Beaumont

Your presence is required at the dark
witch court this evening at midnight.
Return your reply with the messenger
pigeon. Feed the gargoyle with a drop of
your blood.

Sincerely yours,
Magda Ratson, Dark Witch Court, Sec.
Mystic Quarter, NY

"A new job?" asked my grandfather as he drained his new glass in a single gulp.

I shook my head, my insides twisting. "They want to see me," I told my grandfather, watching Tank eyeing the bowl of fruit with his beak open. Was he drooling?

Crap. If it had been a job, the note would have specified that. No. This was different.

"Why do they want to see you?" asked my grandfather, faint worry lines creasing his forehead. "A witch does not get summoned by the dark witch court to swap cauldron recipes, Samantha. Why do I get the feeling you're keeping something from me?"

"It's nothing. Let me worry about this. Okay?" Liar. Liar. Liar.

My guilt redoubled at the fact that I hadn't told him I'd used my gift—the one I'd promised to never use for fear of discovery—to vanquish Vargal. I didn't have the heart to tell the man who'd saved me and kept me safe all my life. I was an asshole.

Greater demons I could handle. Even an ancient vampire skilled with magic. But a meeting with the dark witch court was a little trickier. Plus I'd never been summoned before. Ever. And what did "Feed the gargoyle with a drop of your blood" mean? What gargoyle?

Unease lurched in my chest like a sudden thunder. My grandfather was right. This was no ordinary summoning. Why did they want to see me? Did they know about my secret?

I had a feeling my life was about to change, and not in a good way.

CHAPTER
3

My heart was a steady drum in my chest as I strolled down Wicked Way, my knees a little more wobbly than usual, and my boots kept catching on crevices from the uneven sidewalks. It was almost as though my own legs were trying to trip me, like some mysterious force was trying to stop me from going to meet the dark witch court.

Maybe these forces were right. Maybe I should have stayed home.

But I couldn't refuse the summon. No witch in his or her right mind would refuse, not unless they wanted to end up in the witch prison—Grimway Citadel—a horrid, windowless concrete castle with enchanted walls and glistening with every protection ward imaginable. I'd heard rumors of witches exploding into chunks of blood and guts as they tried to make their escape. Only a fool would even think about trying to escape from the citadel. You had to be mad.

I lifted the strap of my shoulder bag, adjusted the weight, and kept going.

The wind blew through the buildings and the few trees scattered around, bringing forth the scent of sulfur and rot—the telltale sign of half-breeds and demonic magic. Light spilled from the streetlights, and blue-white moonlight pooled around me as I made my way through Mystic Quarter, the paranormal district in Manhattan where witches, vampires, werewolves, faeries, trolls, and all manner of half-breeds mingled.

The district was as eccentric and unusual as its inhabitants situated in the jumble of buildings that made up Mystic Quarter. Vampires sat outside on terraces, drinking maroon-looking liquid, while werewolves stood next to a Meat on the Go food truck, tearing meat from bones, the size of my arm, with their teeth. A cluster of witches lounged in a small garden, drinking from miniature cauldrons. Yeah, it looked weird. But most of the district was just like any other borough in New York, just a gathering of people sitting around eating or drinking and having a good time.

All except for me.

I trudged up Odin Boulevard, pushing my legs faster. I didn't want to meet anyone I knew, right now. My boots clomped with every step while the dark witch court occupied most of my thoughts except for two—Poe and Logan.

Logan because, well, the guy was hot, and his kiss piqued my curiosity, and Poe because I was worried about him.

The raven was a no-show once again. I really didn't understand why he'd gotten all worked up after seeing Tank. It's not like he'd want to be working for the dark witch court as a messenger boy. Or would he? He was hurting, and I had no idea how to help him. He didn't want to share whatever had been bothering him with me, and that stung a little.

Poe was my support system, and without my buddy, I felt empty as I made my way through the dark streets of Mystic Quarter. With Poe perched on my shoulder, I always had a sense of security, of him having my back.

I walked up Twilight Avenue and slowed as I passed my aunt's shop. I thought about stopping by to get her opinion on this meeting with the dark witch court but then quashed the idea because I knew it would only upset her. Worse, she'd probably demand to come along, which wasn't a great idea since most of the court members despised her. She would say it was because she was more powerful than them, and I would say the members didn't like her because she *thought* she was.

I let out the breath I was holding just as I heard the familiar flap of wings.

Poe flew to me and landed on my arm. I gave him a tight smile and found that I was unable to get angry at him for leaving like that after Tank's message. A dull sadness was growing in me, like I was losing him.

"Gordon told me I might find you here," said the bird as he moved up to my shoulder and shifted his weight until he was comfortable. "What? Cat catch your tongue?"

I'd always hated that expression. I pulled my eyes away and continued walking.

"Aren't you going to yell at me or something?" pressed the raven, and I heard the tension in his voice as though he'd been preparing himself for the battle of words we were about to have. And on any other night, I would have.

"No."

"Damn, then you really must be nervous." The bird was quiet for a moment, and then I felt the brush of feathers against my cheek. "Don't be nervous, Sam. It's probably just the usual job request. I'm thinking it has something to do about that vampire killing you told me about last night."

My breath came fast. "Then why didn't they say that in the note? If it is a job, they would have left the message with Tank. I've done hundreds of jobs for them. And not once did they ask to see me. It doesn't feel right. You know what I mean?" Nerves bubbled up again, making my stomach clench.

"Well, for one," began the bird, "you said the vampire had magic. That has to have the witches all worked up and tripping on their brooms. You know how they don't like to share their magic."

"No. This is something else. I can feel it."

Poe settled closer to my neck. "Like what?"

My heart did a somersault inside my chest. "What if this has something to do with my gift? Secrets always have a way of coming out. Maybe they found out."

Poe made a sound in his throat. "I doubt it. No. I think this is about a job. Think about it," he said, balancing his weight on my shoulder. "All the jobs you've ever received from the witch court were always sent by a flying chicken. Right?"

"Right."

"Which tells me," continued the bird, "that this is a job—or something along the same line. Who knows, maybe they're going to offer you one of those stiff seats at court."

I laughed. "Right. Like that's *ever* going to happen. The Beaumont witches never had a seat in that court and never will. We're not... court material," I added, knowing we Beaumont witches hated to follow rules and regulations. We preferred to break them.

"You never know," commented the bird.

"I do," I said, though the smile I felt on my face was a welcomed distraction from the mountain of stress I had been feeling a few minutes ago. I felt marginally better with Poe by my side.

After a three-minute walk, we came to a two-story building with a large metal door that looked like it belonged in the medieval ages, which was really out of place here in New York City. I could still read the faded, weatherworn sign above the door: OAK PARK THEATER.

Glass display windows flanked the entrance door on either side, reflecting the moonlight like silvery mirrors. There was nothing in the windows now, just black curtains. The stone façade was dark and eroded from years of exposure to polluted air and acid rain. It had that old theater feel to it, but it had clearly been a graceful and luxurious theater, once upon a time.

I stood for a moment, my legs seemingly cemented to the walkway and not wanting to move.

"We could make a run for it," said the raven after a moment.

"You know I can't." I shook my head. "You know as well as I do what will happen if I don't make that appointment." Like boiling me alive in their cauldron. I'd heard the rumors.

"Just as obeying the court could have lethal consequences," came Poe's breath, rubbing against my cheek.

"I don't have a choice," I replied, as I took another step forward.

My skin pricked with ribbons of dark magic. It was everywhere—coming off the walls, the door, the roof. The entire building was heavily sealed and warded. The smell of sulfur intruded but then vanished.

The door knocker was an iron-cast gargoyle's head complete with large ears, horns, a squished bat-like nose, glaring eyes and a mouth filled with canines that looked like they belonged to a Great Dane large enough to fit your hand. An iron ring hung from its open mouth. The face was carved in the likes of pain, its mouth appearing fixed in a silent scream. But the proportions were off: the mouth too wide, the forehead too high, the eyes warped.

It was the ugliest thing I'd ever seen.

There was nothing remarkably witchlike or remotely interesting to look at. It was just... warped and grotesque and ghoulish.

"This looks more like something you'd see in the Netherworld," I commented. "Like something the demons would carve."

"Even demons have a better understanding of art. This is... just wrong." The bird gave a huff and said, "So, what happens now? Do we knock?"

I stared at the thing's mouth, and its very large teeth. "Feed the gargoyle with a drop of your blood," I said, recalling the instructions from the note. Damn. That was creepy.

"Excuse you?" said Poe.

My mind raced. "It was written on the note." I drew a nervous breath and held it, stifling a shiver. "The building's heavily protected with wards. You can't just walk in." I reached into my bag and pulled out a small Swiss Army pocket knife, the one I used to cut herbs from my garden.

"You can't pick a lock with that," said the bird.

"It's not for the knocker. It's for me," I said and sliced a small cut on my left finger. A fat drop of blood seeped from the cut like a gleaming red pearl. Before it trickled down my finger, I moved my hand toward the knocker and squeezed my finger so the thick drop of blood fell inside the gargoyle's mouth and splatted on its tongue.

Dark witches. Only they would come up with something so disturbing.

"Now what?" moaned the bird. "I'm not seeing anything."

I stepped back and waited. "Just wait," I said, my nerves making me shake.

Energy hummed in the air, my hair lifting and floating around my shoulders as dark magic glided over me, whispering of power and domination. Damn. Those were some powerful wards.

My pulse quickened. "I'm feeling something."

Poe shifted his weight. "Like what? Indigestion?"

"Halt, mortal! Halt, intruder upon the gates of the secret court of the dark witches!" boomed the door knocker in an ancient voice like the grinding of rocks. Its mouth moved and worked in a disturbingly human way. I watched transfixed as the face shifted, not smoothly like a human face, but jerky and erratic as parts of the iron came together to form expressions.

I smiled. A human would have passed out at the sight of a talking gargoyle door knocker. I thought it was awesome. I loved being a witch.

"Great, it speaks," grumbled Poe.

"Of course I speak, you insolent genus corvus," barked the door knocker, its voice a slightly higher pitch and sending waves of goose bumps over my skin.

This was a whole new level of weird.

"Can you just shut up and open the door, already," commented Poe. "We're going to be late."

The gargoyle's eyes moved up to Poe, and his face screwed up in a contemptuous frown. "Only a dark witch can enter. The nonmagical are not permitted."

"He is magical," I interjected, a small feeling of panic twisting in my gut. I didn't want to enter without Poe. If something were to happen to me, I needed him to go tell my grandfather. "He's my familiar. We share our magic. We're magically connected. He goes where I go."

The door knocker made a face. If it had arms, it would have crossed them over its chest. "I'm afraid that is not possible," it said in a matter-of-fact tone. "As I said, the nonmagical cannot enter," it added, just as a wind howled down the street, sounding a lot like a big fat *no*. "I didn't make the rules, but we all must abide by them."

"Like hell I am." An awful feeling of dread settled in me, and my gut clenched. I frowned. This door knocker was starting to irritate me.

"It's okay, Sam," said Poe. "I'll wait for you here—"

"No." Tension pulled through me. My voice rose as I took a calming breath. "He's coming with me," I told the door knocker. "Or you'll have to explain to the dark witch court why I wasn't allowed entry after they specifically asked for me. I don't think they'll be pleased with you. Is that what you want?" I wasn't exactly sure how a witch could harm a freaking iron door knocker, but it was worth a shot. Perhaps they would melt him.

Its face cracked in an attempt of a frown but came out looking like a grimace. "I'm a door knocker. I have no *wants*. I'm a magical being created for the simple purpose of guarding this door and letting *only* the magical step through. Your blood is the key." His eyes shifted to Poe. "I'm sorry, but familiars are not on the list of magical beings. He simply cannot pass."

Anger slowly burned in my gut. "Fine. Then I'm leaving." I turned to leave and took three steps—

"Wait!" came the gargoyle's terrified voice, and I whirled around, trying hard not to smile.

"Yes?"

The gargoyle's expression shifted from worry to contempt and finally twisted into something that looked like resolve. I could have sworn it looked a shade darker.

"Fine," grumbled the door knocker in a voice reminiscent of Poe's when he didn't get an extra piece of fruit. "Your familiar may enter. But only this once."

"Thank you."

"Jackass," whispered Poe.

Sure enough, a tingling rolled across my skin, and the air thickened with a pulsing energy. I heard a sudden loud click, like the sound of a dead bolt slipping into place.

The tingling lifted. And then the door swung open, revealing high, arched ceilings and floors of polished stone laid with strips of red carpet that led past a grand foyer.

"Welcome," said the door knocker, "to the dark witch court."

I took a shaky breath. "Here we go," I said and stepped through.

CHAPTER
4

The thick red carpet stifled the sound of my boots as I stepped into the foyer as though I were walking on grass. The door shut behind me, and I jerked as I felt the sudden prickling of the protection wards closing around the building, shutting it off from any supernatural access.

The foyer was large and decorated with elegant wood panels. A grand, winding staircase, richly carpeted in red and leading to the second floor, served as the centerpiece of the room.

But I wasn't going to the second floor. The stage was on the ground floor. That's where I was headed. I passed the grand staircase and moved toward another set of double doors with a sign above that read MEZZANINE.

"You know where you're going?" came Poe's voice next to my ear.

"It's a theater. There's only one place the witches would convene."

"The stage?"

"The stage," I agreed as I made my way toward the large double doors. When I thought about it, the dark witches choosing the old theater as their headquarters was perfect. They were all drama queens and in need of a stage to perform.

I was both flattered and alarmed that the dark witch court had asked to meet with me. The sheer notion of it all was staggering. Worse, I was five minutes late. The fiasco with the door knocker had taken longer than I'd expected. *Great first impression, Sam.*

I strained to keep from shaking and tried to keep my face neutral, taking it all in. I was a Beaumont witch after all. I could handle a group of wrinkly old witches.

Bracing myself, I pushed open the double doors and strolled through.

The muffled noise hit me first, and then the musty smell of old carpet. The air thrummed with dark magic, and I knew it was a show of strength and power. They wanted visitors to know they could kill with a snap of their fingers.

All righty then.

The magic reached out around the room, circling me and resonating different strains of the craft. Each one felt utterly different from the next.

The theater looked like any old theater in New York City of moderate size, lit by hundreds of candle sconces along the walls and a great candelabra that hung from the ceiling with three rings of candles. I could totally see it hanging from the entrance hall of a great medieval castle.

By human standards, the room would have fit hundreds of people comfortably in the seats. However, they now sat positively empty, save a few dark witches lurking along the aisles or standing along the walls. I didn't recognize any of them, and that somehow added another layer to my unease.

I walked down a slight slant between the rows of seats toward the stage. A half-moon table rested in the middle of the stage, holding six chairs and facing the audience.

In each chair sat a black-robed dark witch.

There were three males and three female witches. Was it equally balanced on purpose? Who knew?

The female on the far left could've easily passed for my aunt's older sister—frail, bent, and emaciated. Her one hundredth birthday had come and gone long ago. She was bald, and the black robe accentuated it even more. She sat hunched in her chair, but dark eyes stabbed me with sharp intelligence.

The female next to her was equally old, though she had a head full of black hair that spilled over her front. The last female witch didn't look a day past fifty. Plump with coffee-colored skin and short, curly black hair, she watched me with a knowing half smile. Creepy.

The males, well, the one on the far right looked older than the two old witches combined. The male witch next to him was plain and forgettable, middle-aged and slightly overweight, with short brown hair streaked with gray at his temples. Oscar Lessard.

He was the only dark witch I'd ever met on the court. He'd showed up at my home five years ago to offer me a full-time job—to watch the Veil on behalf of the dark witch court. Kind of like private security for the witches.

Red spots marred his pale face like he'd been arguing. Either that, or he'd had a hard time climbing up the stairs to the stage.

The last male witch, with gleaming black hair, looked only a few years older than me. His dark, almond-shaped eyes watched me accusingly.

And suddenly my warning flags tripped.

My legs felt like they were made of cement. But I never stopped moving and kept my face blank. Poe's grip on my shoulder tightened as he sensed my unease.

Darting my eyes around the room, I made mental notes of the exits—the one I'd just come from and two more emergency exits that flanked each side of the stage.

"You know any of them apart from Oscar?" came Poe's voice as the stage grew bigger and bigger.

"No." Oscar and I weren't friends, though it would have been nice to get a heads-up concerning this meeting. At least I could have come prepared. I tried to make eye contact, but he wouldn't meet my eyes.

When I reached the stage, the young male witch jumped off his chair and pointed at me, making me halt.

"Do you see? She's brought her demon with her," he shouted, the anger in his tone igniting my own. "She has no respect for the court. I told you she was the wrong choice." A murmur of consensus reverberated about the table.

Swell. Things were starting out great.

The elderly male witch with four strands of white hair left on his bald head cleared his throat. "Samantha. Were you not told to leave your familiar outside the theater?" he demanded, his voice low though kind and with a lilt of an accent I couldn't place. His white beard was long enough to tuck into his belt if he'd had one. A thick scar started from his forehead and slashed all the way to his chin on the right side of his face, as though the claws of a bear had ripped his face apart. Though his eyes were small, kindness shone from them.

Knowing he must be referring to the gargoyle door knocker, I opened my mouth and answered, "Yes."

I'd barely gotten the word out of my mouth before several of the court members and the witches standing in the aisles rose to their feet with outraged shouts. The court broke out in a cacophony of cries, threats, and disapproving grunts from the ancient ones.

41

Like I said, they loved to perform.

A scowl creased my forehead as I watched their performance. I felt like a child standing before a group of disapproving parents. Screw them. I didn't come here to be scolded, and now they were starting to piss me off.

And yet seeing them bothered like I'd just opened the gates to the Netherworld on purpose also made me feel slightly less nervous. No one paid any attention to my gloves. That's when I knew this had nothing to do with my gift.

This was something else, perhaps equally as important in their eyes. Curious.

Still standing, the younger male witch made a loud judgmental noise and placed his hands on his hips. "She disobeyed the simplest of instructions—to *leave* her wretched demon at the door," he accused with an overdone dramatic flair in his speech. "And you think she'll keep her mouth shut? She won't. She's just like that old Evanora Crow. She can't be trusted."

Oooh. You're going down, buddy, I told him with my eyes. No one talks badly about my aunt without a little broom beating.

I hated this guy. He had the wild eyes of the ambitious wanting to climb the dark witch court ladder and fast. His stance said he wasn't afraid to eliminate everything and everyone who stood in his way. I hated the overzealous, the kind who stepped over the weak to get ahead.

That's it. I'm making him into a voodoo doll.

Poe shifted on my shoulder, feeling my discomfort. "Maybe I should have stayed outside."

"It's too late for that now," I whispered. The female bald witch looked as though she wanted to cook Poe in her cauldron later.

"Sit down, Tran," ordered the older male witch, with a beard. "You're giving me whiplash." A wave of force echoed out from his words, giving the feeling of a gust of wind.

Tran gave me a foul look as he let himself fall in his chair, looking like a spoiled brat who just got his time-out.

Small, pale eyes found me as the old male witch lifted a bony arm and pointed to the row of seats behind me. "Take a seat, Samantha Beaumont."

I cast my gaze about the court. A nervous energy hung about them with the way they shifted in their seats. It was almost as though they were scared. But scared of what? This wasn't a trial either. This was something else.

I turned and lowered myself in the nearest seat facing the stage. "Who's the old guy?" I whispered to Poe, resisting the urge to wipe my sweaty hands on my jeans.

"That's Darius Gruenwald," answered the raven, his voice low so only I could hear. "Head of the dark witch court."

Ah-ha. So this was the infamous witch Darius.

"He took a turn for the worse three years ago when he summoned the demon Beleth," continued the raven. "The demon turned on him, and he barely made it out alive. Beleth gave him that scar on his face to remember him by, so he wouldn't be summoned again. The old fool's never been the same since."

Old fool was right. Another witch playing with demons, thinking they could control a mighty powerful demon. He probably had no idea who Beleth was. I did.

Beleth was a mighty and terrible king of the Netherworld, who had eighty-five legions of demons under his command. Demons like Beleth didn't take kindly to being forced into a summoning circle. Darius was lucky to be alive.

Darius shifted in his seat, and a pained expression flickered across his face for a second, as though just that small movement caused him great amounts of pain. Seems like Beleth left the old man some scars on the inside as well.

"Thank you for coming to meet with us on such short notice, Samantha," said Darius as he folded his hands on the table. His gnarled fingers looked like they'd been broken too many times to heal properly.

I wasn't sure what to answer. "Sure." It's not like I had a choice. They knew it. I knew it. My eyes found Tran, and he was glaring at me. I glared back. "Why am I here?" I didn't even attempt to hide the irritation in my voice. I hated not knowing what was going on. If this had nothing to do with my gift, why was I here?

Darius nodded his head. "James, if you please."

A male witch stepped from the shadows next to the stage, making me flinch. I'd never even noticed him. He wore a dark gray robe similar to the ones from the court members, though he was down here in the shadows while they were up on display.

He disappeared through a wall of heavy red curtains to the right of the stage, and when he came back, he pushed a gurney.

"What is that?" I whispered, leaning forward.

"Cake?" prompted Poe, excitement in his voice. "I'm starving."

The gurney was covered with a black sheet, and under it was a bundle that had the right proportions to be a body.

"That's not a cake," commented Poe.

"That's not a cake."

"A cake would have been nice."

"Definitely nice," I agreed.

James pushed the gurney on the lower level and parked it at the front of the stage. Then he stepped back, leaving it covered with the black sheet.

Darius cleared his throat again, and I pulled my eyes from the gurney to his face. "An unfortunate incident has been called to our attention," he intoned. "Of a somewhat... *delicate* nature. It is the reason we called you here tonight, Samantha. The court needs your assistance."

I stood up, Poe balancing on my shoulder with his wings tickling my neck. I moved toward the gurney, the thumping of my boots on the carpet forming a rhythm with the drum of my heart. I clenched my jaw, already knowing what I was going to find under the sheet.

Standing where I'd assumed was the head, I gripped a handful of the sheet and yanked it off.

Shit.

A wave of nausea hit as I stared at an emaciated, mummy-like face and withered hands, delicate and small. Tiny chunks of flesh were missing from the neck next to the jugular vein.

And behind the dried and emaciated skin was the face of another woman.

I blinked into a smaller, more petite face than the one I'd seen in the alley. It had withered from life but was different all the same.

"What is it?" Poe whispered in my ear. "Something's wrong. Isn't it?"

I stilled my face to keep from showing any emotion. "This isn't the same victim," I whispered back, my lips barely moving.

The ancient vampire had killed another human.

CHAPTER

5

When people say they "require your assistance," it usually means it'll be bad for you. It's a way for them *not* to get their hands dirty and for you to get all muddied up in whatever they wanted you to do. Me. Well, I had no choice. I was screwed.

Okay, so the situation wasn't great, but it wasn't disastrous either. If they knew I'd come across this vampire and hadn't reported it, I'd be in deep in the crapper. It was part of my job to report suspicious half-breed activity, not to mention killings. However, vampire killings were not our problem. The vampires were responsible for taking care of their own. Or better yet, it was the Gray Council's responsibility. I knew I'd better keep that bit of information about the other killing to myself.

Relax, Sam. They still don't know.

Darius leaned forward on the table, his face wrinkling in anger. His small eyes blazed with scorn and fury. "A vampire did this. On that—we can all agree. The proof is undeniable."

And *I* saw him.

"Though it was hard to identify her in this state of... *disintegration*," continued Darius, "her family was able to recognize her by her clothes. Her name was Audrey."

Her family? Edgy, I shifted my weight. "You knew her?" Strange how the dark witch court would know a random human by name. Maybe she was a friend to the witch community. It wouldn't be the first time a human and witch alliance was formed. Usually the human wanted to become a witch. I didn't blame them. Witches were awesome.

My eyes darted back to the victim, and I thought about the horrible death she probably suffered at the hands of that vampire. With that kind of powerful magic and strength, this poor human female had no way of escaping. I swallowed the bile rising at the back of my throat.

And yet the vampire had let me live...

"She looks like a dried-up prune," noted Poe, a hint of concern in his voice. "Must have been painful."

"Very." I looked up and met Darius's eyes. "Okay, so we can all agree a vampire did this," I said and stepped away from the gurney, my hands on my hips. "I still don't understand why you called me here and why the dark witch court is involved. If there's a rogue vampire killing off humans, you should contact the vampire court. Let them deal with this."

"Because," said the head of the witch court, the wrinkles around his eyes deepening with anger, "a vampire is killing our own."

It was warm in the theater, but I felt a shiver roll up my spine, magnified by the sudden stillness of the room.

The vampire was killing witches? Oh, hell no.

Again, the room descended into a chaos of shouts and wails and arguments with Tran, the loudest of them all. The witches stirred, leaving most of the noise to be swallowed up by the space.

Darius leaned back in his chair, letting the witches fuss a little more, and then, "Order!" he called out in a ringing voice as he slammed his hand hard on the table.

Silence.

Impressive. I wish I knew how to control a room like that.

Frowning, I blinked slowly at Darius. "She's a witch?" My head whipped back to the dead woman, the dead witch. It was impossible to differentiate witch from human now. There was no substance to her anymore. No blood. No essence. No magic. I couldn't sense the witch energies that all witches were born with. Not anymore.

"She *was* a witch," interjected Tran, a slant to his eyes. "She's dead now."

"No shit," I said, wondering if the other victim had also been a witch.

Darius's lips moved, but no sound came out at first. "This is the fifth victim," said Darius after a moment. "We found Emma's body in an alley just last night."

I'm so sorry, Emma. I met the old male witch's eyes. "And you're sure all the victims are witches?"

"I'm afraid so, yes," he answered, and I stifled a flinch as he answered my question. "And they were all dark witches."

My stomach was a flurry of emotion—anger, doubt, fear, and regret. I was angry at myself, thinking if I had moved a little quicker, I might have saved Emma's life. I feared an old vampire powerful enough to kill off witches, and finally I regretted I hadn't said anything.

Would Audrey still be alive if I had contacted the court about Emma?

My emotions were all mixed together until I felt as if I was going to throw up. A quiver went through me. If an old vampire was targeting witches, there had to be a reason. Why would a vampire go after a witch who could fight back with powerful spells and hexes when an easier, weaker human was right there for the taking? It didn't make any sense. Why was the vampire targeting witches?

My eyes jerked to Darius. "What does the Gray Council think about this?"

"They don't know," answered the old male witch, his face wrinkling in a deep frown. "We want to keep this between us witches. We would appreciate your... discretion in this matter."

"Yeah, right," muttered Poe.

Darius moved his gaze along the members of his court before settling back on me. "We don't want a mass panic. If word got out that a vampire was killing witches, well…"

"All hell would break loose," I offered, knowing the panic it would cause within the witch community. Let's not forget the tension and animosity it would create between the vampires and the witches if the dark witch court accused the vampires. It would get ugly. And then there'd be a war. Shit, this was really bad.

"Quite right," said the old witch as he shifted in his seat. His face was partly cast in shadow, adding a new layer of grotesqueness to the scar on his face. "Which is why we couldn't risk sending you a messenger pigeon with the detailed information."

"Right."

"The relations between the witches and vampires have been on good terms for over a hundred years," continued Darius. "Before we can make any accusations or even bring this to the attention of the vampire court, we need to be certain. We need to be *absolutely* sure. Without a doubt. So you see, Samantha. We need to keep this quiet. The fewer who know what's going on—the better."

I took a breath. "Yes, I get it." I was already involved, whether I liked it or not.

But something didn't settle well with me. If the vampire was targeting witches, why hadn't he killed me?

I looked to the stage, my eyes traveling over the members. "What exactly do you want me to do?"

"To track and kill it," commanded the bald female witch, surprising me. Her voice was harsh and cold like a winter storm.

I gave the old witch a knowing smile. "Okay, then." So, this was about a hunt.

"Ask them for a pay raise," said the bird, and I had to agree with him on that.

Darius cleared his throat. "There are rules about this sort of thing, Magda," he said, a hint of warning in his tone. "We can't go around killing vampires," he added. The name rang a bell as I remembered reading it from the note sent with Tank. The bald witch was the dark witch court's secretary. Magda Ratson.

Magda bared her three teeth. "Do you see this vampire following any rules? It's killing witches." She pointed to Audrey's dried out corpse. "Five dead already. How long do you want us to wait before more witches are killed? And I'm not the only one here who wants to see its head on a plate."

At that, the other witches all mumbled their consensus, all apart from Tran and Darius. Interesting.

Once the members quieted, Darius's scarred face turned toward me. "Samantha. The court would like you to find this vampire—"

"Make it disappear, Samantha," barked the old witch Magda, her eyes fierce and determined. I was starting to like her.

Nothing like shoving vampire bodies under the rug. "No problem."

Darius's posture shifted to one of nervousness. "The court would appreciate your silence on this matter." He looked to Poe, and a ribbon of fear slid behind his eyes before he mastered it. "I would like your word that your familiar won't spread stories. We all know ravens are fond of tales."

"Bite me, you old fart," muttered Poe.

"I promise," I said loudly, hoping to hide the bird's voice. "He can keep his mouth shut."

"No I can't," said the bird.

"Shut it, Poe," I warned.

"So, that's it?" exclaimed Tran. "You're just going to give her the job?" he yelled, stirring the witches into a buzzing murmur.

Now I'd had just about enough of his crap. "Don't be such an infant." I glared at Tran. "If you've got a problem with me, be a man and spit it out," I growled, making Poe laugh.

The smile Tran gave me was truly feral. "Problem?" his smile widened. "Yes. As a matter of fact, I *do* have a problem with you. I don't trust you. You're an outcast. You don't have any friends in the community. Nobody likes you."

I pressed my hands on my hips. "I like me."

"Me too," answered Poe.

Tran's jaw clenched. "Witches like you can't be trusted," he added, his dark eyes gleaming with belligerence.

"You mean the pretty ones?" I took a challenging step toward the stage. The nerve of this guy. I couldn't see his fingers. If he was starting up a dark curse, I was going to hex him.

"Tran. That's enough of that," ordered Darius, a hint of frustration in his voice. His gnarled hands were clenched into fists. "We've already discussed this. The matter is closed."

The young witch glared at Darius. "It's not."

How did he get a seat on the dark witch court? I stood with my legs apart and tapped into the energy of my rings. Just in case.

"Out with it, then, little witch. What's gotten you all worked up?" I flashed Tran a brilliant smile. "Is it because you like me? It's not your fault. I'm irresistible."

At that, Tran let out a long and spiteful laugh. Then another one.

Damn. I never thought I was *that* ugly.

A savage light lit Tran's eyes, and his chin lifted. "You know nothing."

"Well, then," I said with a breath. "I'm not going anywhere. Tell me."

With a sliding sound of wood, the young witch jumped up from his chair, and his expression became almost taunting. "You're a pity hire."

I stilled. "Excuse me?"

He let out a rough cackle. "You barely have any skills as it is. I wouldn't even call you a witch. More like a human playing a witch."

"I've got plenty of skills." *You black-haired bastard.* "Want to see 'em?"

"Please," exclaimed Tran, his face a shade darker. "A dead mother, and your father abandoned you. You only got the job because the members here feel sorry for you."

My lips parted, and a flush rose from my neck to my face. It hurt. Everywhere hurt, and I felt as though Tran had hit me with a dark curse. Was it true? Was that the only reason the dark witch court hired me in the first place? Because they felt sorry for me?

I met Oscar's eyes, and for a moment I saw pity there before he mastered himself. Then it was gone. But I'd seen it. It was all true.

I stood feeling like an idiot, like the biggest fool in the world, the butt of a universal joke. Me, Samantha Beaumont, a big ol' fool.

It had been a pity offer. All those years of working for the dark witch court, just because they felt sorry for me.

Anger and frustration filled me, and I curled my fingers into fists to keep them from shaking.

"Don't believe him, Sam," said Poe, the anger in his voice triggering mine tenfold. "He's a liar."

I gritted my teeth, unable to answer. Not because I feared I would break down in a slop of tears but because of the anger simmering in my gut. I might do something stupid. Very stupid.

Tran watched me with a sour expression. "No offense," he said.

I bared my teeth. "None taken." Anger stirred in me. I took a steadying breath and looked at Darius. "Is that all?"

Darius watched me for a moment, his eyes pinched and his expression weary. "It is." His lips moved in anticipation of what he was about to say next. "We'll have a pigeon sent to monitor your progress. The dark witch court thanks you for your service..."

I spun around, Poe gripping my shoulder to balance himself, and trudged back up the aisle. The last of Darius's words were merely a muddled whisper behind me, and I caught a few gasps of outrage from the witches over the loud pulsing of blood in my ears. I didn't care how rude this looked. I didn't care about any of them. I just wanted to get the hell out of here.

My eyes burned, but I would never let any tears fall. Never in the presence of this witch court.

Poe was silent on my shoulder. He knew better than to try and speak to me when I was like this. Smart bird.

My body was tight with emotions as I fumed. I was beyond humiliated. I wasn't a failure or an incompetent witch, not by any standards. Okay, so I needed a little magical boost with my sigils—sue me. It's not like other witches didn't borrow their power or direct their energy from magical objects as well. What set me apart was that I didn't borrow magic from demons. Instead, I used them for whatever skill they mastered.

But I had another skill—the one I'd kept a secret my entire life. I had discovered it accidentally when I was eight. I'd touched my father and tapped into his inner magical power—and took it for my own. Then he'd tried to kill me.

If the court were to discover my secret—that I had the ability to borrow magic and use it as my own with a simple touch—they would kill me.

I had two choices. Let them think I was weak or die.

And I hated it.

My mind was a turmoil of emotions. I didn't even remember making it to the front door. With a shaking hand, I yanked it open and rushed out into the street.

And then the tears fell.

CHAPTER
6

By the time I'd left the theater and stopped by the local witch pub for two glasses of wine to clear my head, it was nearly five in the morning. I was surprisingly awake, high on adrenaline and emotions. The thought of a large pepperoni pizza and being curled up on the sofa with a soft blanket and the latest Netflix series to binge-watch had my legs on overdrive as I strolled up the streets of Mystic Quarter and headed toward Witches Row, my neighborhood.

The night was warm and humid, smelling of rain. I could almost feel the water in the clouds, the electric charge of the lightning waiting and contemplating where to hit. The sky was completely covered, and I had to rely on the sporadic streetlights in the quarter to help me see. Tires whispered on the pavement, and light appeared in the street opposite me, evolving into headlights.

My jaw hurt, and I unclenched it when I realized I was grinding my teeth. Damn the dark witch court. Damn them all to the Netherworld.

My blood pressure spiked, making me dizzy. Screw them. I'd been in worse situations than this. Hell, I'd been in plenty. And my experience had taught me that no matter how bad things were, they could always get a whole lot worse.

Whatever emotions I felt about the dark witch court meeting, I pushed them back. I wasn't about to have a meltdown because a few witches thought me weak and frail. There'd be time to think about all that tomorrow—specifically, how many hexes and dark curses I could use on Tran. I had a few of my favorites in mind. I'd discovered Casual Castration and Forever Impotent three months ago in my aunt's dark grimoire collection. Yeah, my aunt had an awesome dark hex collection. Love her.

Right now, though, I had a date with whatever new hottie was on Netflix.

Thinking of hotties, Logan's lips emerged in my mind's eye, and my pulse increased. I couldn't help it. The angel-born did that to me.

My stomach fluttered—actually fluttered, as though butterflies and moths were fighting over my guts—at the thought of his soft, warm lips on mine. It had only been a kiss with no real feelings behind it except my own selfish pleasure and my uncontrollable hormones. And yet I'd seen the desire in his eyes that had matched my own. He'd wanted something from me at that moment. But it had been just a moment, instant bliss, and had lasted but a few seconds.

Still, it had been some damn good seconds. I wondered what he looked like naked...

"You okay?" came Poe's voice suddenly, yanking me out of my thoughts about Logan's fine imaginary front.

I halted and looked to both sides of the street. "I'm fine." The wind was warm, blowing up and against my back as my blood hummed in my ears. Pulling my head up, I crossed the street and stepped onto the cracked sidewalk.

"No you're not." The raven shifted on my shoulder, beating his wings for balance. "I felt your heart rate increase. It does that when your emotions spiral out of control."

And when I'm thinking of Logan's hot ass.

"You can't let that group of witches get you down, Sam," said the bird, and he rubbed his head against my ear. "Let them think what they want. As long as you get paid for it, who cares. Right?"

"I care," I said, my boots clomping on the sidewalk. "Maybe I'm too proud. But I don't like anyone—especially witches—thinking I'm weak. You heard them. They only gave me the job because they think I'm a useless moron. I can't live with that. I've got my pride, you know."

"I know," agreed the bird, and I felt his hot breath on my neck. "So what are you going to do? Quit?"

"Yes," I answered, surprising myself at how quickly I'd made that decision, and how right it felt. "That's exactly what I'm going to do. The hell with them." I knew it was the right thing to do. Especially after what they'd pulled, they probably expected it. I couldn't work for people who didn't respect me. How could anyone?

"What about the vampire?" the bird insisted, a hint of worry in his tone. "You told them you'd look into it."

A faint warning stirred in the back of my thoughts. "I know I did. I was there."

The bird chuckled. "You lied to your own court? I'm impressed."

"Don't be. I didn't lie," I said, looking sideways at the raven. "I'm still going to find the vampire. He—because I have a feeling he's a *he*—is killing witches. I can't just let that go. Even if I despise every witch on that court."

"Even Oscar?"

My breath escaped me in a huff. "Yes. Even Oscar," I said, twisting my sigil ring on my left index finger with my eyes focused on the sidewalk. "He started this. He conned me into thinking the court needed me in the first place. He went on and on about how I was helping them keep our community safer."

"But you were in a way," informed the bird. "Even if they don't see it."

61

"It doesn't matter anymore." I shook my head, my tension growing. "I'm doing this last job for me. Not the court. And after that... I'm done."

The bird was silent. "What are we going to do for money? You know I can't live without my sunflower seeds."

My gut tightened with worry but I pushed it away. The utility bills were a huge amount of cash—half my pay actually. "I'll think of something. Maybe I'll open up a shop like my aunt."

Poe made a sound of disapproval in his throat. "That's never going to work," said the bird.

I let out a frustrated breath. "Why not?"

"Have you looked around lately? There are at least *twelve* witch shops alone in Mystic Quarter. There's way too many."

"I'll be lucky number thirteen." Yeah, that sounded lame.

"I hate to rain on your parade, but it costs money to open a business. Do you have savings? No. You don't. So who's going to lend you the money? A human bank when you have no record of employment? Not going to happen."

Right. I hadn't thought about that. "I'll figure something out. I always do." Which was the truth. I always got myself out of sticky situations. "Maybe I can work for the angel-borns. I've heard they'll hire witches sometimes. And they pay well. They're loaded."

"Sure," cawed the bird. "You'd like that. Wouldn't you? Being so close to Logan. Admit it. You have the hots for him."

"That's not the reason." Damn that bird. "And I don't have the hots for him. I barely know him."

"Uh-huh," said Poe, a smile in his voice. "You go ahead and tell yourself that, witch. I saw the way you two kissed. You wanted to jump his bones. Admit it."

"Don't start with me, bird," I warned. My boots thumped dully on the sidewalk as I slowed my pace. "I'm not in the best of moods. I might do something *crazy*," I added with wide eyes.

Poe laughed. "You going to tell your gramps?"

"I'm not sure." I was embarrassed enough. I didn't want to see the expression on his face when I told him the dark witch court hired his granddaughter only because they pitied her.

"I think you should," Poe said lightly. "I think he deserves to know if he can't afford to eat anymore."

Right. I was the main breadwinner in the family. "It'll be fine, Poe. Stop worrying."

I clenched my fists as I walked, a fierce determination filling me like a shot of adrenaline. I could do this. I knew I could. I would find the bloody vampire, vanquish him, and then make plans to take care of my family.

I was in control of my life. I was strong. Nothing could stop me.

And then something from the shadows jumped me.

CHAPTER

7

Everything happened at once.

There was a hissing sound, a thump, the scent of rot, and then I pitched forward onto the pavement. An instant later, the sound of Poe's wings told me he'd flown away before I hit the ground.

No more than three seconds went by before I rolled on the cold pavement and pushed myself to my feet to face my attacker, a spell forming on my lips as I tapped into the power of my sigil rings. I felt a gentle whisper and an effort of will as the power of the rings answered back.

I was ready.

A darkness spread around me, thickening swiftly as it pressed in like a thick, black mist rolling with a gust of wind, until I could barely see maybe twenty feet around me. Beyond that was just a murky vagueness, shutting out all the light. Not so much as the soft yellow light from a streetlamp or even the light from the neighboring buildings pierced through. The black mist began to press in closer, and it became an effort not to panic and bolt as the air grew colder.

He's back.

"Come on, you bastard vampire!" I growled, readying my spell. "Show yourself!" I wasn't about to let this bloodsucker dry me out like a thousand-year-old mummy. I was going to fry his ass.

The soft scuff of shoes on pavement was my only warning.

And then out from the darkness stepped three men.

No, not men, but humanoid demons by the smell of rot that rolled off of them. They were all dressed in the same expensive-looking gray suits, like they'd just stepped out of a high-end lawyer's firm.

I raised a brow. "Okay—*not* vampire." Crap. Where did they come from?

Heart thrashing, I struggled to ignore my sudden panic and focused on these demons. A smart witch always knew it's best to *know* your enemy if you wanted to *defeat* your enemy. It was the first rule in the Witch Club—not really. I just made that up.

I took in all their details. Broad shouldered, they were all the same height and build, maybe six feet with lean and agile bodies under their expensive suits. The same short white hair topped their heads, their faces gaunt and eerily identical like clones. At first glance they looked human, but the grayish-blue skin and faint black mist that emitted from their bodies were all demon. Black midnight eyes glared back at me with so much hate and promise of pain the hairs on the back of my neck stood up.

Oh. Shit. I knew what these baddies were.

Higher demons.

Though I'd never faced one before, I knew only one demon race paraded as clones, as doppelgangers, because, well, in some sick demonic way, they felt like it.

Higher demons were a race of humanoid demons from the Netherworld. They were demon lieutenants, leaders of demon troops and high in the demonic army rank. They were also powerful bastards with the authority over lesser demons like ghouls and imps.

I also knew they had supernatural strength, speed, and enhanced endurance. Adding to the fact they were highly intelligent left me with an extremely dangerous combination. Double crap.

My gut clenched. I should have stayed home.

"If I had known this was a costume party," I said, happy my voice was even. "I would have brought my broom and pointy hat."

Higher demons were usually out for angel souls. Something about the thirst for their angel essence, kinda like a vampire's thirst for blood. So why were they all looking at me with that hunger in their eyes? I ain't no angel.

One of the higher demons broke free from his brethren and stepped forward. "It *is* a party," he said, his voice disturbingly human. An evil grin flashed across his face. "A fête for your witch soul. The celebration of your death."

Figured he would say that. I looked to the sky, saw only black shadows and mist and shouted, "Poe! You all right?" Damn it. Where was that bird?

"Right here," answered Poe, making me jump. His voice was just a few feet behind me, though I couldn't see him. "Sam, I don't like this one bit," said the raven from the darkness.

"That makes two of us," I answered, squinting through the dark haze while trying to find his shape.

"Uh, Sam? I'm not feeling so hot," he added, his voice low and tired, like he was about to pass out.

I froze, alarmed. "What do you mean?" I tried to look for the raven while keeping my focus on the higher demons in case they did something stupid, like lunge at me.

"There's something in the black mist," I heard the bird say. "It's making me... dizzy."

I felt the blood leave my face. "Poe? Poe! Answer me."

But I only heard the blood pounding in my ears. *Oh my God, Poe!*

I glared at the demons. "What did you do to him, you bastards!"

Together, the higher demons laughed, sounding like a pack of hyenas, and my anger skyrocketed.

"Sam," breathed Poe, his voice barely a whisper, "I think I'm going to take a little nap."

"Poe!" I took a step back toward his voice. "Poe, where are you?" I scuttled backward, straining to see through the mist and trying hard not to step on my familiar. That's all I needed—squishing my raven to death.

Was he going to die? Fear was sharp and hit deeply.

The higher demon's low, mocking laugh grew in depth but then faded with a bitter sound. "Don't worry," he purred. "Either he'll wake up just as he was in an hour, or he'll die."

Keep it together, Sam. "You did this on purpose. Why? What the hell do you want?"

Fear slid through me, but I pushed it away. Hatred nearly dripped from me through my pores as I eyed the demons. If they'd killed Poe, I was going to repay the favor.

"You higher demons are a long way from home," I said to the closest higher demon.

The same higher demon smiled, his gray teeth matching his skin. "We're here to collect your soul, little witch."

"You already said that." Reaching my awareness to my rings, I tapped into their magic, readying the power I was going to use if they moved another inch.

My shoulders stiffened. It was three against one, and with odds like that, with a different kind of opponent, I wouldn't have given it a second thought. But with three higher demons, things just got a lot more complicated. I knew if I shot a spell at the first one, by the time I'd even thought of conjuring another—I'd be dead.

I was so screwed. Why were these situations always happening to me?

"Vorkol says hello, by the way," said the nearest higher demon, a snicker in his voice. He was so very close now, he only had to leap, and he'd be on top of me.

Vorkol? "Never heard of him. Is he a black-eyed bastard like you?" At that, all the higher demons laughed, and a chill dropped down my spine. Damn, they were creepy.

The higher demon flashed me his teeth. "I haven't tasted the soul of a witch in a very long time." He lifted his chin and sniffed the air, as though he were trying to catch my scent. "Not as sweet as the angel-born," he commented, his black eyes on me, "but we'll make an exception tonight."

"We're here on business," said the higher demon on his right.

"Nothing personal," added the higher demon on his left. His hard body was poised in anticipation.

So, the bastards wanted my soul, eh? Not going to happen.

"Too delicious to pass up," intoned the closest higher demon, and with a flick of his wrist, a dark dagger slipped into his hand. Black mist emanated from the shaft, the blade as sharp as a scalpel.

I shuddered at the sight of two more blades appearing in the hands of the other two higher demons. Death blades.

Death blades were believed to have been forged in The Black Wastes of the Netherworld. But that wasn't what had bile rising up in the back of my throat. It was the fact that their demonic power was derived from the souls the blades destroyed. That's what the black mist was—the remains of previous victims' souls.

The blades were also poisonous to angels. Again, I wasn't an angel. But that didn't seem to matter to them.

If they thought I'd just stand here and let them kill me, they were even more stupid than they were creepy.

The higher demon in the middle brought his blade to his face. His gray tongue flicked along the blade in a suggestive way, licking it slowly while keeping his black eyes on me the entire, disgusting time.

Cold seeped up my back. "Yikes. Now, why the hell did you do that? You think that's going to turn me on? You sick, creepy demon."

"Perhaps," he intoned. "Perhaps we're going to have a little fun with you before we kill you." He gave me another deviant smile that put me on edge and had my head screaming—*run!*

"I haven't had the taste of a woman's flesh in quite some time," he sneered. "The pleasures of humans can be the pleasures of demons as well."

I threw up a little in my mouth. "You're never going to touch me," I growled, my blood pounding in anger.

The higher demon just smiled, showing a slip of teeth. "But we will, little witch." Watching me, the demon rolled his eyes slowly over my body from my breasts to my groin.

"Never," I said, my voice final.

"We'll see about that," answered the same higher demon.

Tension pulled me stiff, and hearing the pleasure in his voice, I felt a snarl escape from me.

I'd rather die than be raped by a gang of higher demons. Nothing male touched me without my permission.

And then something inside me snapped.

A slow burn of fury took root. "I'm having a really bad day," I began, all the emotions from the court meeting rushing back into me. "So, if you don't want me to fry your ugly, rapist asses, you should get the hell away from me. 'Cause I'm feeling a little *crazy* tonight."

The middle higher demon chuckled, and his eyes took on a satisfied glint. "Let's play, little witch."

And then they did.

CHAPTER

8

Did I mention that higher demons had super-supernatural speed?

In a blur of motion, the higher demons attacked, their death blades whistling in the air in a song of death and destruction and blood.

But I was ready for them.

"Feurantis!" I shouted. Energy rushed out of me into my hand, and I hurled a fireball at the nearest higher demon. The blast exploded on his chest into a roar of flame, and for an instant it turned that black mist as bright as though I were standing under an afternoon sun.

I didn't wait to see if my spell worked on him. The bastard had two brothers. And they were coming at me.

I raised my right hand, my sigil ring blazing with energy.

"Dis caeli!" I cried, waving my arms as the magic of my rings roared through me. A blast of powerful kinetic force hit both higher demons, slamming them back through the blackened mist and to the ground with a satisfying thud.

"Ha!" I shouted, feeling a burst of pride at my own skill. And Tran said I wasn't even a real witch. "Take that. You want some more, eh? You black-eyed, mother—"

With a pop, the fire on the first higher demon went out. His shoulders rocked up and down as he laughed. He looked at me, his ebony eyes glistening with amusement.

Damn. There wasn't a scratch on him. Not even a scorch mark on his suit. They either had wicked tailors in the Netherworld, or he was immune to my magic.

I gave him a nervous smile. "Can't blame a girl for trying," I said as I took a step back.

He wiped the arms of his jacket with his free hand. "No. And you can't blame a demon for killing a mortal either. It's in our nature."

The sound of shoes scuffing the pavement reached me, and his brothers appeared through the wall of black mist. Swell.

The higher demon bared his teeth in an evil grin before lowering himself into an attack stance.

I took another step back. I wasn't stupid. Straining my mind, I searched for a spell or dark curse that would actually work on a higher demon. Which were slim. I focused my will on my rings, concentrating, and I felt a gentle pull on my core.

His fist came out of nowhere and hit me in the side of the head. It threw me hard to my left, and if I hadn't planted my legs at the last minute, it would have thrown me to the ground. And then I'd have been finished.

My concentration vanished. I stumbled and whirled around, blinking the black and white spots from my eyes. God. That. Hurt.

"Amateur little witch," snarled the higher demon. "You'll have to do better than that if you want to defeat us with your little witch tricks. Think bigger."

"All righty, then." I blinked, my head throbbing with pain, and shouted, "Sphaeras!" A sphere-shaped shield of golden energy rose up from the pavement and pulled to a close just over my head.

"There you go," I howled. "*Bigger.*"

Okay, so it wasn't a sphere of fire or some dark demon magic, but I needed to think. I needed time to contemplate how I was going to get out of this mess—alive.

My shield wouldn't last forever, but I needed to protect my ass in order to *save* my ass.

Think, Sam. Think!

If I couldn't defeat them on my own, I'd have to find someone or something that could.

And I had just the demon in mind to kick some higher demons' butts.

Pulling out my chalk from my pocket, I fell to the hard pavement and began to draw a summoning circle.

When in doubt, always summon a deceitful demon from the seventy-two listed in the Ars Goetia that you can control. Or one with a giant mouth, full of sharp teeth.

Through the shimmering golden energy, I saw the two other demons join their brother just as I finished my circle. The three of them stood facing my golden sphere, their body language confident and sly, and I didn't like it.

I smiled and waved my fingers at them. "Oh, boy, do I have a surprise for you guys." I laughed, and I began to draw the summoning triangle-shaped sigil. These fools had no idea who they were messing with.

Next, I wrote the name Buné in the center. Buné was a massive, three-headed dragon demon. Three giant dragon maws to each fit a higher demon's head. It was perfect.

No way could these higher demons take on a two-thousand-pound dragon. And he was cute too, purple with a fiery red mane of hair that spread from the tips of his heads to his tail. But he did have a temper, especially when someone stepped on his tail. Love dragons.

Heart thumping, I shot to my feet again while channeling the magic from the summoning circle and triangle. "I conjure you, Buné, demon of the Netherworld—"

There was a sudden snap, and my protection shield fell.

Ooops.

My bravado plummeted as I watched the last of my golden energy shimmer and disappear around the edges of three death blades pointed at me.

I stilled, and then I glowered. "You bastards burst my bubble."

The higher demons grinned, their gray teeth like that of cadavers. They made odd little gestures with their death blades, and threads of black mixed with gold light leaped toward their arms in spiraling paths. It was almost as though their blades had consumed my sphere like they consumed souls.

I knew I had seconds to react before they did. I never stopped drawing on my rings, pulling the energy into me.

"For that, I will break every bone in your body, and then I will take your witch flesh over and over again," said the middle higher demon. His gaze jumped to mine, his delight lighting his black eyes. "We are going to have some fun, witch bitch."

I seethed. "Call me that again, and I'll have to agree." My frustration gave my voice some anger.

The higher demons moved.

And so did I.

In a smooth motion, I pushed the energy from my rings and threw it. "Vento!" I shouted, and a blast of powerful wind hit the higher demons, throwing them back and giving me those precious seconds to turn around and run. I knew my spells wouldn't hurt them, but what else could I do? Give a witch a break!

I wasn't known for my great bursts of speed, nor my talent to see in the dark. So I didn't get very far—five feet, give or take a few inches—before I felt the pain.

Agony exploded from nowhere inside me, and I screamed. It felt like my lungs were on fire. My concentration shattered, and the bits of the spell I'd pulled from my rings vanished. My knees gave way, and I hit the pavement beside what looked like a metal garbage bin.

The pain concentrated toward my lower back. Instinctively, I reached out, my fingers finding wetness under my T-shirt. They'd stabbed me with one of their death blades. It was enough to cause extreme physical misery with its poison but not enough to kill. Teeth clenched, I lifted my head to find the higher demons standing above me, the black haze moving around them like eerie black capes.

Great. That's all I needed, *super*-higher demons.

I grabbed the sides of the bin and pulled myself up, trying not to hurl at the stench of garbage that assaulted my nose. "You know," I said, struggling to my feet and taking their not-attacking-me as a sign I could actually do just that. "Three against one," I panted, trying to hide the fact that I felt as though my spinal column was melting. "That's not exactly fair."

"We're higher demons," said one of the gray-skinned clones. "We don't *do* fair. We do whatever we like."

"Not with me, you won't," I hissed as another wave of pain hit me. "You're all going to die." Blocking out as much pain as I could, I pulled on the energy from my rings.

In unison, the higher demons laughed. The sound was as unpleasant as if they'd scratched their fingernails on a blackboard. I hated that.

"How sweet of you to think you can best us," said one of the higher demons, coming closer and causing the stench of sulfur to fill my nose and mix with the week-old garbage stench. He carved the air with his death blade and said, "You should take comfort in knowing you won't die alone."

The higher demons blurred and came at me in a rush, but I'd been expecting that.

Since I knew my magic did diddly squat to them, I did the only other thing I could.

I reached in the bin, grabbed handfuls of garbage, tried not to vomit at the cold, squishy substance between my fingers, and hurled it at them.

It worked like a charm.

The three of them froze, disgust plastered on their faces as they screamed something incoherent and bestial. They struggled against chunks of rotten meat and fruit all mixed in with a brown and green slime. Their shouts became lost in their attempt to wipe themselves clean. The three of them started clawing at their clothes and faces in a frenzy.

It was the strangest thing I'd ever seen. The great and powerful higher demons had a weakness. And that weakness was cleanliness. Go figure.

As for me? Well, I took it as my cue to get the hell out of there.

I spun around and ran through the black haze toward what I hoped was the street. I just needed to get to a safe place for now. I'd come back for Poe. I was no good to him if I was dead.

My legs, heavy with the pain in my lower back, burned with every step. I knew it was the poison. If the cut had been deep, my legs wouldn't have moved at all.

I kept going. I could see a break in the haze, a spot where the darkness wasn't so dark, as if someone had turned on a light. Always follow the light. The sense of freedom pushed my legs harder. I was going to make it.

A fist came out of nowhere and connected with the side of my head.

I pitched sideways, my hip exploding with pain as I hit the hard pavement.

Well, my escape didn't last long.

Head throbbing, I felt a presence above me. Twisting, I snarled and kicked out with my leg as hard as I could, hitting a higher demon in the shins and taking him down to the ground. No sooner did he crumple and another higher demon appeared in my line of sight.

Before I could move, he grabbed me by the throat and lifted me up, my boots grazing the ground as I stared into his black eyes.

"Not bad for a witch," said the higher demon, his face smeared with what looked like pea soup. If I could have smiled, I would have. "That some martial arts or something?"

I struggled to breathe. "It's called asshole."

He squeezed harder. "You shouldn't have soiled us with your human waste. You're going to pay for that."

"You shouldn't have tried to kill me," I wheezed, and the other two higher demons appeared at his side, looking equally pissed and covered in slime. Boo-hoo.

I tapped into my rings, willing the magic to come, but it didn't answer. Either my magic was spent, or the death blade's poison was keeping me from reaching it.

The higher demon with his hand wrapped around my neck smiled wickedly, seeing the fear in my eyes.

Was this it? Was this how I was going to die? Killed by some demon thugs in a dark alley? Talk about a cliché way to die. There was nothing honorable about dying in that way. Especially for a Beaumont witch. What would my Aunt Evanora say?

If only I could reach Poe...

"That's how the big boys do it, little witch," said the higher demon with satisfaction as he pulled me closer.

I pursed my lips and spit in his face.

The demon lost his smile, and a snarl replaced it. "You're asking for it," he said, and he used his free hand to wipe his face of my white foamy spit. I'd gotten him good. Yay for me.

"Poe?" I gasped, praying that my familiar was still alive somewhere in that horrid black mist. "Poe! I need help!"

The higher demons laughed, mocking and hissing, thick with something wet and bubbly erupting from them. When it came to spooky laughter, they were the champs, hands down.

Fear coursed through me like an icy ribbon and settled into my core. I was going to die.

And what image flashed before my eyes? Logan's lips. Damn. I was such a girl.

A blade with a coiling black shadowy mist appeared before my eyes.

"I'm going to cut out those pretty eyes of yours," said the higher demon. "Then I'm going to eat them, one by one, while you watch until you can't see anymore. But you will feel the pain."

Terror slid to my middle, and his black eyes darkened. "Time so say bye-bye, little witch," he said in warning.

His blade grazed the skin on my neck, my flesh tingling as the cold metal slipped along my jawline and then back, tracing a line along my neck. I felt the demon's grip tighten in anticipation of my death.

I struggled in his grasp, in my panic, and then a new fear slid into place behind it. I didn't want to die. Not like this. Tears welled in my eyes.

Cauldron save me...

The blade pricked the skin on my neck—
And then retreated.

With my lungs burning from the lack of air, I blinked through my tears as the higher demon whipped his head around at something behind him.

An orange glow broke through the black haze. Even from my limited vision I could feel its rays upon my skin, warming my face with its presence.

Morning was approaching.

The demons hissed at the sun—a hateful enemy, the one that would destroy them.

The pressure around my neck released, and I dropped like a bag of sand. My feet did nothing to break my fall, and I hit the pavement hard on my left hip.

The higher demons squealed and scrambled like frightened rats as they jumped around seeking shadows and trying to avoid the sunlight, their black eyes wide in panic. It was a glorious sight.

I knew they'd be demon toast if they stayed a second longer. There was nothing more deadly to a demon than the sun. It was equivalent to the myth about vampires and the sun. Vampires *could* go in the sun because of the mortal blood in their veins, whereas higher demons would combust into ash, just like an expensive Hollywood visual effect.

Squealing in protest, the higher demons dispersed before the light. They scurried down the street and scampered away into the last of the black haze, back to whatever Rift they crawled out of.

I smiled. "Bon voyage, bastards," I wheezed and rubbed my neck.

With a last shimmer, the unnatural black haze lifted and evaporated like dew in a morning sun. A few seconds later, there was only me.

And Poe.

Poe!

I picked myself up and stumbled into the alley, not really recognizing anything I saw since just a few moments ago everything had been covered by a black mist.

A small black bundle the size of a house cat lay on the pavement next to one of the building's brick walls.

I rushed over and fell to my knees. A moan escaped me as the cut on my lower back ripped. The skin on my fingers burned as I scraped them on the asphalt, gently slipping them under Poe's body. Carefully, I picked up the raven with my hands, rubbing my thumb across the feathers on his belly.

"Poe?" My throat tight, and I swallowed, trying not to cry. *Please, not my Poe. Not Poe.*

His eyes opened. "What did I miss?" asked the raven. He shifted to his feet, shook his feathers, and climbed up my right arm.

I sighed in relief. "Thank the cauldron." I ran my eyes over the bird. "I'm not seeing any visible marks. What did they do to you—"

The clink of scraping boots jerked my attention behind me.

The air was bitter despite the bright morning sun, and I squinted at two human males walking briskly toward me. The two men wore navy uniforms, black boots, and finished the look with navy caps.

Cops. I swallowed the nausea in my mouth. It looked like New York City's finest were coming to greet me. Swell.

CHAPTER
9

I liked nothing better than finishing a night where I'd almost died in the hands of higher demons by pulling out my acting chops and playing the innocent human to the police.

"Oh shit," I breathed.

"Oh cops," said the bird.

Damn it. My stomach quailed a little bit, but I pushed it away. Who knew? Maybe they weren't here for me. I was tired, in pain, and just wanted to go home. Straining, I got to my feet and started walking in the opposite direction, hoping they'd just ignore me. I hadn't done anything after all—nothing that concerned the human population.

"You there. Stop right there!" said one of the policemen.

I kept walking with Poe balanced on my arm like a hunting falcon, as every step sent a wave of jarring pain through my lower back.

"I said *stop!*"

Okay, then. He said *stop*. Guess that meant I had to obey. My mood soured, and I felt I was going to lose it. Damn the human police. I really didn't need them nosing in my business right now. I had enough going on in my own paranormal world, thank you very much.

Resolute, I turned slowly and raised my hands. Poe jumped to my shoulder, his feathers tickling the side of my face.

"Is walking in an alley a crime nowadays?" I asked, pulling my face into the sweetest smile I could muster, which probably looked as fake as it felt. It was all I had.

The policeman with the beard, which he kept clipped close to his face, glanced down at his cell phone and then back at me, his fortysomething face pinched in a frown. He had a strong jaw, and his dark eyes flashed. Even with his cap, I could see his hair was cropped close to his scalp, Marine length.

I clenched my jaw, fighting with the alarm bells setting off in my gut. I didn't like this.

Still holding my hands in the air like a fool, my gaze darted to the other officer. He looked to be in his twenties, with a Latino flair, and a plain, forgettable face. His mouth was slightly open, and he wore one of those quizzical expressions, like he was waiting for the other guy to give him orders since he had no idea what do to. Great. A rookie cop. This was just getting better.

Seeing as they weren't pointing their guns at me, I took it as a sign they weren't going to shoot me and lowered my hands. I swallowed. So far, so good.

"Why don't you spell their asses," muttered the bird. "A few memory charms, and we're golden."

"Can't," I whispered, my eyes never leaving the older cop. What was he looking for? "The demons stabbed me with one of their blades, and now I can't seem to draw any magic from my rings."

I forced a blank expression on my face, trying to keep my concern from showing. Two cops in Mystic Quarter? Not good. Even more disturbing was their interest in me.

Poe shifted on my shoulder, and the younger cop flinched, his jaw clenching as he tried to keep his face from showing any emotion. Amateur. I bit my tongue hard so I wouldn't laugh. It was obvious. The cop was terrified of Poe. It was smeared all over his face. I'd seen that look before, the one that said, if you looked at the raven, you'd be cursed with something foul and irreversible, or worse, if the raven happened to touch you—well—you'd drop dead right there and then. Humans. Such scaredy-cats.

The rookie cop's eyes were glued to Poe. "Do you have a license for that animal?" asked the young cop.

"Who's he calling a bloody animal?" cawed Poe, his talons biting through my shirt and into my flesh.

87

Reaching up, I stroked Poe's chest, trying to calm him before he did anything stupid, like poke the young cop's eyes out.

"Since when do I need a license for having a pet raven?" I asked. "Do you need a permit for a goldfish?" I added, laughing. They didn't laugh.

"Ma'am, under federal law, it's illegal to keep crows as pets," said the rookie officer importantly, his expression transitioning from sly to unpleasant.

"Raven," I corrected. Bummer. I had no idea. But human laws didn't apply to us witches and half-breeds. Granted, Poe wasn't even a *real* raven. He was a demon, so that didn't count.

"He's not a pet," I remedied, securing a low *thank you* from Poe. "He's my friend. He comes and goes as he pleases. He's not in a cage, if that's what you mean. So there's really no problem."

The young cop snickered. "What kind of a freak are you?"

The kind that would have you piss blood for a week. I glowered, not caring one bit that he could read the hatred on my face and loathing in my eyes. I wanted him to see how I felt.

"What's this about?" I asked instead.

The young cop's face was blank as he avoided my gaze and glanced at his partner as though waiting for the more experienced cop to take over. His posture and expression both said he was way too cool to care what I thought, but I could practically smell the uncertainty he was working hard to hide.

"He smells like a rookie," snickered Poe, pulling that thought out of my head. He had to stop that. The bird shifted closer to my ear and whispered, "What are they doing on our side of town anyway?"

"That," I mumbled under my breath, catching the frown on the rookie's face at my conversing with my bird, "is something I'd really like to know."

Still, the dark witch court was on the outskirts of Mystic Quarter, which made it easier for cops or a roaming human to wander into our community without really knowing. Still, something had drawn them out. I glanced back at the rookie, seeing nothing to help me understand why they were here. The older cop was going through his phone again.

"You haven't told me what I've done?" I began, irritated. "You can't just go around harassing decent folks for nothing. I'm just walking here."

A sly, satisfied grin appeared on the rookie's face. His eyes narrowed as he thought about his answer. "You look pretty suspicious to me. You look like you've been in a fight or something. Care to tell me what happened?"

Hands on my hips, I glared at the young cop. "Nothing happened," I said, not appreciating the way his smile widened. Creep. "I'm just on my way home. That's all."

Eyebrows high, the rookie cop asked flatly, "What's your name?"

I clamped my mouth shut. This wasn't my first time being stopped by human cops nor would it be my last. But I'd always managed to get away before I had to give them my name—usually aided by some magic. Trouble was, if they got my name, they'd know who I was and where I lived. And that would be bad. If human cops started to snoop around Mystic Quarter, in our paranormal business where they didn't belong, it would get *really* ugly—for them.

"Your name," repeated the young cop, his dark eyes narrowing. The first hints of stubble were showing on his chin.

It was my time to raise my brows. "What? You think because you asked s-o-o-o nicely, I'm actually going to give it to you?" What a dumbass. I wasn't giving him anything.

The bearded cop was still scrolling through his phone. What was going on?

I stared at the cops. "I'd really love to stay and chat, but there's somewhere I gotta be." Like my bed. "So if you're not going to charge me for anything—because I haven't done anything—I'm going to go now."

"You're not going anywhere," answered the rookie cop, his hand moving to his gun on his hip.

I frowned. Now why the hell did he have to go and do that. "Then tell me what this is about."

"No."

"Can you give me a clue?"

"No."

I made a face. "Is *no* the only thing you know how to say?" I added, watching as the rookie's face went a shade darker, the rim of his ears reddening. Cops were so easily provoked and jumpy. Under different circumstances, they were my favorite humans to play with. But not tonight.

"Sam," warned Poe, "if you keep pissing them off, it won't go well for us. Just play dumb. Dumb always works."

I let out a sigh through my nose. If only my magic could work, I'd be on my way home right about now, with two oblivious cops on their merry way out of Mystic Quarter.

My anger deepened when I realized the higher demons had stabbed me on purpose. They knew cutting me with their death blades would render my magic obsolete. I hated those black-eyed bastards.

Plus I knew they'd be back. They were sent by this Vorkol to kill me. But I wasn't about to let that happen. I was going to find out who Vorkol was, and I knew just the demon to ask.

"It's her," said the bearded policeman as he neared, and my heart gave a thump before settling into a faster pace at my sudden panic. He stared at his cell phone and then his gaze fixed me. "Yeah. That's her, all right."

"What about me?" I narrowed my eyes, not liking the triumphant tone in his voice or the recognition that crossed his face. It was almost as though... almost as though he recognized me.

"What's going on, Sam?" Poe's voice rang loudly, drawing the attention of the cops. But I wasn't worried about that. To them, Poe's voice was just a regular raven's caw and not an actual language. Sucked to be human.

"I don't know." I strained to control my breathing, my mind sifting through thoughts as I scrambled to find a plan of escape but came up short.

Poe's claws gripped my shoulder hard making me flinch. "You need to run. Run, Sam!"

The urgency in his voice had my tension rising. "I can't," I said, though my posture had shifted subconsciously, "If I run, they'll shoot me." And I seriously doubted I'd get two paces before I'd be tackled by the rookie. Hell, he looked like the type who'd love to tackle a female.

"Cuff her," said the bearded cop to the younger policeman.

Oh. Hell. No. "Excuse me?" I shouted. "You can't do this. Not until you tell me what the hell is going on!"

The rookie cop started forward but then halted. He glanced at his partner. "What about the crow?"

The bearded cop's eyes moved to Poe. "Kill it if it bites you."

A vicious snarl escaped me. "I'll kill you first if you touch a feather on my bird." Immediately, I knew that was the wrong thing to say as I saw the deepening scowl on the bearded cop's face. Oh well. Too late to take it back. Not that I really wanted to.

"Did you hear that, Sergio?" The bearded cop slipped his phone into his pocket. "She just threatened the life of a police officer."

"And you just threatened to kill my raven, you prick." A sound of disgust slipped from me, and for a second I really wished my magic rings worked, if only to hex these cops. The Casual Castration hex came to mind.

"Hands behind your back. Do it," snarled the rookie, though his eyes remained on my familiar. "We're charging you with assault on a police officer."

Bastards. "Poe," I whispered. "You're my one phone call. Get help."

"Got it." The bird leaped off my shoulder and took off into the morning sky, his wings beating strong and true. I took a half second feeling of comfort knowing he was safe.

Lips pursed, I glared at the cop. "I know my rights, copper," I growled, though not entirely true. "I—I have a right to a lawyer." Didn't I?

"You do," answered the young cop, his jaw muscles tensing as he stepped forward. Metal handcuffs hung in his right hand, winking in the morning sun.

My blood pressure spiked to a new high. I took a step back. I couldn't let these cops arrest me. I was a witch, damn it. Not some street thug. I had to do something. And whatever it was, I had to do it fast.

"If you resist," he said, seeing my intention as he made a show of the cuffs by spinning them around his finger, "it'll only get worse for you."

Not as much as it'll get worse for you. I gritted my jaw. "How can it be worse than being arrested by human cops when I didn't do anything?" Oops. That kinda just slipped.

A frown marred his face at the mention of *human*. "You are a *freak*."

93

"I'll take that as I compliment, coming from you." I stood there with my legs cemented to the pavement. Without my magic, I was out of options.

He took my silence as a sign that I wouldn't run. He moved behind me and yanked my arms hard behind my back. The bastard did that on purpose.

Shit. Shit. Shit.

I felt the cold metal around my wrists and heard the clamping sound of the cuffs snapping around them. I didn't even move.

Heat rushed from my neck to my face. Feeling like the biggest fool in all of Mystic Quarter, I threw my gaze around the streets, hoping no half-breed was witnessing my utter humiliation. I didn't see anyone, but that didn't mean no one was watching.

I wiggled against my restraints, watching as the older cop walked back to his police car with the stride of a confident and satisfied man. It seemed as though he'd saved the city from harm by arresting a serial killer on the FBI's Ten Most Wanted List.

"You're making a mistake," I hissed, my tension rising and mixing with my fear of the unknown and my anger at these foolish cops. "I haven't done anything!"

"Yeah, you have," came the rookie cop's voice from behind me. The air shifted behind me, and I felt him move closer. Then he said in my ear, "You're under arrest for the murder of Emma Woods."

My face went slack. My heart stopped, sank to my feet, and splattered against the pavement.

"You have the right to remain silent," said the cop, and he shoved me hard, making me stumble. "Anything you say may be used against you in a court of law. You have the right to an attorney before speaking to the police and to have an attorney present during questioning now or in the future. If you can't afford an attorney, one will be appointed for you..."

The rest of his words were lost under the pounding of blood in my ears. I was being arrested for the witch murder I was trying to solve.

And there was nothing I could do about it.

CHAPTER
10

Human jail sucks.

I sat on a hard metal bench, my back against the brick wall in a six-by-eight cell. Surprisingly, I was alone. The only other person in the holding cells was a man lying down on the floor in the neighboring cell across from mine. He hadn't moved for the past twelve hours, so I figured he was sleeping—or perhaps dead. His clothes were torn, shabby, and smeared with brown stains, like he'd pulled them from the dumpster. His face was so filthy and covered by so much beard and hair it was impossible to tell his age.

The holding cells were made up of four different blocks, stuffed in a hallway and tucked at the other end of a room through a steel door. The only window in this damn place was secured to that steel door. And through the tiny window was our jailer.

He sat behind a desk, his eyes heavy with boredom and maybe even a little irritation. He was bald, large and soft, an indication that he'd spent way too many years sitting at that desk.

The only way out was through my cell's barred door and then out that steel door. With my magic, I could have blasted it off its hinges, but without my power, I had nothing.

Much to my horror, I'd fallen asleep for a couple of hours here and there in my sitting position, perfect to give me neck pain. The guard had allowed me a bathroom break and some water, but no food. My rumbling stomach was enough to wake the dead in the neighboring morgue just down the street.

I'd been able to assess my wound in the bathroom mirror. As soon as I pulled up my shirt, I'd nearly vomited.

The wound was unlike anything I'd ever seen—a two-inch dark purple cut with black, spidery veins surrounding it like a web. A drift of rotten flesh smell had made my knees wobble, and that's when the nausea hit.

Damn. I was rotting.

It's not like I could ask the human police for help. This was a demonic wound, so nothing the human doctors possessed could help me. I needed magic.

With working magic, I would have summoned Marchosias from the Ars Goetia, a wolf demon with griffin wings, to fly me home. I could have done lots of things if I had a spark of magic in me.

A lick of fear rose in me and stayed. I knew if I didn't get this wound looked after soon, I'd be in big trouble—the dying kind of trouble. I couldn't even perform a healing sigil. Nothing worked. So I did the next best thing. I washed it out with soap and hot water. Once I was out of this jail, my grandfather or my aunt could heal it for me.

They couldn't keep me in here forever... could they?

When the fever set in, I knew I was in worse trouble.

Sweat ran down the sides of my temples, but my face still blazed with a fevered intensity. I was hot and cold all at once, shivering as though I'd stepped outside naked in the middle of March in subzero temperatures. My teeth clamped together with a chill, and panic filled me. The pain was almost unreal as the fever pitched, hitting me with another wave of nausea.

Vertigo hit me next, and I clutched at the edge of the bench, trying not to fall over. If the higher demons had stabbed me twice with their death blades, I would have died of its poison by now. The poison was deadly to angels and the angel-born, and apparently it didn't do us half-breeds any favors either. It was the mortal blood. It had to be.

Where are you, Poe?

Twelve hours was an insane amount of time to have to wait for a rescue from my familiar. Yes, he was wild and sometimes forgot his place when something sparkly grabbed his attention, but he'd been there when the human police arrested me. He knew I was in trouble. So why wasn't he here yet? Had something happened to him? Had the higher demons' black mist finally killed him?

I clenched my jaw and swallowed the bile that rose in the back of my throat. My thoughts were rambling now, fear and dread making them scamper around like a mischief of frightened rats. I couldn't let myself fall into despair. That would be turning my back on who I was—a dark witch. We didn't despair. We got shit done. I needed focus. I needed to concentrate and think of a plan. If only I could get that jailer in here, I could use my Goddess-given boobs to win him over. Possibly even convince him to let me go free, with more persuasion.

Granted, that would be hard to pull off right now, seeing as I felt like I'd contracted the Ebola virus.

I felt the presence of eyes on me and swept my gaze to the window. The jailer was watching me, his eyes lit with curiosity. A satisfied smile wrinkled his face when he saw me looking. The bastard could see I was sick, and he chose to sit there and do nothing.

Was it even legal to keep me locked up for so long without so much as a phone call? I doubted it. These guys were shady.

I raised my trembling hand and gave him the finger. His scowl made me feel a tad better, but my minor feeling of elation was quickly drowned by another wave of fever. Yup, I was going to die in this wretched place.

Cauldron be damned. I could do nothing but wallow in my pain. Was this how humans felt? Powerless? Normal? Boring? Thank the cauldron I was born a witch.

Sleep encroached on the edges of my mind, and I let it in.

I closed my eyes and tried to calm my breathing to better suppress the fever. I thought of Logan's lips—such fine, glorious, and kissable lips. Such a fine and glorious behind. My own lips curled into a smile as I pictured the angel-born without any clothes on, which was surprisingly easy considering all his clothes were molded snugly around his tight, athletic body.

What? I was single. It was perfectly acceptable to fantasize about hot angel-borns even though I was a dark witch.

Yup. He was even more glorious naked— hairless, with six-pack abs, and thick, solid biceps that could pick me up and pin me to one of these walls...

My fever spiked.

Was Logan a tentative lover? Or was he wild and tantalizingly dangerous with an insatiable thirst of desire. A hot thrill spun through me. But then the feeling faded almost as soon as it had appeared. I might never see him again.

I sighed heavily. "I hate this place."

"Then let's get you out of here," came a familiar male voice.

My eyes flashed open, and I forgot to breathe.

Logan stood in my cell.

He wore his usual black—black pants and black leather jacket over a black T-shirt. His dark hair looked black in the dimness of the room. His brown eyes searched my face, and I found myself incapable of looking away. Those were such pretty, pretty eyes. He had that effect on me. He was every bit as handsome a bastard as I remembered. Perhaps a tad more.

And yet I wasn't the type of female who was easily persuaded by a pretty face and tight behind. But it *was* a dream, so why the hell not?

I let out a feverish giggle. "You're not really here. I'm dreaming." And it's a very good dream...

"She's losing it," came another voice, and a black bird fluttered into the cell and flew to Logan's shoulder. "Look at her. She's delirious with fever. We need to get her out of here before the poison spreads to her brain."

Another giggle escaped me. "Poe? Get out of my dream." He was probably only showing up in my dream because I was so worried about him.

"Looks like it already has," said Logan, his voice deep with concern.

The raven leaped off Logan's shoulder and landed next to me on the bench. "Wake up, Sam. This isn't funny."

"Get out of my dream, Poe," I said again, annoyed that I couldn't even control my own dream. I reached out to push him away but missed.

101

"It's not a dream, you idiot. Wake up!" The raven clamped his beak around my index finger and bit down hard.

"Ow!" I yelled, and snatched up my hand, my heart pounding in my finger. "You little shit. You bit me! That's twice you bit me!" Wait a freaking second. That was *real* pain. If I felt real pain, then...

That sobered me right up.

Holy hell. Logan was actually here and real, and I'd nearly said something really, really stupid.

The Goddess must still love me.

Using the wall as support, I balanced myself to my feet, trying to gain back some of what little self-respect I had left. "How did you get in here?" I asked, my eyes flicking past Logan's shoulder to my cell's open barred door and finally to the steel door. That one too was open. The desk was also empty of its guard. "What happened to the guard?"

"He went for a nap," answered Logan. He hurried forward. "We don't have much time before he wakes up and is really pissed. I've got a car parked outside. You think you can walk?" He reached out for me, but I brushed his hand away.

"Of course I can walk." I pushed off the wall. My legs wavered a moment before I straightened myself. "Just not for very long." Now that my delusions were gone, the pain and the nausea came rolling back in. Note to self: never get stabbed by a death blade again.

"We would have come sooner," said Logan, his features pinched in worry, "but we had to wait for the shift change. Less witnesses. Less mess."

I nodded as I strained to keep from falling over. Made sense. But something didn't. I looked down at the raven. Strange that he'd gone to Logan instead of my grandfather or even my aunt.

Worse, I had morning breath—or evening breath—depending on how you looked at it. I hadn't brushed my teeth in more than twelve hours. It was what I liked to call, mud mouth—when I actually felt a thin layer of mud on my teeth and gums.

This was just fantastic.

And Logan, well, he looked good. Too good. His stubble and the heavy weariness on him made him look damn sexy. And he was just too close, too tempting. He was just a tad taller than me, and I was suddenly a hundred times more nervous.

Get a grip, Sam. He's just a man.

I glanced away before I started to drool because that would seriously cramp my style.

"Logan. Why are you here?" My voice came out in a grunt as I attempted to rid myself of my idiotic thoughts.

"Poe told me what happened with the higher demons." Logan shrugged. "Isn't it obvious? I came to rescue you. And... it looks to me like you needed rescuing." A sly smile crept across his face as he took in my sore state.

If I wasn't so red in the face from my fever, I would have felt a gargantuan flush right about now. My free hand wanted to tap down any misplaced hairs, but I stopped myself before I made myself look like a fool. If I did, he'd think I cared what he thought of me. I didn't.

Logan's gaze moved to my lips, and a faint smile quirked the corner of his mouth. The memory of our kiss apparently amused him to no end. When our eyes met, his widened a fraction, and I knew he was thinking of the kiss we'd shared.

Okay. So *this* was what this was about. He obviously thought I wanted to sleep with him because of one, teeny-weeny kiss. Okay, maybe, just a little. But he didn't have to know. And I wasn't *that* easy, either. I didn't rip off my clothes at the sight of a pretty face. After five glasses of wine—maybe.

Arrogant male. If he thought I was going to fall all over him because of a kiss, or his drool-worthy physique, he didn't know me at all.

My anger rocketed, replacing my fever and lameness for a moment. "I don't need your help. I was doing fine on my own." *If I can just keep the room from spinning.*

Logan grinned. "Right."

Keep breathing. "The human police were just about to let me go," I lied, my voice coming out a little angrier than I intended.

"Sure."

"They have nothing on me."

Logan raised his brows. "Really?" He turned toward the guard's desk. "So all those photos of you kneeling next to the dead witch on his computer are fake? That's some damn fine Photoshop work if they are."

Poe snorted and I shot him a look.

Crap. Why didn't I take that human woman's phone?

I heard a flap of wings, and Poe landed on my shoulder. I turned and looked at the bird. Seeing the question on my face, the raven said, "Don't kill the messenger raven," he whispered, just out of Logan's earshot. "I'm here. Aren't I?"

"Why is *he* here?" I mumbled. The room started to spin again as some of my anger was wearing off.

The raven let out an exaggerated sigh. "I looked for your grandfather *all* over Mystic Quarter. Nobody's seen him. And your aunt is gone to Louisiana for some dark witch convention. He was the only one available."

Great. My familiar sought help from an angel-born before looking to another witch. What did that mean? And what did it mean that he actually came?

Poe made a noise in his throat. "Did you know he's one of the top angel-borns here in New York?"

My eyes went to Logan. "Yeah. He's an operative. I know."

"No," said the bird, and he leaned against my cheek. His breath was warm. "I mean, yes, he's an operative for the angel-borns, but he's also the new Head of House Michael."

I shifted position to get a better look at the angel-born. I'd remembered seeing his P-shaped birthmark on his neck—the archangel Michael's sigil—branding him not only as an angel-born but also from that specific house. I couldn't see it now under his jacket, but I knew it was there. Looking at him now, he seemed too young to hold such an important post within the angel-born hierarchy.

Well. Looks like Logan wasn't just a pretty face with a nice tight behind after all. Interesting.

But it also made him even more dangerous.

What was also dangerous was the rate in which I was about to keel over if I didn't get some healing magic in me soon.

I took a step forward, and it was all I could do not to spew the remnants of yesterday's meal all over my cell floor. This was not how I wanted the Head of House Michael to see me—weak, sick, and a total mess.

"I might throw up in your car," I added, not looking at Logan as I took baby steps toward the door.

"It's not my car," answered Logan, a smile in his voice.

Okay, then.

Walking like a hundred-year-old witch, bent with arthritis, I left the jail behind me, praying I'd never see the inside of it ever again. But my mind was racing and jumping with questions.

Why did the Head of House Michael come to rescue me?

CHAPTER
11

"Are you almost done?" My voice sounded impatient. I was hungry, and the intoxicating smell of the grilled cheese with tomatoes and onions simmering in the frying pan had me salivating. Fatigue rolled over me in a sluggish wave as I lay on my stomach on the kitchen island, the granite cool against my skin.

"I would be if you'd stop fidgeting," barked my grandfather, standing next to me. "This is a complicated spell. You just don't remove the death blade's poison like you would a wart from your ass. It takes concentration, technique, and expertise. One wrong move, and the infliction could get worse. There are levels to peel off, if you will, before reaching the poison."

"Like an onion," came Poe's voice as he landed on the stool next to the counter. A large watch hung from his left foot. "He's basically saying you're like a vegetable."

I made a face. "Where did you get that watch?" I asked, not remembering seeing it before now. Must have been the fever.

"From our friendly neighborhood jailer," said the bird, puffing out his chest proudly and looking like an overgrown pigeon. "I took it as payment for wrongful imprisonment. I could have gouged out his eyes, but taking the watch was a lot less messy."

On any other night, I would have scolded my feathered friend for stealing from a human, and a police human at that, but I was too tired to care. All I knew was that Logan had somehow managed to knock out our jailor and two other policemen who were working the night shift. I'd never even noticed Poe taking the watch from the unconscious human. Probably because I'd been too busy trying not to vomit all over myself.

Logan. Now he was a curious one. He could have refused to help, or better yet, have sent someone in his place. But the angel-born, the new Head of House Michael, had come on his own to bust me out of jail.

I let out a sigh. I'd been on the bloody counter for more than two hours, and although my grandfather's wizardry had managed to remove most of my fever and had suppressed some of the pain in my lower back, I was running out of patience. He promised minimal scarring, not that it made a difference. It would only add to the litany of scars I carried.

"You said it would take five minutes." Yes, I sounded ungrateful, but I was starving, my hunger turning me into Godzilla the witch, without the lizard skin.

My grandfather made a disapproving grunt in his throat. "If I don't remove *all* the poison, it will spread farther into your blood and eventually kill you. Are you willing to risk that?"

"You don't have to be so grumpy. I'm the one in pain here. I'm the one who got stabbed." I turned my hip to look at him and groaned at the pain. I gritted my teeth, feeling light-headed and more tired than angry.

"Stop moving!" shouted my grandfather, his finger pointed at my eye as he moved around and appeared in my line of sight. "If you don't stop moving," he warned, "I'm going to hit you with a sleeping spell."

My mouth fell open. "You wouldn't dare."

A wicked grin spread on the old witch's face, the smile of a madman contemplating an evil scheme. "Try me, my dear girl. I might be old, but I can still whip your ass with my magic. Don't temp me."

A smile tugged at my lips. "Fine." I settled back down with my chin resting on the hard counter. "I'll *try* not to move."

Poe snorted in a way only birds could snort. The raven looked positively happy, watching me on display like this. Thank the cauldron Logan wasn't here. Though I didn't know why I cared. He'd already seen me at my worst.

My grandfather wrinkled up his eyes at the corners. "You should be thankful I'm not sticking you with a needle," he said as he tightened his blue bathrobe and moved to the counter next to the island.

If you stuck me with a needle, I might have to kill you, Gramps.

My grandfather wiped his brow, and the fine seams and wrinkles around his face deepened in the shadows, making him look old and frail in the kitchen light. "Never quite understood the logic with human doctors and their needles," he said. "Why inject a foreign solution into the body when you're supposed to take out what's making them ill? They're just pumping the body with hazardous cocktails instead of removing the illness. Strange medicine, that is."

I had to agree. I could never understand human medicine myself. How could you heal anything without magic? It sounded like lunacy. Magic made sense. Needles did not.

I gestured to the frying pan. "You think I'll manage to taste that grilled cheese in this century?"

"That's gratitude for you." My grandfather sighed. "In my days, we respected our elder witches. Disrespect and insolence? If we spoke out of turn, we'd lose a finger. Sometimes two fingers. Sometimes an ear or an eye. My best friend, Ludwig, lost his eyebrows. Never was the same after that."

"I'm glad things have changed and evolved from the more barbaric ways of treating each other," I grumbled, glad I wasn't born in that generation. Otherwise, knowing my attitude, I would have lost more than a few fingers.

My grandfather made a huff. "Not really. And we most certainly didn't disrespect a witch while they were *trying* to help after spending *hours* repairing your body."

"Okay, okay." I sighed. "You've made your point. Please proceed with the healing, O Wise One."

My grandfather made a face before turning around and rummaging through the vials and jars on the counter next to the island. He picked up a glass jar and whirled around, the ghost of a smile on his face as he looked at me. I knew that smile. It was a "you're going to get it" kind of smile. What was he playing at?

My pulse increased. "What is that?" His large hand covered most of the jar, and from the angle of my head, I couldn't see much.

"Leeches," informed Poe.

Leeches? I gave a start. "Leeches!" I pushed myself up and spun around, my legs hanging down from the counter as I positioned strategically, in case I needed to run. The pain was forgotten at the idea of slimy, disgusting leeches coming anywhere near me.

Oh. Hell. No.

Grinning, my grandfather held up the glass jar for me to see. Packed on the bottom were a colony of black, slimy, flat-looking worms. Leeches.

My grilled cheese erased from my mind, I nearly threw up right there and then, the moving leeches sending another wave of nausea coursing through me.

111

I'd seen my share of disgusting, slippery, demon guts and entrails, but this? This was another level of disgusting, hitting my repulsive meter to the very top.

I gripped the sides of the island counter. "You *cannot* be serious," I said, hating how scared and weak my voice was. I was a dark witch. And yes, I had a problem with creepy tiny leeches. So, sue me.

"How do you suppose we remove the poison?" asked my grandfather, his free hand on his hip. "By asking it nicely? Don't be stupid, Sam. Leeches have been used for centuries for medicinal purposes. Even human doctors have used them." He moved forward—

I raised my hand. "You're not coming near me with those things," I said firmly. "No way."

"Sam." The wrinkles on my grandfather's face deepened. "If you don't let the leeches do their job, you will die. I don't think you understand how serious this is."

"I do."

"Apparently not. The poison in your wound will spread if we don't take it out now." He hesitated. "If I don't take it out now, it will be too late."

He looked every bit the mad scientist. The crazy white hair flowed just past his ears, the thick white eyebrows, the manic gleam in his eyes, and let's not forget, the witch was wearing just a bathrobe.

"There must be another way," I said, trying to keep the panic from my voice but failing miserably.

"There isn't." My grandfather's expression turned into a scowl. "Now, be a good witch and take your medicine." He stepped forward.

"You come near me with that jar," I warned, "and I won't be responsible for what I'm about to do to you."

My grandfather let out an exasperated breath. "By the cauldron, I swear. You are a *Beaumont* witch, Samantha. We do not run away scared of a few leeches. Now, just suck it up, and let me do my work."

"Easy for you to say." My eyes went to the glass jar. It wasn't enough that I'd nearly been killed and then imprisoned all in one night. Now he wanted to mess around with leeches? "I'll take the sleeping spell now."

"Can't," said the crazy old witch holding the jar of leeches. "You need to be awake for this."

I frowned. "But you just said—"

"I lied. Get over it." He twisted the lid and tossed it on the counter. *Do they look bigger?*

"Just do it, Sam," encouraged Poe. "What's the big deal? They're just leeches."

"Exactly."

"They're excellent with a bit of salt," informed the bird. "And sautéed in garlic. Can't forget the garlic."

The ground wavered. "I think I'm going to be sick."

"You're already sick, Samantha," noted my grandfather. "You'll die if you don't let the leeches do

113

their job." Seeing the panic on my face, he added with a softer voice. "They are tiny miracle workers. I promise it'll be quick."

I knew he was lying. But what choice did I have? And yet I knew he was telling the truth about the death blade's poison. If I didn't get it out of me, the poison would eventually kill me.

"If I do this," I said, pointing my finger first at my grandfather and then to Poe, "we'll never, *ever*, speak of it again. Got it?" *I can't believe I'm actually thinking of going through with this. I must be mad.*

Poe lifted his right wing. "On my honor as a demon."

I pursed my lips. "Demons don't believe in honor."

The raven shrugged. "I know."

I glanced at my grandfather, raised my brows, and waited.

"Oh, for cauldron's sake," began my grandfather, but then with one look at me, he added, "fine. I will never mention you and leeches in the same sentence. Now shut up and turn back around."

I swallowed back the bile and did as I was told. I barely felt the cold counter as I lay down, bracing myself at the thought of tiny suction-cup-like mouths on my skin.

Did you ever jump into a lake and come out full of leeches? Me neither. So when I felt a cold, wiggling creature plop against the skin on my lower back for the first time, I flinched, my legs kicking out behind me.

I'm going to pass out. I'm going to pass out. Please, let me pass out!

Plop. Plop. Plop. Three more leeches wiggled their way around my wound until their tiny mouths fastened onto my flesh, sucking out the poison like miniature vacuum cleaners. I gagged. It was the most disgusting sensation I'd ever felt.

Oh, God, I'm going to barf.

"Breathe, Sam," came my grandfather's voice behind me. "It'll be all over soon."

I clenched my jaw until it hurt, not trusting my voice, especially all the foul things I wanted to call my grandfather.

I'm going to throw up. Then I'm going to punch my grandfather in the face.

"I've gotta see this," said Poe as he leaped in the air, his wings fluttering, and landed on the kitchen island somewhere behind me.

I scowled. "Glad you're enjoying the freak show, Poe."

"That's disgusting," said the raven, after a moment's hesitation.

"Poe. I'm going to make a stew out of you," I threatened through gritted teeth.

The bird was quiet after that.

I swallowed hard, flinching at the rhythmic suctions. The little bastards were drawing in my blood in harmony, like vampire worms. With my hands fisted, my breathing slowed and steadied as I fought to bring the terror under control.

"So, Logan bailed you out of jail, eh?" said my gramps. I knew he was only trying to distract me so I wouldn't jump off the counter, screaming like a banshee.

"More like busted me out," I answered, my voice tight with tension, sounding shaky. The hairs on the back of my neck stood up, and it felt like every inch of my skin was covered in goose bumps.

"Why were you there in the first place?" inquired my grandfather, his voice tinged with worry.

I took a breath and recounted the events leading up to my arrest, including what happened with the dark witch court.

"Well, you're not going to like what I have to say," declared my grandfather, his tone grim, like he was about to give me bad news.

My breath hissed out. "I'll probably like it more than the leeches."

"There's been another death," he said. "Another witch died this evening while you were... *indisposed*. And from what you've just told me, it appears to be from the same vampire. Vera's description was quite vivid, to say the least. The body was... well... dried up, if you will."

Vera Wardwell was a witch and my closest neighbor. She was nosier than a bloodhound on a trail. If there was information to be had about the murders, Vera was all over it.

The sickness that rose in my throat had nothing to do with the leeches this time. "At this rate, there'll be no more witches in Mystic Quarter at the end of the month if we don't stop him."

Poe cursed. "Then we better find him."

"I just wish I didn't have these higher demons on my ass. I could do my job and not have to look over my shoulder the entire time." A leech gave a tug on my skin, and I winced.

"Blasted higher demons," said the old witch, his voice rumbling behind me. "I don't like that. I don't like that one bit. Why do you suppose they came after you?"

"It has something to do with a demon named Vorkol." I hated what these bastards had done to me. And now I had to suffer leeches because of them.

"Vorkol," repeated my grandfather, his tone pensive and his feet shifting on the floor next to me. "Never heard of him."

I shook my head. "Me neither. But if he's out to get me, I want to know why." I wasn't going to spend the rest of my life looking over my shoulder. I was going to find out who this Vorkol was. And I knew just how to do it.

"There," came my grandfather's voice. "All done."

My mood lifted as I turned my head and looked at my grandfather. "Really? The leeches are gone? And the poison? It's over?"

The old witch gave me a shrug and spoke to the floor. "Unfortunately, I'd be lying if I said *all* the poison was gone from your system. The blade's poison can never truly be removed," he said and quickly added at the frown on my face, "but enough of the poison was removed that you'll never even notice it's there."

I clamped my mouth shut. I wasn't sure how I felt about still having that demonic poison in me. But he was right. I felt good, better than good, and had no more pain. I could live with that.

My grandfather gave me a nervous smile. "How do you feel?" His voice had held a faint ribbon of worry at the revelation of some of the poison remaining.

I pulled my shirt down, swung my legs off the counter, grabbed the still-warm grilled cheese from the stove and took a bite. "Ravenous," I said between chews. I let out a moan. "God, that's good." I was surprised I was actually still hungry after the ordeal with the leeches. I looked at the jar in my grandfather's hand, seeing the dark leeches wiggling inside, engorged and twice their size.

I took another bite. "You got all of them out. Right?"

My grandfather made a face as though I'd just insulted his new batch of gin and held the jar for me to see. "Of course I did. Who do you think I am?"

"Good." I pushed the last piece of the grilled cheese in my mouth, making Poe laugh, and darted for the stairs.

"Samantha Beaumont! Wait just a minute. You haven't told me how you feel?" called my grandfather.

"Like spelling some demon's ass," I called back and climbed the stairs two at a time.

Like hell I'd let myself get jumped by higher demons again. No. This time I was going to be prepared. This time I was going to fight back.

A smile reached my face.

Showtime.

CHAPTER
12

I knelt on the floor, my heart slamming against my rib cage as I finished drawing the Goetia triangle with my chalk. I drew the unique sigil of the demon I wished to summon and wrote its true Latin name in the center. Taking a calming breath, I stood up and stepped in the Circle of Solomon.

Poe, perched on the chair next to my cauldron, tutted at the name I wrote. "He's going to think you enjoy his company," lamented the raven.

I let out a sigh and pocketed my chalk. "You've got a better idea?" I countered.

"Yeah," said the raven. "Logan. I think we should call him."

I frowned at the bird. "What is your obsession with the angel-born? He shouldn't even be involved in this. But unfortunately, he is."

"He did save your ass from jail. Give him some credit."

Ouch. "One time," I said. "But he can't help me now. Besides, the higher demons were after me, not him."

"I'm with Poe. This is perplexingly stupid, Sam," said my grandfather, his voice scornful and winning an approving caw from Poe. With his arms crossed over his bathrobe, he leaned against his worktable. "The more you summon the same demon, the less power remains in the circle that keeps him in submission until it won't hold him anymore. You won't even notice his knife at your throat until it's too late."

"He won't do that to me." God, I hoped I was right.

My grandfather let out a frustrated breath. "You've only just recovered from your ordeal with the higher demons. Can't this wait until tomorrow?"

I shook my head. "It can't. If it hadn't been for the rising sun, you wouldn't have a granddaughter anymore. They'll be back. They're going to try again, to finish what they started. Only this time I'll be ready for them." I needed ammunition. I needed to know why Vorkol was after me and how to kill these higher demons. And I was going to find out how.

"Besides, I have a job to do." Like finding the ancient vampire who was killing off witches in New York City and killing him. "I can't exactly pay the bills if I'm dead. Now, can I? I'm running out of time."

The whole fiasco with the dark witch court's revelation of why they hired me in the first place had my stomach twisting. It hurt, damn it. And whatever plans I had would have to wait. Sunrise was just three hours away, too short a period of time to do much of anything if this should fail.

My life had quickly gone from bad to worse in a matter of weeks. Not only had I nearly been killed in the hands of the Greater demon Vargal, as he'd tried to raise the pagan god Nergal, by sacrificing a few psychics, the dark witch court had been lying to me all these years. I felt like a fool.

My dream of a simple witch life, a few paranormal cases thrown in, with the steady dark witch court paychecks had vanished.

Everything was different now. There was no going back.

I took their silence as my cue to begin the summoning. I pulled the energy from the circle and triangle, channeling the magic.

"I conjure you, Farissael, demon of the Netherworld to be subject to the will of my soul," I chanted, focusing on my will, the circle, and triangle. Yes, I was taking a risk summoning him again—and for what I was about to ask him—but I had no other choice. "I bind you with unbreakable adamantine fetters, and I deliver you into the black chaos in perdition. I invoke you, Farissael, in the space in front of me!"

There was a pop of displaced air as the lights flickered and went out. A wind rose, lifting my hair around my face and shoulders.

When the lights flickered back on, a man stood in the triangle before me. Tall and fit, he had a pleasant face and striking dark eyes framed with thick lashes over an olive complexion.

And he wore nothing but a pair of tight red briefs.

Holy hell.

Faris, the mid-demon, smiled, like the devil himself had just been awarded the prize of the century. His dark eyes met mine, and he said, "What's the story, morning glory?"

I rolled my eyes. *Here we go.* "Faris," I said, in way of greeting. "Where are your clothes?"

Faris's smile widened. "My dear, sweet, edible, Sammy. You do realize I have a life outside of this"—he looked down at the floor—"confinement. If you must know, I was in the process of pleasuring the Barbie twins with my—"

"Stop!" I shouted, doing my best not to picture it in my mind. "Don't want to hear about it."

"Why ever not, dearest?" Faris moved his hips in a sexual manner, making me flush. "Jealous? Don't worry, Sammy baby. There's enough of me to go around." He made a show of his chiseled, tanned, and hairless chest, and finished with a wink.

Cauldron help me. It didn't help that I had seen what those tiny undies were trying to cover and doing a piss-poor job of it, I might add. It was hard to keep from staring.

As a mid-demon, Faris ranked higher than a lesser demon but not quite up the demon ladder to be comparable to a Greater demon.

"You better watch yourself, demon," said my grandfather, his tone suggesting the demon's behavior was groooly inappropriate, if not outright impolite. He pushed off his worktable and came forward, his fingers moving in a spell. He would have looked threatening if he wasn't wearing a bathrobe. Now, he just looked mad. "That's my granddaughter you're speaking to," he growled.

"What? You're going to smother me with that hospital gown?" chided the demon with mock surprise.

"Bathrobe," corrected my grandfather.

Faris twisted his face in a sour expression. "Yes, well... for all our sakes. Please keep it on."

"Grandpa, it's fine," I told him. I was used to Faris's antics. Poe, well, he was quiet. Too quiet as he watched the scene unfold, eyes on the mid-demon. "Let's focus on the real issue here, okay?"

"Yes, let's." Faris dragged his gaze from my grandfather. "Sammy baby," declared the mid-demon. He lowered his eyes and said, "you look like shit."

"Thanks."

"What happened to you?"

I took a breath and looked at the demon. "Faris, you have something I need." Damn. I knew that was the wrong thing to say by the way Faris was looking at me.

His lips curled into a sly smile, and I swear I saw a star twinkling on his teeth. "Why, you wicked, wicked witch. It's about damn time."

"Information," I blurted, though the damage was done. Shit—I glanced at his crotch again. "Something happened to me last night."

"That's putting it lightly," grumbled Poe, and Faris's attention snapped to him.

The mid-demon's gaze darted back to mine. "Sam, darling. If you're going to tell me you had sex with someone else and didn't invite me," he said, hands on his hips, "I'm going to be a little disappointed. I've acquired some new toys, and I think you'll appreciate the soft—"

"I was attacked by higher demons," I exclaimed, impatience making my voice rise. Lack of sleep with a handful of leeches sucking on my flesh would do that.

Faris's smile faded a little. "What are you talking about?" He barely reacted, pausing to glance at my grandfather before looking back at me.

"I'm talking about those black-eyed, clone bastards," I told him. "That's who."

Faris raised a brow. "I know the type. How many?"

"Three."

He watched me with rapt attention for a beat longer. "You're alive. Why is it that you're alive if—like you say—three higher demons attacked you?"

125

I shivered at the memory of how close I was to dying. "The sun. The morning sun appeared and they took off."

Faris made a soft whistle. "Yes, that should do it," answered the mid-demon, the faintest bother in his expression as he took in my disheveled appearance again. He sighed and said, "This is all very exciting, and I'm glad you're not dead, but what's it got to do with me? I have the Barbie twins waiting for me back at my apartment," he added smugly. "They get pretty nasty if they don't get their weekly... *release*."

"I get it," I said. I never had imagined him having an apartment in the Netherworld. I'd never really imagined the Netherworld having any kind of structures. I'd always pictured it like any version of hell—endless firepits, burnt rubble, millions of demons torturing human souls, all the clichés. Perhaps I'd been wrong.

Damn. His crotch was in my line of vision again. Damn. Damn. Damn. I pretended to be interested in his feet. Turns out they were meticulously manicured.

"Barbie twins," said Faris again and gave me an exasperated look. "Unless you have something *other* in mind," he said and his smile widened, "I really must go."

"The higher demons were sent to kill me by a demon named Vorkol," I said and saw the recognition of the name flash in Faris's eyes. "You know who he is. Don't you?" I shifted, nearly stepping out of my circle. "Who is he? Tell me, damn it."

Faris slid his hands over his perfectly styled, short black hair. "You know how this works, Sammy, darling. You can ask, but I don't give information out for free."

Crap. This again. I let out a long breath. "I know."

"What's in it for me?"

"So you do know him?" I asked. When he didn't answer, I pressed. "I need to make sure."

The demon gave a nod of his head. "Yes. The name rings a Netherworld bell."

I met my grandfather's shocked look—part worry, part anger, part disbelief.

"He could be lying," accused my grandfather. "You can't trust him."

Yup. All true. But I had no one else to turn to.

"Relax, you old bag of witch bones," said Faris. His eyes found mine. "It's simple." He smiled like a man who knew he had me. "I know who Vorkol is. But the question is... *what* will you give me in return?"

Cauldron be damned. I knew he was going to ask this again. "I'm not sleeping with you."

"Can't blame a demon for trying," purred the demon. He sighed dramatically. With his hands on his hips, he added, "I want another night off of this triangular confinement. If there are higher demons after you, you're going to need my help."

I watched Faris, seeing the underlying plans behind his eyes. "What about the Barbie twins?"

Faris flashed me a smile. "They can wait."

My jaw clenched, seeing I could never truly trust him. "Why do you want to help me?" I asked, knowing full well he wasn't doing anything for me, but for him. There was something in it for him. Always was.

"Isn't it obvious?" said the mid-demon, a smug smile on his face. "I happen to like my nights out of my confinement. If you die, who's going to give me my free passes to the mortal world? I like it here," he added, looking around. "And the mortal women happen to enjoy my company. I'd rather not lose that."

I knew he was lying. That couldn't be the only reason, but I also knew there was a bit of truth in it. Plus I needed all the help I could get. If Faris was willing to help, I'd take it.

"Done." I knew I shouldn't be trusting this demon, but so far, Faris hadn't let me down. However, my chest tightened in sudden doubt. Faris was a demon after all, and he could easily kill me.

Oh God. What was I thinking?

My grandfather let out a cry of outrage, but he quickly squelched it at my scowl.

"So? Who is he?" I leaned forward in anticipation, breath held.

Faris smiled at me with seductive delight. "Vorkol, my dearest Samantha... is not a *he*, but a *she*. And she's the Greater demon Vargal's wife."

CHAPTER
13

How do you catch an ancient vampire skilled with magic? With bait. Want to guess who the bait is? Yours truly.

Okay. So this was at the top of my stupidest plans list, but I didn't have much else to go on. I was desperate, and guilt gnawed at my gut.

Witches were being murdered because of me.

As I connected the dots, it was all making sense now—the recent murders of female witches, the higher demons trying to kill me. The two were connected. I was sure of it. I just didn't know how exactly.

This all had to do with Vorkol. Somehow, she'd hired a vampire to kill me too.

I'd killed the Greater demon Vargal, and now his demon wife was out to get me. Fantastic. I could add that to my list of accomplishments. I'd pissed off a creature of the Netherworld while trying to save human lives. What else was new?

If the dark witch court found out the killings were my fault, I had no doubt they'd hand me over to her. I was to them, after all, something pitiful, lame, and weak. But I wasn't going to make it easy for them. Or for anyone

According to Faris, Vorkol was a ruler of sorts with many demon armies under her. And of course, she was also a Greater demon. If Faris was telling the truth, she had a higher rank in the demon hierarchy than her late husband. I was all for female empowerment—just not for lady demons who wanted to kill my ass.

But first, I had to stop the vampire from killing any more witches—including me. Then I'd deal with the higher demons and Vorkol.

I pulled on my boots, zipped up my leather jacket, and turned to Faris, who'd thankfully demon-magicked a pair of black pants, shirt, and polished shoes. He looked ready for a night out on the town, not dressed for vampire decapitation.

"You ready?" I asked, standing in the foyer as I adjusted the strap of my messenger bag.

Faris raised his brows suggestively. "For you, Sammy baby, always."

Poe made a disgruntled sound in his throat from the coatrack on the wall and rolled his eyes. "This is going to be a long night."

I caught a glimpse of my grandfather's white hair down the hall before he disappeared into the kitchen. "I'll be back soon, Grandpa," I called. I waited a few seconds, listening. "Giving your granddaughter the silent treatment is very childish," I yelled.

"Going on a hunt with a mid-demon is also very childish," he called back, and I heard the clink of a glass hitting the marble counter.

I smiled. Yes. We were both very immature, and that's how we liked it.

I flexed my fingers, the leather gloves cracking. My sigil rings shone in the soft light. I'd performed a few pre-spells before getting ready to leave. I needed to make sure I could still do magic with a small trace of the death blade's poison still in me. As it turned out, I could.

Smiling, Faris stepped closer to me, way too close. I was expecting the scent of sulfur, the normal demon smell. Instead, an aroma of chamomile and honey filled my nose. Whatever glamour he was using was damn good. Clever bastard.

I didn't want to give Faris the satisfaction of knowing his closeness was making me uncomfortable by stepping away, but I needed to open the door.

"You think I'm right, don't you?" I asked the mid-demon. "About the vampire?"

Faris inclined his head. "She knows higher demons are useless under the sun. So, she's put a vampire on your tail. It doesn't surprise me. When she wants something done, she goes all out. She's not taking any chances with you. She must really want you dead."

"Maybe," I said, unease trickling through me. "Then why is the vampire killing those witches? If he wants me, why kill them?"

The demon shrugged. "I'm not sure. I think perhaps now that he's tasted witch blood, he can't stop himself. Or maybe Vorkol told him to kill all witches that match your description. That's more like her. Go out with a bang, that sort of thing."

I felt ill, but something still didn't fit.

I sucked in my breath through my nose to get rid of some of my tension, grabbed the doorknob, and pulled open the door—

My heart leaped to my throat and stayed there.

Logan stood on the platform.

Why was he always doing that? Heat rushed to my face before I could control it. Cauldron be damned. Why did he have that effect on me? And those snug blue jeans were making it harder. That's what happened when a girl hadn't been on a date in months—hormones out of whack and all.

"Logan?" I said, trying to formulate complete sentences with my heart in my throat. "What are you doing here?"

The handsome angel-born stood facing me, his brown eyes searching my face. He wore a black motorcycle jacket over a tight gray T-shirt that looked painted on. Jaw clenched, his face darkened when Faris stepped into view beside me.

"Have no fear, the Boy Scout is here," teased Faris with an obvious, underlying threat in his voice. "A baby angel-born. How nice. Did you forget your pacifier?"

"I came to see how you were doing," said Logan. His eyes were back on me, though the irritation was clear in the tone of his voice at seeing Faris with me.

For some reason, I believed him. Granted, it just made things a lot more complicated.

"She's fine," interrupted Faris, stepping closer to the doorframe. "Can't you see? Now, run along. I think I can hear your mommy calling."

Great. I didn't have time for this. A tingle of worry brought me stiff. "It's late, Logan. You shouldn't be here."

"That's right, Boy Scout," said Faris, his eyes wide in mock concern. "Is that... is that Gerber on the side of your mouth right there?" he added, as though speaking to a small child.

Logan didn't move. "I'll leave," he said, his gaze sharpening on me, "if that's what you want."

Crap. Now, why did he have to say that?

"Yes," answered Faris before I had the chance. "Please leave," said the mid-demon with a tone of finality.

"We could use your help," declared Poe suddenly, and I turned around to shoot him a look.

"Help with what?" Logan's posture stiffened. "What's going on?"

"Nothing that concerns the likes of an angel-born," replied Faris as he straightened.

133

I let out a breath. "We think the vampire attacks on the witches and the higher demons that tried to kill me are connected," I said quickly. "The higher demon Vorkol—"

"Vargal's wife," interjected Poe.

"Is trying to kill me," I finished. "Payback for killing her husband." Yada yada yada.

Logan's eyes squinted. For a moment he just stared. "What vampire attacks?"

Right. He didn't know. "There's been a string of vampire attacks on witches," I told him, seeing Faris cross his arms over his chest. "Six dead so far. All female. We think he's under Vorkol's control."

"Fits the bill," said the raven.

Logan's eyes flicked to him and then back to me.

"And you're going after him tonight?" asked the angel-born with a certain amount of incredulity.

"We are," I answered.

Poe leaped off the coatrack and fluttered to my shoulder. "Sam's the bait."

I cringed, seeing how stupid this plan sounded when he said it out loud like that. But I had nothing else to go on. I'd fought a rogue vampire once, a female. She'd been on a killing spree in Queens—human children—which was a big no-no. I did the only thing I could. I burnt her to a crisp. But this time it wouldn't be so easy.

Logan's eyes were intense as he said, "I'm coming. You're going to need me if you want to kill this vampire. I can help."

Faris got in Logan's face. "Listen, Boy Scout. We don't need you. Sammy and I are perfectly capable of vanquishing a tiny vampire on our own. We wouldn't want your precious angel hands to get dirty."

"Like yours, demon," Logan shot back, winning a snarl from Faris.

I pushed Faris out of the way before he did something stupid, like start a fight in my doorway. "It's fine. He can come if he wants," I said, pulling my eyes from Logan's satisfied smile and stepping on the porch. "If fact, I don't need either of you. So if you don't shut up and pretend to get along, you can both stay here. I don't have time for this pissing contest. And if you mess this up"—I warned, pointing my finger at both of them—"I'll turn you both into twelve-year-old girls with pimples. Got it? Good. Let's go."

I shut the door with a bang, and without waiting for them to follow, I climbed down the front steps and jumped onto the sidewalk with Poe balancing on my shoulder. The curtain from Vera's bay window shifted, and I caught a glimpse of red hair before it disappeared again.

Damn it. My tension rose. How much of that conversation did the witch hear? All of it? I didn't have time to worry about that right now. I had much bigger fish to fry—like a vampire.

I pushed the thoughts from my head and rushed down the street.

CHAPTER
14

We walked in silence for a while, Faris and Logan on either side of me, trying to outwalk each other as though this was some sort of competition. Chests out, their legs moved awkwardly like both were trying to speed walk and slow walk at the same time.

I'd never noticed how similar and yet dissimilar they were. They were both tall, though Faris was an inch taller than Logan. The demon was dressed in an expensive-looking shirt and pants, whereas the angel-born was dressed more casually. Both were dark in terms of their eyes and hair color, but where Logan had more of a soft complexion, Faris was all hard angles. There was also an age-old intensity in Faris's eyes that Logan didn't have, no doubt the result of being a demon for thousands of years.

I'd been surprised that Faris had decided to accompany me on my vampire stakeout, and more so that Logan had volunteered as well. Granted, with the infinitely more suspicious and concerned way the angel-born was watching Faris, I had the feeling he had come to help me, yes, but he also came to watch the demon. He didn't trust him. And I didn't trust either of them.

We were an odd foursome.

My boots clonked on the pavement. I sighed, trying to shake my tension. This was going to be a long, long night.

Together we spilled out into the dark streets of Mystic Quarter. The night air was warm and saturated with the scents of humans, half-breeds, alcohol, blood, coffee, exhaust, all of it mixed in with the smell of sulfur. It was Friday night, when the quarter came alive. Noise hit me, including the occasional werewolf cry and fluttering pixie. Four vampires lumbered past us, their eyes on Logan. No surprise there. Most half-breeds despised the angel-born. Something to do with how superior they felt to the rest of the half-breeds, as though their angel essence gave them that right.

I didn't think so.

A cloudless black sky loomed over us with a collection of brilliant stars. It was a glorious night, but the beauty did nothing to quench the guilt eating a hole through my stomach walls. Somewhere in my city, a vampire was killing off witches because of me. How many more innocent witches were going to have

KIM RICHARDSON

their essence drained out of them by a crazed vampire? How many more witches were going to die before he was stopped?

I felt a heightened anxiety along my spine, in my pulse, and in the beat of blood in my ears. The faint drone of distant cars seemed very far away as our tread echoed on the sidewalk.

We walked in silence for several moments until Poe finally said, "Do you know where to find this vampire?"

"I have an idea."

"Feel like sharing?"

I shrugged. "What? And ruin the surprise?" I answered, making my familiar grunt his disapproval.

"You are one strange witch, Samantha Beaumont," said Poe, making me smile. I thought so too.

We hit Odin Boulevard. A small park came into view, decorated with four stone benches and two draping crabapple trees. A fountain, the size of a ten-by-ten pool, stood silently in its center.

It was the same fountain Kyllian had used to travel back to Horizon, using its water as his transition to that other world. A tug pulled at my chest. I missed that big angel. I hoped the Legion was good to him this time around. If not, they'd have me to deal with.

"There," I said, and both Logan and Faris turned to look at me as I pointed straight ahead. "The park." I wanted to make myself available, so what better

138

place than in the middle of a park—open and quiet where everyone could see me?

Logan raised a questionable brow. "You think this vampire is going to come look for you here? In this park?"

"I do," I said and crossed the park to the bench that faced the fountain. Water poured into a dark pool in the display's center, looking like oil. I turned and sat on the bench, the cold metal seeping through my jeans. "He's hunting witches that match my description in Mystic Quarter. Most witches are sleeping comfortably in their beds now. I'm right here."

A wicked smile creased Faris's face as he sat next to me and crossed his leg at the knee. "I can tuck you in later, if you want. I'm an expert tucker."

Poe made a sound in his throat, fluttered to the fountain, and began drinking some water.

Logan's expression darkened as he took in Faris's proximity to me. "I don't think it's going to work."

My mood soured. "It will," I said, not appreciating his tone, his lack of faith in me, or Poe gargling water in his throat that sounded like he was reciting the alphabet. "See. I'm making it easier for him. I'm making myself available."

"Sammy," purred Faris, as he scooted closer until our thighs touched. He draped his right arm around the back of the bench behind me. "I'm right here."

Lips parted, heat rushed to my face as I moved over and turned to face the mid-demon. "Look. I appreciate you being here and all, but if I want to catch this vampire... you need to make yourself scarce or he won't come."

"Hear! Hear!" agreed Poe.

Irritation flickered behind the demon's dark eyes, and a chill fluttered through me. For a moment I thought I'd gone too far. His demonic magic was far superior to mine. He could probably turn me to ash with just a snap of his fingers if he wanted. I started to second-guess my decision to let the demon come here.

My attention alternated between Logan and Faris, my tension growing as Faris mumbled, and a black haze enveloped his hands.

"As you wish," declared Faris as he forced the irritation from his face and stood up, the haze gone. He tugged the sleeves of his shirt and said, "I'll be right over there, where the fun is." His eyes moved over to the Dusk & Dawn Vampire Pub across from the park, lingering on the three female vampires sitting out on the terrace as they sipped their red-colored drinks. They were practically undressing the demon with their eyes. Figured.

Faris's mood shifted, seemingly pleased. "Looks like I'm still in business. The business of sex," he added, his teeth showing and raising his brows suggestively.

Cauldron help me.

"And that goes for you too," I said with an exhale, and Logan's smile vanished. "If he gets a whiff of your angel-born smell, he'll never show."

A frown creased Logan's handsome face, looking appalled. "I smell?"

I rolled my eyes as I let out an exasperated breath. "I don't have time for this," I said, annoyed. "As a matter of fact, you do. All angel-borns smell. Everybody knows that."

Faris snorted, looking smug. "Don't fret, Boy Scout. Samantha smells too, you know."

I made a face. "Yeah, well, October is my bathing month."

The mid-demon's expression shifted to one of satisfied appreciation as he ran his eyes over me. "I knew you were a dirty little witch."

"Look," I said, feeling a giant migraine coming on, and pinched the bridge of my nose. "Just stay out of sight. Okay?"

Logan's lips parted, and for a moment I thought he was about to argue. "What if he overpowers you with his magic?" he asked instead. "You said he was very powerful. One of us should stay close."

"What am I? A figurine?" said Poe as he jumped around the fountain. "That's why I'm here. I've got her back. You can go now."

I shifted in my seat. "Listen. He wants me, and it's me he'll get." I lifted my gloved hands. "I can handle an old vampire on my own." I was ready for him. I clenched my jaw. "This ends tonight. I'm going to fry this pointed-tooth bastard."

Logan's shoulders stiffened with tension, the rims of his brown eyes growing in frustration. "What about the higher demons?" he said, and Faris's attention snapped back to mine. "You nearly died the last time. They'll kill you."

"They won't."

Logan gave me a sharp look. "You need me."

I clenched my jaw. Boy, he was annoying me tonight. "There's only about an hour and a half left before sunrise."

"All the more reason for me to stay."

Faris coughed and muttered, "Boy Scout."

"I'm not dead yet, so let me do my job." Now I was pissed. I wasn't some weak female who needed rescuing from a man. I was a dark witch, damn it. I had badass magic. I controlled demons and bent them to my will.

Logan's jaw tightened, belligerent to the end, and I forced myself to relax. I knew better than to piss him off. I might never see him again. Okay, that was selfish, and his coming here tonight had me confused as hell, but there was no time to wrap my head around that. If I survived tonight's ordeal, that was another story.

A sigh slipped from Logan. "You're crazy."

"So I've been told." I smiled. "Living life on the edge and all that crap." Not really, I'd much rather be home with a glass of wine and be binge-watching something on Netflix, preferably with a hot angel-born with dark, sultry eyes... and preferably naked.

"Come along, Boy Scout," said Faris. "I'm sure we can find a female desperate enough for your company."

I watched as a demon and an angel-born walked side by side and crossed the street toward the pub, both here to protect me. Didn't see that every day.

"I'm going to scout around the area," declared Poe, and I pulled my attention from Logan's perfect behind. The raven ruffled his feathers. "Be right back." With a strong beat of his wings the raven soared into the inky black sky and was gone.

Now I was truly alone. Good. I exhaled long and loud, focusing my will on my sigil rings and tapping into that power. The metal warmed as they answered. They were fully charged, so all that was missing was a target.

Where are you, you vamp bastard.

My heart thrashed madly, every beat pushing my tension higher. Yes, I was anxious for the vamp to show up. But that's not why I was leaning on the edge of the bench, hands clenched, ready to throw a spell.

I remembered the higher demons and how powerless I'd been. I'd just bumped shoulders with death.

I'd pissed off the Greater demon Vorkol by killing her husband. I'd be pissed too if someone had killed my husband. But he'd started it.

Adrenaline pounded through me, feeding off my fear. I let out a breath and clenched my fists, trying to stop them from shaking but failing. The realization of what I'd just agreed to dawned on me, my knee bobbing up and down.

I was purposely sitting by myself in the park at night, hoping the ancient, witch-killing vampire found me. Yeah. I was insane.

I leaned back, enjoying the familiar smells and noises. Nothing was out of place, if the bizarre and the unusual was your sort of thing. It was mine.

Across from me, I spotted Logan leaning on the pub's brick wall, arms crossed over his chest, and his face in a grimace, looking pissed. He was staring at the ground. Either that, or he liked the way his boots flickered in the pub's light.

Faris, well, he sat at the table out front, a female vampire on his lap while another stood behind him, massaging his shoulders. The third female vampire was leaning on the table across from him, and even from a distance I could see the hunger in her eyes. She looked like she was about to jump him right there. Damn, that demon was good.

He caught me staring, winked, and lifted his glass in a toast. I gave him a smile. I couldn't help it. He must have demon-spelled them.

I checked behind me, breathing deeply for the distinctive scent of vampire but getting nothing except the smell of trees and pavement. The sound of wings hit me as Poe landed on the fountain.

He shrugged and said, "All clear. No higher demons and no creepy old vampire either."

"Thanks, Poe," I answered, not liking the relief I heard in my own voice.

Minutes went by and still no sign of the old vampire. Nothing. Nada. Soon, minutes turned to an hour, and still nothing. Still no vampire. And no higher demons. The only thing I had was a numb butt from sitting on the hard bench.

"Sunrise is in less than two minutes," said Poe.

I pulled out my phone and checked the time. "Yeah. Well, I better let Faris know before things start to get too hot for him."

"Nothing's ever *too* hot for me." I looked up from my phone to find Faris walking toward me with Logan next to him.

I stood up and stretched, noticing that his vamp girls were gone. "Looks like the higher demons are a no-show." I cast my gaze around the street. "I don't think the vampire's coming either."

"You sure?" asked Logan.

"The murders were all committed at night," I said, feeling like a fool and having had witnesses to my shame. I'd been certain he'd come. "He's not coming."

Faris clamped his hands together. "Well, I really must be going. Let's do this again sometime. Not really." He gestured grandly. "But do let me know how you fare with this vampire."

A haze of blackness rose around the mid-demon. "Later, darling," he said, and with a wicked smile, he vanished.

Faris disappeared just as a row of pinks painted the horizon.

Logan yawned, and I had to clamp my jaw shut so I wouldn't join him. Only then did I notice how exhausted I was too.

"If you don't need me to stick around," said the angel-born, "I think I'll go too."

"Sure, you should get some sleep," I answered, knowing part of him had stuck around just to keep an eye on Faris.

"I'll come by later and check on you," declared the angel-born as he turned around and strolled down the street to whatever curb he'd parked his car next to.

"Did he just invite himself over?" asked Poe.

Damn. I watched his shoulders sway as he walked away and turned down Odin Boulevard. "Yeah. He did."

"Well," said the raven as he shook his feathers. "I'm starving. Mind if I go and catch my breakfast down on Blood Drive? I hear the rats are as big as cats."

I grimaced, trying not to imagine Poe eating a rat. "Go ahead. I'm going home to bed," I said, too tired to care. Besides, he needed to eat, and I hadn't packed anything for us in my bag.

"Later." And with that, my familiar took to the air, banked to the right, and vanished behind a three-story building.

I sighed through my nose. This had been a huge waste of time.

Feeling like an idiot, I wrapped the strap of my messenger bag over my shoulder and hit the street.

The sun was arching toward the horizon, painting the rooftops in Mystic Quarter in pinks and yellows as I headed for Witches Row, my district. The sky was a mixture of deep pinks and violets. It was going to be a gorgeous day. But even the idea of a glorious day ahead did nothing to lift my spirits.

A vampire was hunting witches, and I'd failed to catch him.

I needed to come up with a better plan. This had been a total bust. My only other option was to go to the vampire court and see if I could get a name out of them. Probably not. If a vampire from their court was killing off witches, they wouldn't tell me a thing. Instead, they'd go off and deal with him on their own. Plus the witch court had forbidden me to tell anyone.

Shoulders hunched, my boots clomped on the pavement like they were cement blocks. I yawned. God, I was so tired I could barely lift my feet. Shadows loomed. The soft light from the sun hadn't reached high enough over the tall buildings and the majestic oak trees, leaving me in the dark.

The air around me suddenly shot down ten degrees cooler, and I halted.

A flicker of something cold and dark rippled in the air. It tugged inside my chest as an icy shudder ran through me.

A black mist rose and leaked between a row of parked cars, heading south on Grim Avenue. And there, moving with it, was a hunched silhouette of a man with short, calculated strides.

The vampire.

Gotcha, you son of a bitch.

I sprinted after him. I wouldn't let him kill anyone else. He was mine.

I ran down Grim Avenue, just as the vampire disappeared around the corner. I reached the end of the block and turned the corner.

By the time I saw it coming out of the corner of my eye, it was already too late.

My instincts kicked in, and I pitched to the side as fast and far as I could, but I barely had time to register the movement as I lunged.

The higher demon came at me in a blur of rustling, guttural whispers, carrying the scent of rotten fruit, blood, and carrion. I blinked at the undulating black hole looming behind him, rippling like black water. A Rift. A demon portal, a doorway into the Netherworld.

My heart jumped, and I gasped, unable to cry out.

The higher demon grabbed me by the throat and pulled me into the Rift with him.

CHAPTER
15

Have you ever wondered what hell truly looked like? Have you really taken the time to imagine what the realm of demons and other unruly creatures looked like? Really looked like?

Well, scratch that.

Take your worst nightmare and the scariest movie you've ever seen. Multiply that by a thousand and you might be close to what the Netherworld resembled.

And I was there.

I, Samantha Beaumont, dark witch extraordinaire was in the Netherworld. The *freaking* Netherworld!

I knew I was in the demon realm. I felt it in my thoughts and my bones, and in the primitive, skin-crawling part of me at the base of my brain. I was in a different world than my own.

149

But why was I there? And how was this even possible?

I sat on my cage's floor. The metal was a dull black and reeked of sulfur. Through the metal bars, scattered around my line of vision, was a world of smoke and blood and ash—and cages.

Everywhere I looked was another cage, the same size as mine, occupied by twisted creatures, demons, or what I believed had once been humans. It was impossible to count them all. Ten thousand? A hundred thousand?

And just like them, I was a prisoner.

The cages hung above a dirt-packed ground by thick chains made of the same black metal, hundreds of feet in the air, to a distant ceiling out of sight in the darkness overhead that was lost in shadow. It was dimly lit by growing flames from a few wall torches. A cave maybe?

It was cold, and I wrapped my arms about myself as an acidic wind pushed the hair from my face. My bag was missing. Either I had dropped it when I was grabbed or the higher demons had taken it. All I had were my rings. As soon as I had opened my eyes and realized where I was, I'd tried to tap into my rings to bust out of this cage.

But my rings were cold and dull. Their magic wouldn't come.

And then I saw why. Etched along the bars of my cage were winding spirals of demonic symbols and runes—wards to keep whoever was in the cage from using magic. Great.

I licked my dry lips and took a breath, wincing at the burning in my lungs as though I were breathing the fumes of a mixture of bleach and ammonia. It was toxic. The Netherworld was toxic to mortals.

So how was it possible that I was here breathing their air? It shouldn't be possible, yet here I was, sitting in a damn cage. I knew I wasn't dead. If I were, I wouldn't feel pain. Pain was my only indication that I was, in fact, still very much alive.

I had no idea how long I'd been in this cage. One minute I was being strangled by the higher demon, and then everything went black. The next thing I remembered was waking up in this cage, in the Netherworld.

I could hear screams drifting through the interior of this place. I'd heard rumors that the Netherworld was similar to our world, perhaps even like a mirrored version, only twisted and perverse. I guessed I was in some dungeon or prison. The constant cacophony of cries and moans made it very clear. This was a *bad* place.

The cries grew louder, and then the sound of a heavy door opening and closing reached me. I heard sounds of a heavy tread and the crunch of dirt and gravel. Fighting a dizzy spell, I wiped the tears from my eyes and peeked through the bars to the ground below. With the constant wind and acidic air, it was hard to see, but I could make out a shape. Big. Grizzly bear big. My vision cleared, and I saw dark gray fur and horns, a thick chest with a great sword strapped to his back, and strong human legs. A minotaur demon.

My breath slipped from me. I knew that demon. Hell, I'd summoned him. He was one of the seventy-two demons in the Ars Goetia.

Andromalius.

He was a mighty great earl of the Netherworld, and as evil as evil got. Swell. He had been one of my first successful demon conjurings. And by successful, I mean only that I had conjured him and he didn't escape the triangle to kill me. Though he tried. Many, many times. It had scared the shit out of me.

Andromalius walked over to a raised platform to a metal contraption. He pulled on a lever and then pushed it back. The squeal of metal grinding metal pierced over the loud howls and screams, followed by the rattling of a chain. A metal cage only twenty feet from me dropped to the ground like a rock in a pond.

The cage rattled on impact. There was an instant yelp of pain, and then a green body jerked itself back to the edge of the cage followed by a whimper.

From a series of keys around his waist, Andromalius unlocked the cage's door, yanked it open, and pulled out a small, green, humanoid-looking creature with large bat ears.

The creature fell to the ground, its ribs showing through its thin skin. It knelt on the ground, its clawed hands up in surrender, pleading in some demonic language. I had no idea what it was saying, but it was obvious the demon was pleading for its life.

Andromalius focused its eyes on the skinny demon. Then he pulled out his sword, and with a mighty swing, decapitated the demon in a spray of flying bits of bone, a head, and a mist of black blood.

A mixture of screams and shouts erupted in the cave. I couldn't tell if they were screaming in fear or excitement. Maybe a little bit of both.

A chill that had nothing to do with the icy air scuttled up my spine. This wasn't a prison. This was death row.

The sound of the door opening and closing again reached me, followed by the sounds of many feet. I stared as a mob of squat, flat-nosed, sallow-skinned creatures with wide mouths and glowing red eyes pushed a wheelbarrow the size of a small car. Thick, leather-like gray skin covered their repulsive, hairless bodies. Imps. Horrid little bastards.

They scuttled to the body of the dead demon. Their red, evil eyes crinkled with amusement, and the sound of wet chuckles rose from their throats. The hairs on the back of my neck stood on end. The smallest of the group waddled over to the head and kicked it like a soccer ball. It hit the side of the wheelbarrow, and the imps let out a howl of laughter.

I hated these little freaks.

A deep growl escaped from Andromalius's throat, causing the imps to jump up in a panic and scurry around the dead demon's body. They picked up the head and body, dumped them in the wheelbarrow, and then were off again.

It was all over in less than two minutes.

I watched, horrified, as Andromalius went back to the platform and wrapped his hand around one of the levers, pulled, and pushed it back.

I barely had time to register as my own cage rattled. It plummeted toward the ground like an elevator from the tenth floor whose cables had snapped.

Cauldron help me.

I screamed all the way down—which lasted a mere two seconds—and hit the ground.

Ouch.

My right arm, shoulder and hip screamed in pain, as my body smashed to the ground a few seconds behind the metal cage. My head was tucked in against my chest, and my instincts to do that had probably saved my life.

The rattle of keys reached me, and I jerked my head up. I blinked as a thick hand grabbed me by the throat and hauled me out of the cage. Andromalius released me, and I fell hard on the dirt floor.

I knew I had seconds before he swung that sword at me. Rolling to my knees, I took a steadying breath—and coughed. Not a good idea. The air was as foul as though I'd breathed in Satan's astray.

Now that I was out of my cage, I tapped into the magic of my rings. A small tug answered, but at the same moment, an overwhelming feeling of nausea hit me, and I stumbled to my knees, losing my focus.

If I couldn't use my magic, I'd have to use my next best skill. I had to talk my way to survival.

Footsteps neared, and I blinked through my tears. "Andromalius! Wait!" I cried, my voice harsh and low, sounding like I'd just swallowed acid.

The minotaur halted at the sound of his name.

I knew one of two things was about to happen—one, the demon would recognize me and decide not to kill me because I was pretty; or two, he would recognize me and proceed to cut my head off. I was hoping for the first.

The minotaur demon stood facing me and adjusted the key at his waist. Old, faint scars marred his face, adding another level of badass to his appearance. He was naked, save for a tan leather loincloth that barely concealed his hairy malehood.

His sword was still sheathed. So far so good. Maybe I would live to see my world again. A fetid smell of decay, manure, and worse flooded out from him. He'd smelled awful when I'd summoned him, but this was way worse. Being in the Netherworld, his lovely stench was magnified a hundredfold.

With a Herculean effort, I got to my feet. The pain in my shoulder and hip were still white hot, threatening to make me pass out.

I gave him a little wave with my gloved hand, knowing I was probably the only witch who had ever summoned him. "Hey, there. You remember me?" Damn, he was a big sonofabitch. He had to be at least seven feet tall. How could I have forgotten that?

Andromalius's eye twitched, his nightmarish canines lengthening as his lips peeled away from his teeth into a snarl.

I took that as a yes. "I was a junior witch when we first met. So you see... I can't be responsible for any... mishaps that happened. I mean, you did return to your world in one piece. Right?"

The minotaur's yellow eyes blinked.

I pulled my face into a smile. "No hard feelings, eh?"

Andromalius's nostrils flared, and a deep growl escaped from the demon's throat.

"Okay, then. Good talk."

Please don't kill me. Think, Sam, think! If only I could hit him with a sleeping spell. Would my magic even work in this world? I had no freaking idea.

I braced myself for something horrible but...

"Follow me, witch," said Andromalius in a heavily accented but clear and deep voice. I nearly fainted.

"You can speak English!" I stared stupidly into the demon's face, all of it—the hideous asymmetries of the minotaur's bull head, his large, bulging, yellow eyes, his repulsive, wet muzzle, the curve of his sharp, deadly horns. "You never spoke to me before. At least, not when I summoned you." The minotaur demon flared his nostrils, and I saw him make an effort to stay calm. I took a careful step back. "Please don't eat me," I said, swallowing back the bile that rose in the back of my throat. "Aren't cows herbivores?"

Andromalius breathed through his nose and said again, "Follow me, witch."

He wasn't going to kill me. Interesting. But it also scared the crap out of me. There were worse things than suffering a clean, instant death. Try torture. Being tortured for hours. Being tortured for years.

Still, out of this place was a plus. Maybe the air would be cleaner wherever he was taking me.

"Lead the way, cowboy," I wheezed, my mood brightening a smidgen. Maybe there was still a way to get out of hell.

Screams of protest shouted from above, and things I didn't want to admit I saw hit the ground at my feet in stinky bombs.

So, what's a witch to do? Give them the finger, of course. So I did.

Holding my breath, I moved closer to Andromalius and walked alongside him, straining to match his speed even though every step sent jarring pain through my spine. Anywhere was better than this shithole, literally.

We walked in silence across what I could now see was a gargantuan cave, the size of a football field—less the cages. Lights played in soft colors on the walls, mostly shifting in reds and yellows. The cave was made of black rock, and the walls were jagged and sharp like razor blades. I made a mental note to not touch the walls if I didn't want to lose a finger.

"Where are you taking me?" I was a curious creature. I couldn't help it. All witches were. How did that saying go? Curiosity killed the witch—*and* her cat? Yeah, we were always meddling in things that didn't concern us.

The minotaur demon's muzzle clenched, but he said nothing.

"How come I'm still alive and breathing?" I waited a beat longer. "I'm mortal. I shouldn't be alive. How is it that I'm still alive?"

Andromalius shifted his gaze down to me, and for a moment I thought he was going to answer. His yellow eyes blazed, but then he looked away and kept walking.

"Not much of a talker." Grimacing, I trudged forward, my hip and shoulder throbbing as another wave of nausea hit me, making me stumble. I caught myself before I fell flat on my face. I refused to show this demon how much pain I was in as I followed him.

The floor sloped slightly up, where a mound in the cave floor gave rise to an enormous steel door.

Andromalius pulled open the door and beckoned me to follow.

So I did.

With a curious sideways shuffle, I stole a peek behind the giant minotaur's back, but I saw only darkness and shadow. As soon as I crossed the threshold, I felt it.

For one breathless moment, I felt as though my entire soul chimed with sound of dark laughter. Demonic magic.

The air shimmered before me like heat waves. The pull of magic was strong, and it was making me feel even more nauseated.

When the world stabilized around me, I stood in a ballroom.

What the hell?

I stumbled into the massive room that was easily the size of a grand cathedral. Iron chandeliers hung from twenty-foot ceilings held by pillars decorated with paintings, depicting various demons battling winged angels. Orange light fell from overhead, illuminating the polished black floor into a myriad of colors. Iron tables lined the walls, laden with bottles, decanters, chocolates, cakes, and hundreds of different types of hard and chewy candy.

Across the ballroom, a group of demon musicians with several arms played instruments straight from the dark ages on a dais. The music was dark and medieval, sounding like a close version of Carl Orff's *Carmina Burana*.

The air was not better in here, and I tried not to take deep breaths though my lungs needed it.

The music turned faster, louder, and though I'd grown accustomed to the smell of demonic magic, my nose pricked and burned with the rising tang of sulfur, stronger than I'd ever sensed it.

The dancers were a spectacle on their own. Poe would have loved to see this.

Hundreds of demons danced about the room, mid-demons in their humanoid forms by the looks of them. There were no imps or ghouls here, though I couldn't distinguish any of their features beyond the various masks they wore.

Couples moved about the ballroom floor in blurs of fancy lace, silk, and shadows of swirling colors. They danced expertly, moving to the rhythm of the dark orchestra.

Demons had masquerade balls? How twisted was this?

More disturbing was that none of the dancing demons paid any attention to me, too enthralled in the music and the dancing, as though they were in some kind of trance.

I didn't care how pretty and lavish it all was, in a disturbing way. I just wanted to go home and breathe clean air. I wanted to get back to my life, to my world.

I looked up at Andromalius, and the minotaur demon was still, looking like a statue carved out from Greek mythology.

"If I had known this was a soirée," I managed to get out, "I would have worn my dancing shoes."

And then the music stopped. So did the dancing.

Shit.

My heart did its own beating of music as the ballroom floor dancers parted in unison like a great curtain.

In the middle of the ballroom floor stood a single female demon.

She was dressed in a light blue formal ball gown with a wide, floor-skimming skirt that could have fit five demons under it, a robe à la française. It was open at the front and ended in a flowing train. A long neckline and a generous amount of breast spilled from the top of the fitted and jewel-adorned bodice.

Her white-colored wig was styled in a pouf, piled a foot over her head in neat tresses and decorated with bows and sparkling jewelry.

Her skin was paperwhite and flawless, as though she'd never seen the sun in a thousand years—very vampiric. Unlike the other dancers, she wasn't wearing a mask, revealing a thin face with hard edges. She wasn't exactly pretty, but she wasn't ugly either.

If I were to guess, I'd say she was going for a Marie Antoinette look. Though I doubted the late French queen would have sported red eyes with that outfit.

Her blood-red eyes narrowed, and her expression was filled with a stern, almost regal confidence. An amused smile curled her perfect red lips.

The only thing I knew or could be sure of in this godforsaken place at this very moment was that I was staring at Vorkol, the late Greater demon Vargal's wife.

CHAPTER
16

"**M**ove!" With a powerful thrust, Andromalius rammed me in the back, and I pitched forward. Unable to stop my fall, I slammed into the cold, hard floor in a jumble of limbs. My chin smacked the cold stone and I tasted blood in my mouth, my bones groaning and barking in pain. Fire blazed across my face and in my limbs. I hurt everywhere.

Harsh, guttural laughter rose all around me, the sound bouncing off the walls and echoing in my ears, nightmarish and endless. Bastards. Pure hatred filled me, and for a moment it consumed my pain. If only I could use my magic, I'd burn them all.

"Get up," growled Andromalius, and a thick hand grabbed me by the arm and hauled me to my feet, sparks dancing in my eyes as I steadied myself.

"Move," he said again and pushed me forward. It was a miracle I stayed upright.

Wincing, I willed my legs forward, moving as fast as I could without breaking into tears. God, it hurt. I didn't want to add to the already self-satisfied smile on Vorkol's face. She was enjoying my pain a little too much—and rightly so. I had killed her husband. But, like I said, he'd started it.

Andromalius's heavy pace and breathing sounded right behind me. He stood ready to slice my head off at the first sign of trouble, no doubt.

A smart and sane witch would have been scared shitless. But I was neither. I wasn't scared. I was angry. Furious. She'd taken me away from my loved ones, my family, my friends, and stuck me in a cage like an animal.

Gritting my teeth, I raised my chin and stared Vorkol in the eye as I walked toward her. The slight narrowing of her eyes at my defiance almost made me smile. Like hell I'd show her fear. Yes, she might kill me right here in her glorious ballroom, but I wouldn't die a frightened little witch. I'd die fighting like a dark witch, with everything I had in me. I had more balls than most male dark witches. *Bring it on, demon bitch.*

The assembled demons flanked me on either side, still like soldiers from hell. The demons were a silent group, straight in attention of their mistress. That kind of control and power was terrifying, and I was a little envious of her.

Vorkol was not the Queen of France, but it was obvious she thought she was the queen of something.

Great. I'd pissed off some version of the queen of the Netherworld, or something close to it.

She never moved, except for the small, horrible smile she gave me. She stood and waited as I trudged forward, her demonic magic sizzling in the foul air between us. She had a lot of it. I was envious about that too.

Finally, I made it to her without falling on my face again. Yay for me. Now that we were a mere six feet apart, she was even skinnier and fouler up close. Her white skin, offset by her ruby eyes and lips, made her even more terrifying. She was scary, but I'd never show it. She wasn't devastatingly beautiful as some of the vamp females I'd seen in my world, but her eyes held the power of some demoness of darkness and malevolence. I could tell no one screwed with her.

It was clear she wasn't the queen of her legion on account of her looks. No, this female got her power by taking it.

Vorkol opened her mouth and said, "What's this? The little bird is out of her cage?" She spoke with a faint accent that was impossible to pinpoint. From her neck hung a long, thin chain—and from it dangled a single, black jewel the size of a golf ball. Like my rings, I could sense the magic pulsing from it. It was a magical artifact, a tool that helped her channel her magic.

I was glad she was using English and not the old demon languages. My Enochian was rusty. But why even bother? Why hadn't she killed me already?

The demonesses' face twisted into an ugly snarl. "How is it that a small, worthless mortal witch, such as yourself, killed Vargal? A Greater demon, the highest commander of the Damnation Army?"

Shit. Right to the point. When trying to avoid a question, ask another question. "How is it possible that I'm here at all," I said between coughs, "standing before you, in this place? Andromalius isn't much of a talker. Something tells me... you are."

Her eyes widened, and a sneer marked her features, making her appear false and cold. I braced myself.

I'm dead.

"I made sure my higher demons cut you," said Vorkol, surprising me and enjoying the shock she saw on my face. "The death blade's poison is enough to get you through the gateway to our realm." She shrugged. "Eventually you'll die, but not today. I wanted to see with my own eyes this *great* witch with immeasurable power." She cocked a brow. "All I see is a little birdy out of her cage. Small. Insignificant. Mortal."

Again, her entourage of demons threw back their heads and laughed. It was getting old.

Subconsciously, I reached behind my back and felt where I'd been stabbed. "So, you wanted me here?" I questioned, my voice bitter. It was getting harder to speak because of the burn in my throat, which was closing up. She either wanted to kill me herself or enjoy seeing me die. It was obvious now.

Vorkol took a step closer to me, and the scent of rotten onions filled my nose, making my eyes water. "I won't ask you again," she ordered, angling her head as though her wig was too heavy for her thin neck. "How did you do it? How did you kill Vargal?"

Well, I was in a conundrum. If I told her how I did it, she would either kill me or worse, drain me of my power for herself. I couldn't let that happen. My power would enable her to borrow magic from other demons and gods, bending it to her will and making her into one of the most powerful creatures in the Netherworld.

The realization dawned on me. That's why I was here. It's why she'd had her higher demons drag me here. She wanted to know *how* I'd done it. How a little ol' witch like me had killed her precious Vargal.

No way would I tell her, but if I didn't say anything, she was going to kill me.

So, I decided to do what only I could. I was going to fight. I wasn't a fool. I knew I couldn't win this fight, not against hundreds of demons. But if I was going down, I would go down fighting.

Still breathing this acid-like air, I pulled on the power of my rings. A faint tug answered. There was power there, but barely. Hope filled me. I could do this. I would burn the wig off her ugly head, if nothing else.

Vorkol's lips parted, and her gaze moved to my hands.

I called to the power of my rings, feeling their warmth and the light tug on my soul as I reached out to them. Raising my hands, I shouted, "Fulgur—"

Tendrils of darkness slammed into me. The last thing I saw was Vorkol flicking her wrist before my breath whooshed out and I hit the floor. White-hot pain exploded into me as the heat of the demon's magic burned through me. I screamed and felt as though my soul was trying to burn out from my pores. It was as though Vorkol was pulling it out.

"Is this it? Is this the extent of your power?" laughed Vorkol. I took a deep breath and regretted it immediately as the acid air scorched my lungs.

Vorkol let out a short, rough chuckle. "You think you can kill me? You think you can best me with your witch magic? Go on, then, little bird. Give it your best shot."

The sound of laugher boomed around me, echoing in my ears like the beating of dark drums. Anger swept through me like a fever. I hated demons. Really hated them.

I lifted my head and stared at her through my eyelashes. "Maybe not. But it was worth a try just to see that look on your face that just maybe... I *can* kill you." Yeah. Nice going, Sam.

Silk and lace rustled as Vorkol leaped toward me, her skirts shifting as they brushed the polished black floors. She bared her teeth, inches from me. Her breath came in a snarl, her red gaze crazed and fevered with savage intent.

Did she think she could she scare me in that dress? She didn't.

Adrenaline shot through me as I pulled on my magic again, knowing what was coming. But I didn't care. Energy hummed through me as I willed it to come. I was going to let her have it.

"Feurantis!" I howled as twin balls of fire sprouted in my hands. I flicked them at her.

Vorkol screamed as sheets of yellow and red flames rose from her dress and reached high above her wig. Her howl, guttural, not human, echoed against the walls and reverberated through me.

The bitch was burning. Good. I could still fight my way out of this.

The scent of burnt flesh filled the air around me. I braced myself for the following onslaught of demons, but they hadn't even moved. Their eyes were on Vorkol. Even Andromalius was still, the red and orange flames of his mistress burning reflecting in his yellow eyes.

This was *not* good.

Vorkol screamed one last time. Then through the flames, her eyes opened against the torment just as another sound came from her lips. Laughter.

With a pop of displaced air, the flames that had been burning her a second ago vanished, revealing the perfectly tailored blue silk and lace dress. There wasn't a scorch mark on it, or on her.

Now I was in deep doo-doo.

The ballroom exploded in loud applause and praises, and the demoness took a bow, as though she'd just finished her performance on stage.

I clenched my jaw. She'd just played me.

Vorkol fixed her gaze back on mine, seeing the anger simmering there, and her pale skin darkened.

The smile she gave me was truly serpentine, and it terrified me.

"My turn," she said.

Oh. Shit. Now I felt fear.

I had a second of doubt. I could have tried to protect myself, but what was the point.

She attacked.

Tendrils of darkness shot from her outstretched hands and ripped into me. The world flipped over, and pain lit through me as the demon's magic, raw and unfiltered, ripped through my body to my soul and began to consume it. It was hard to explain, but I knew that's what she was doing. She was eating away at my soul.

Panic surged and I jerked, instinct moving in as I tried to tap into my rings. The pain was too intense and I lost my focus. I fell to the floor as her demon magic flowed in me. The pain was so powerful, black spots marred my vision.

I was dying. Or I was about to pass out.

Laughter reached me, and I looked up to find Vorkol standing over me, her eyes wide with excitement and hungry for my soul. I blinked through my tears and saw a thin white veil, like a mist pulling away from my body and into that black jewel around her neck. In my pain, I could see a part of my soul slipping into her, my strength going with it.

Somehow I knew it wasn't all of my soul, only part of it. But something was different. I felt weak and feverish like I had the flu. If she kept this up, I was a very dead witch.

"Tell me how you killed Vargal," came Vorkol's voice, "and I'll make the pain go away."

"Bite me, princess," I wheezed. Yeah, not the smartest thing to say, but she had just stolen a part of my soul.

The last thing I saw was Vorkol's face twisting in a grimace before she hit me again with her darkness.

I tried to move out of the way, but it was too late. The tendrils hit and lifted me off the ground, flinging me across the ballroom like a rag doll. I hit a pillar—or at least I think it was a pillar, but it could have been a wall—and dropped to the floor. I couldn't breathe. I slid to the floor in a crumpled pile of limbs, my cheek on the cold stone tile.

This was not how I planned to spend my night.

I rolled onto my stomach, clenching in pain. My sight went gray at the pain, and I nearly passed out. My face rubbed onto the hard floor as I coughed the acid-like air every time I took a breath.

Vorkol's skirts swished as she walked toward me, a collection of rustling fabric whispers, carrying the scent of sulfur and rotten onions. "Tell me!" she howled. Her wig slipped over her brow, and she pushed it back. Her red eyes darkened, and my fear slid deeper and twisted in my gut. "Tell me, or I will tear you apart. You can spend eternity down here in your cage, with no arms, no legs, and no soul," she cried, full of an unsatisfied hunger. Vorkol was a predator. She killed to take what she wanted, but she wouldn't take me.

I knew Vorkol would play with me until she ripped me apart and took all of my soul.

But a faint whisper of self-preservation forced me to turn my head and face her, or maybe I was just crazy and stupid. Perhaps a little bit of both.

My lips parted, but nothing was coming out. My body shook with pain. My head lolled to the side because I didn't have the strength to keep it straight. Straining, I tried to spindle the magic from my rings, but I was only an empty shell. The magic I'd felt before was gone, and I didn't have the energy to will it back.

Before I knew what was happening, I heard the sharp sound of flesh smacking flesh. When the pain hit, I realized it had been my flesh. *My* face.

The world lurched, and I hit the cold polished floors again. A pained sob escaped me as I lay on the floor in a crumpled heap, my breath a whisper and my lungs burning with every intake of air.

"Duvali. Take those rings off of her," I heard Vorkol say, and my eyes snapped open.

A maskless demon male loomed over me. Though he, too, shared the humanoid features, they were gaunt and repulsive somehow, like they didn't fit. He almost seemed as though he were still wearing a mask made of flesh. His skin was pale gray, and his large, crooked nose seemed like it might have been broken a few times. He was tall and thin, with mousy-brown hair, and to me, he looked like he might have been a scarecrow in some lifetime past. There was no beauty in his features, just a twisted malice, as though inflicting pain to others was his favorite thing.

The demon named Duvali reached down, yanked my hand forcefully, and pulled off my rings from both hands. Then he placed them in Vorkol's waiting palm.

I looked up at her, and when she was sure I was watching, she made a fist with her hand, her lips moving in some demonic curse. When she opened her hand a moment later, all that remained of my golden sigil rings was a pile of golden dust.

Vorkol laughed and wiped her hands, golden dust falling about her skirts to the floor like sheets of golden pixie dust. "I'm going to enjoy breaking you, little bird."

Well, now I was neck deep in the crapper.

The crowd of demons parted, and then a familiar face appeared among them—one I'd seen only a few hours ago—looking pale and terrified. I'd never seen those emotions on the mid-demon's face before.

Faris's lips moved, but I couldn't understand what he was saying. He stood there, jaw clenched, his expression shifting from shock and fear to something I didn't understand.

He didn't come to me. He didn't help. He just stood there, watching my helplessness and pain.

It was a surprisingly painful moment of realization that he'd just leave me here to die. But what did I expect? He was a demon.

I pulled my eyes away, but before I could stop them, the tears fell. They just did. I was exhausted, and seeing Faris there—watching me get my ass kicked but doing nothing to stop it—was worse than the pain Vorkol had inflicted on me.

I wasn't a robot, and this hurt like a bitch because I thought he was my friend. I thought a demon was my friend. It sounded absurd. I was a fool.

"You *will* tell me how you did it before you die," said Vorkol, her voice a triumphant hiss, and her wig slipped to the side of her head again. "That's a promise." She straightened as though she'd won some victory and said, "Put the bird back in her cage where she belongs."

I turned to the sound of a something heavy approaching and Andromalius stepped in my line of sight, still stinking of sulfur and manure.

"Up," ordered the minotaur. I'd forgotten all about him.

I tried to move, but I couldn't even feel my legs or my arms anymore. The world spun and I strained to keep my head up. I blinked but couldn't stop the darkness that crept into my vision.

Andromalius grabbed my arm, and the darkness took me.

CHAPTER
17

The vampire leaned over the young witch, teeth bared and gleaming in the streetlight.

"Stop!" I howled and ran through traffic to get to the other side of the road. My arms pumped as I gained speed, all the while pulling on the energy of my sigil rings.

The vampire turned at the sound of my approach. A hoodie kept his face in shadow, but I could see his smile well enough.

I reached him and yelled, "Vento!" I threw out my hands and hit him with a wind blast.

It caught the vampire in the chest, and he flew back, away from the witch at least twenty feet. But the pointy-toothed vampire managed to land on his feet, smiling. The bastard was as agile as a cat. He let out a velvety laugh that made me want to punch him.

"You think it's funny, you bloodsucking bastard." *I'm not finished with you.*

I really wanted to kill this vampire. One, well, because he was bad, and two, because after this I'd wanted nothing to do with the dark witch court ever again. After him, I was done with them. With all of them.

I walked over to the witch, saw that her chest was moving, and no puncture wounds or blood marred her, and took that as a good sign. I moved toward the vampire.

"It ends tonight," I said. "You won't hurt any more witches. You're finished."

I lifted my hands, gathered my anger and my disgust as handy sources of fuel, and shouted, "Involuta!"

Furious power rushed out of me, lashing out in a blaze of white and blue fire that spun around the vampire. Ribbons of blue and white fire wrapped around him, burning brighter and hotter, the spell cocooning him in flames.

With a bored expression, he lifted his right hand, and my ribbons of fire disintegrated into puffs of smoke.

Damn. I forgot. He had some magic of his own. Speaking of magic, a dark, black haze lifted around him, spilling behind him like a rippling cloak.

"Okay." I shrugged, closing the distance between us. "So that was pretty cool, but I'm still going to kill your ass."

He opened his mouth, showing his fangs, and laughed. "I'm coming for you, Samantha."

I pursed my lips, still holding on to my magic. "Look here. We've already got something in common." I smiled. "I'm coming for you too. Hasta Feuro!" I threw out my hand and a yellow-orange spear-like fire blasted toward the vampire.

With a burst of impossible speed, he moved, and in a blur of motion, he appeared next to me.

I flinched. "You're a sneaky sonofabitch." And yeah, that was cool too.

I pulled on my magic and held it. He was close enough this time for me to hit him again, and this time I wouldn't miss. This time, he would burn. "You can tell your demon mistress that she can kiss my ass," I said, my rings pulsing with magic and begging to be released.

The vampire's smile grew. "Sam," he said, his voice a harsh whisper, and then he took a step forward and into the dim light.

Adrenaline hit, my lips parted in my readied spell—

The hoodie fell back from the vampire's face, and Logan stared back at me...

"Sam!"

My eyes fluttered open, and for a moment I thought I was in my bed back in Mystic Quarter. But when I took a breath and winced as the acid air burned me, I knew I was still in the Netherworld, and in my cage, no less.

I had no idea what time it was or how long I'd slept. Years, maybe. Who knew? I lay on the floor of my cage for a moment, tired and a little dizzy. I hadn't eaten anything since that grilled cheese, and I was dying to use the bathroom. Did they even have bathrooms? No, the incident with the minotaur before told me the bathroom was right through the cage bars. Now that's going to be interesting.

"Sam!" hissed the same voice I'd heard in my dream.

Slowly, I sat up and peeked down through the bars. Faris stood on the ground, staring up at me. He wore his signature body-snugging black shirt and matching pants. With his dark hair styled to perfection, he looked clean and fresh and ready to go out on a date. It made me sick.

The cage next to me shook. "Sam!" screeched my caged neighbor. "Sam. Sam. Sam. Sam," he repeated, jumping up and down.

The demon was humanoid, maybe four feet tall, give or take a few inches, with a mane of silver, shaggy hair that stuck to his face in dirty clumps and blended with his long, thin silver beard. A gray, weatherworn robe, which I suspected had once been white, hung loosely on his thin frame. His limbs—thin from what I could see of them—were stained and dirty, as was his face. The bones of his gaunt face were sharp, and he was smiling. His blue eyes, lit with fever and madness, were fixated on me.

"Well, I must say," expressed Faris, a smile on his face as he watched the small demon dance around his cage, repeating my name. "Your friend seems excited. What did you do to him?"

Frustrated, I slumped back. "Go away," I hissed and turned around. Bastard. What did he want?

The surrounding demon prisoners screeched and hissed, the sound rising like a sigh of excitement.

"Sammy, darling," pleaded the mid-demon. "Don't do this. You know I love you, you silly little witch. I had to use many of my bribes to get here. Do you know how many souls I had to trade for a little R & R with you?"

"I don't care," I yelled back. My voice shook, and I hated that he was seeing me like this—defeated, abused, and angry as hell. "I should have never trusted you."

"Trust!" squealed the little demon in delight as he clapped his hands. "Trust. Trust. Trust..."

Faris made a loud exaggerated sigh. "Here. Catch."

I turned around just as Faris tossed a package wrapped in a black cloth up toward me. Figuring I had nothing to lose, I slipped my arm through the bars and caught it easily.

I yanked my arm back and peeled the cloth away from the bundle. A moan escaped me. An apple, slices of cheese and cold cuts stared back at me. Fresh by the smell of them. My mouth salivated. But then...

"Did you poison these?" I asked, feeling foolish, but I had to ask. I was in the Netherworld. Maybe food was different here. Maybe it was toxic to mortals.

Faris's face twisted in annoyance. "Don't be stupid. Here. Water."

I caught the water bottle and even before putting that glorious slice of cheese in my mouth, I had the bottle open and drank as much water in one gulp as I could without being sick. I smacked my lips. Damn that was some good water—the best water I'd ever tasted in my life.

Next, I tore into that cheese. "Thank you," I said, my mouth full. "I was starving."

Faris was shaking his head. "Higher demons, right?" he questioned. "When?"

I took another bite of cheese and washed it down with some water. "On my way home. Just after you left." I felt eyes on me and looked up to find my neighbor still, hands wrapped around the bars. His forehead was pressed against the bars with his blue eyes following the cheese in my hands. He looked like he hadn't eaten in years. My chest tightened, and I felt sorry for him.

"But it was sunrise," said Faris. The surprise in his voice softened my anger a little, but not enough.

Irritation pulled my muscles tight. "Yeah, well, they jumped me where the sun hadn't hit yet. In the shadow of a building. I didn't know they could do that. They had a Rift there waiting for me." I should have known they'd try something like that. I should have been better prepared. I took a bite of cheese, watching the little demon stare at my mouth, drool slipping at the edges of his lips.

"Yes. That would do it," commented Faris, drawing my attention back to him at the nonchalant tone of his voice. He pulled at his sleeves and picked off what I'd assumed was lint. Then I lost it.

"How could you? How could you just stand there and let her hurt me!" I screamed. "You let her take a part of my soul! My soul! And did nothing."

Faris put his hands on his hips, which only infuriated me more. "Sammy, baby. If I had interrupted Vorkol at her own party—if I had *intervened*—she would have had her entourage shred me to bits," he said, his voice low and controlled. "First. I happen to like myself very much. And second, how am I supposed to help you escape if I'm dead?"

I let out a huff. "Why should I believe you? You're a demon." I was pissed off, hurt, tired, and feeling the beginnings of a claustrophobia attack if I didn't get out of this cage soon. Or I'd simply go mad, a blabbering idiot, like my neighbor.

"I wouldn't have risked my reputation if I didn't care," he said, a hint of anger in his voice.

"Reputation?" I laughed, feeling ill. "I'm in a damn cage, and all you care about is your reputation." I frowned. Part of me wanted to throw his food back in his face, but the other part, the smarter part, won. I kept the food right where it was.

"You're a mortal. You can't possibly understand."

"Try me," I growled, my stomach aching from too much stress and not enough food.

Faris sighed and shifted his weight on his feet. "It's all I have. Here in the Netherworld, your reputation either makes you or breaks you. Unlike the mortal world, it's not about the money or how many fancy cars you have in your garage. Here. It's what you can do with the little power you have."

"You mean souls?" I was starting to hate him.

"Yes." He shrugged like that wasn't supposed to be disturbing to me. "I'm a demon. Souls are my business."

"It's a sick business." I swallowed the last of my cheese, savoring the taste on my tongue and knowing this might be the last time I'd taste cheese ever again. That was so very sad.

Faris was silent, and he sent his eyes over my cage. "What about your magic? How much of it can you use? Obviously most of it is tied to your home world, but as a witch," he was saying as though he were talking to himself, "you have demonic blood, which means it is still operational. Just not at a hundred percent. Rusty. Like an old Buick."

My gut tightened, and I felt like I was about to vomit. "You were there, Faris. You saw what she did to my rings. Without them... I've got nothing." Except for my gift, but I wasn't about to announce it to the world right now. Besides, I didn't even know if it'd do me any good. If Poe were here, maybe he could have helped me. But how does one get out of the Netherworld? Rifts were used to get into my world, so perhaps it was the same thing here. It made sense to me. If I wanted to get out, I needed to find a Rift to my world.

"The rings can't be the only source of your power. You're a dark witch, for demon's sake. I've seen what you can do. There's more magic in you than you think."

"Not enough." My voice was final. He didn't have to know the rest.

"Mmm," grumbled Faris, apparently dissatisfied. "That does pose a significant problem. Without any means of magic, it won't be nearly enough."

I snapped my attention back to him, the remainder of my meal forgotten. "What are you talking about?" I demanded, not liking the hint of fear in his voice. "Faris?" The distant look in his eyes and the way he was looking at me made me more nervous.

Faris's expression twisted and he looked away. "Vorkol likes to be entertained, as you witnessed tonight. She has a healthy appetite for flaying and torture parties."

I shrugged. "Your typical stereotypical female villain. So what?"

The mid-demon shook his head. "She's worse," he said. His eyes met mine, and they looked completely black in the dim light. "Much worse."

"Figures."

"How does that mortal expression go again?" he added thoughtfully as he cocked his head. "Make love, not war? If you ask me, I prefer sex over torture. Unless there's a bit of torture *with* the sex. Then all is well." He grinned.

I rolled my eyes. "How nice of you to be thinking about sex when I'm about to be killed."

"Sammy, darling," drawled Faris, a sly smile on his face. "One can never stop thinking about sex. It's unhealthy."

"Not as much as *not* having sex," I grumbled, and Logan's face flashed in my mind's eye before I quickly quashed it away.

"Vorkol is ancient and powerful," Faris was saying. "She was here long before me and long before many of the lesser demons. Her favorite thing is to see suffering. She has plans for you."

"Swell."

"She likes to play games with mortals." He stiffened, a muscle feathering along his jaw. "If you think today was bad, you'll want to slice your own wrists when you see what she has planned for you."

"You're just full of sunshine. Aren't you?"

Faris lifted his hands dramatically. "Why did you have to go and piss her off by killing her mate? Couldn't you have just... ignored him? I mean—how bad could he have been?"

My jaw dropped. "He was trying to *kill* me," I said incredulously. "He was also killing innocent mortals to raise some pagan god. Remember?"

He made a face, eyebrows high. "Nobody's perfect."

A loud boom shook the cave's walls, and then my cage shook. My heart gave a beat before settling into a normal pace. In the distance, the sound of the grinding of rocks grew and died, like the tremor from an earthquake. Or it could have been two gargantuan demons fighting each other.

Faris whirled around toward the sound and then looked back up at me. "Sammy, darling. I don't have much time left. I'm going to do my best to get you out."

"Your *best*?" Was he freaking serious? I wanted out of this cage just so I could kick his stupid, condescending demon ass.

"I mean"—his smile faltered and he cleared his throat—"I'm going to get you out. No need to get all pissy and emotional. It's not going to be easy for me."

"So don't bother." He was really starting to piss me off. Granted, he had brought me some food and water. I let my shoulders fall. "You're deluding yourself. I'm never getting out." The thought of spending the rest of my days locked up in this cage had my insides twisting.

The mid-demon scowled at me. "You know I think you are a hot-blooded female. But right now, you're acting like a child."

I let out a tired laugh. "I'm exhausted, Faris. I'm tired and I hurt and I think I'm missing a part of my soul. So forgive me for being a little *pissy* and *emotional*." The memory of Vorkol reaching into my chest and pulling a piece of my soul had my cheese threatening to come back up.

I just wanted to go home...

The sound of a stomach rumbling reached me. I looked down at my middle and realized it wasn't me. I glanced up to find the haggard demon still with his face stuck to the bars of his cage, his big blue eyes pleading and teary.

God, he looked pathetic. But he *was* a demon. I didn't even know why I cared. He was probably in here because he didn't bring in enough souls or did something *really* bad—in demon terms. Or maybe he was another victim of Vorkol's injustice. He reminded me of that scruffy old dog I'd seen once at the local pound. I never did get over his sad eyes. I always regretted not taking him home with me. It still pained me to think about what happened to him.

I let out a shaky breath and looked down at my cold cuts, turkey from the smell of them. I was still ravenous, but somehow, it didn't feel right to eat them.

Resolute, I folded up the remaining food in the cloth along with the rest of my water bottle. Still holding on to it, I stuck my arm through the bars toward my neighbor.

"Here," I said, dangling the bundle before him. "Take it."

The gaunt demon jerked back, surprise flashing on his face, and his bottom lip shook.

"Sam? What are you doing?" hissed Faris. "Don't give him any food. He's going to die anyway. You're going to waste that on a dead demon?"

"I am."

"Do you know how many souls I had to trade for that?" he added, clearly pissed.

"I don't care." I met the scrawny demon's blue eyes. "Take it," I urged him, ignoring Faris's cry of outrage. "It's okay. You can have it."

In a blur, the demon snatched up the bundle, faster than I would have thought possible in his miserable state, sat in the corner of his cage and began to eat. I sighed. Poor little bastard.

"You do realize he would have probably killed you for it," said Faris, his tone dry and accusing. "You have no idea what you've just done."

"I just gave a little bit of food to someone who really needed it." Maybe Faris was right, but I was too tired to care. I sat back and wiggled to a comfortable position, if you consider having metal bars pressed up against your ass and back comfortable. "You should go, Faris. The minotaur will be back. You don't want to end up like us."

"I'd kill myself," stated Faris, his face squished up in disgust as he took in the other cage tenants' ragged physiques and dirt-smeared cages. His eyes found mine. "I'll get you out, Sam," he said. "I promise."

"I thought demons didn't make promises," I said, watching the scrawny demon eat his meal with shaking, gnarled hands. "Not unless it was a promise to kill you."

"I'll get you out."

I glanced back at the sound of determination in Faris's voice. I almost believed him. But if what he said about Vorkol was true, he was wasting his breath. I was never getting out.

And with that, the mid-demon, dressed in his finest, turned on his heel and left.

I watched him go with a heavy heart. He was the only demon I knew in the Netherworld.

Now I felt truly alone and utterly hopeless.

CHAPTER
18

I woke to the sound of my cage bars rattling.

And then I was falling. With me still in the cage.

Great. Here we go again.

Together we hit the ground. I'd barely had time to register the pain of impact before the minotaur opened my cage's door and pulled me out.

Andromalius tossed me on the dirt-packed ground like a used cloth. I spat the dirt from my mouth just as a chaos of shouts and cries erupted above me. The cave was filled with screams as the other prison guests shouted their outrage at me being out of my confinement again. But I wasn't stupid enough to think this was a good thing. I knew being out of the cage was bad. Really bad.

Vorkol was going to question me again, and when I didn't answer, she would take more of my soul. It was hard to keep from shivering, and I had the sudden insane impulsive thought to make a run for it.

But where would I go? A Rift. I needed to find a Rift.

"Up," roared the minotaur demon.

Grimacing in pain, I did what I was told and staggered to my feet. If Faris hadn't given me any food and water, I don't think I could have stood, not with the constant burn of the acidic air.

"Move," ordered Andromalius, his yellow eyes gleaming with contempt and his nostrils flaring.

He didn't have to tell me twice.

I walked toward the steel door, the only exit I could see in the giant cave. I stole a covert glance over at Andromalius, but his dark fur, retracted muzzle, and permanent scowl gave me no indication of what was about to happen to me. Except, perhaps, more pain.

The minotaur pulled open the door. Behind the threshold more of the dark mist fell, but all I could make out was simply darkness. I followed him and stepped through to the other side. Darkness and demonic magic were a heavy cloak around me. My core rang with demonic power, dark and cold like a malevolent intent spilling over me, telling me I didn't belong. I held my breath and padded forward in the thick shadows.

As soon as the darkness lifted, I gasped.

I blinked. And then I blinked again, waiting for my brain to acknowledge what I was staring at. I was not standing in a ballroom.

I was standing in an arena the size of a hockey rink, oval shaped, with circular rows of seats on the upper levels. Double steel doors stood across from me on the ground level. A hot wind that smelled of rotten flesh fluttered across the golden sand. Black flags mounted on high poles rippled, displaying a black serpent within a red circle. I could see a white, flourlike line had been drawn on the sand. One step outside of that ring and I'd be disqualified, or dead.

Fantastic.

Okay. So, Vorkol had some heavy-duty magic. I thought only gods and goddesses could change realities. Boy, was I wrong.

The rows of seats were filling up, and across from me, on the upper levels, lay a small balcony. And on a thronelike chair sat Vorkol.

She'd ditched her Marie Antoinette guise for a tight, red pantsuit that showed off her lean frame, complete with red shirt and tie. Now that the wig was gone, I could see her hair was blonde and slicked back into a tight low bun. She finished her look with ruby-red lipstick that matched her six-inch red pumps. She looked more like a colorful lawyer than a demon.

Pillows, cushions, thick woven carpets, and low, narrow tables were positioned on the balcony. A mix of six male and female demons lounged on the balcony floor among the cushions. They all had something in common. Fake smiles marred their faces, and their eyes were locked on to me, cementing my belief that *I* was the entertainment.

The demon Duvali stood behind Vorkol. His white suit only made his pale, pasty skin whiter, but it did nothing to remove that gangly, gaunt scarecrow look about him. Damn, he was vile.

Vorkol's her red eyes stared into mine. Her lips curled into the kind of knowing smile a psychopath would give right before slicing someone's throat.

My heart threw itself backward and clung to the bars of my rib cage.

This was no ordinary arena. It was a fighting pit.

I'd seen my share of fighting pits in the werewolf community. The only difference was this one was enormous, and in the Netherworld.

When Faris had told me Vorkol enjoyed playing games, I had no idea he'd meant it literally.

I threw my gaze around the rows of seats. The noise of the crowds rose in excitement—the high-pitched laughter of the females and the hoarse cries of the male demons calling out each other with what looked like bets. Great. They were betting on me—or against me.

The reassuring weight of my sigil rings was gone, so I had nothing.

A lone figure stood in the first row of the seated demons. Faris. Our eyes met, and only then did he seat himself, his eyes never leaving mine. He sat between two pretty demon females. Both were blondes, leggy, and with enough boobs to have the average college boy drooling.

The only thing out of place was his face. Faris wasn't smiling, despite the voluptuous females who were practically sitting on his lap. Thin lipped, the mid-demon's frown had my pulse rising. His expression said it all. This was going to get ugly.

He said he would get me out, but would it even matter if I didn't survive this? Whatever this was?

Nausea gripped me, but Andromalius took me by the elbow and escorted me to the far end of the pit.

He let me go, and I turned and looked up at him. "No rest for the wicked, eh?"

The large minotaur's nostrils flared as he looked me over and then walked away.

"Nice talking to you," I grumbled as I watched him disappear through another set of doors. Then I heard the sound of a latch closing.

Heart thrashing, I looked around the arena and cringed. I hated being the center of attention, and now I had hundreds, possibly thousands of demon eyes on me. Worse, I recognized two demons I'd summoned before sitting in the seats—Paimon and Barbatos, both in their human forms. Their angry expressions told me they were anxiously waiting for me to get what I deserved.

I had no idea what that would be, but when the steel doors burst open and flew off their hinges, I knew.

A low, loud bellow erupted from inside the lower level of the arena, and then a tiger-sized spider came scuttling out of the doorway.

"Oh, crap," I breathed, goose bumps riddling my skin. I hated spiders. Especially really big, hairy ones that looked like they could bite my head off.

Thick black hair and bristles covered its body, except for its eight legs. They were covered in red hair, and each ended with a sharp claw. Fangs the size of my arm dripped with yellow venom. Two large yellow eyes sat in the middle of its head framed by three smaller ones on each side.

The spider stopped inside the white outline across from me. Its head shook from side to side, and it looked really pissed off and hungry. It had to weigh at least five hundred pounds, maybe more. Though this demon wasn't part of the seventy-two demons listed in the Ars Goetia, I knew what it was.

It was an igumo.

A giant spider demon. One of the more deadly of the lesser demon species, they were wild. No one could really control an igumo. They were too stupid. They were programmed to kill and then eat.

Every part of my body and brain told me to run. Run away and hide. I couldn't fight this demon, not with my bare hands. My legs trembled from the rush of adrenaline, yet my feet wouldn't move. My eyes found Faris. He leaned forward in his seat looking pale—almost as pale as I felt.

My stomach twisted on itself. How was I supposed to fight this thing without my magic rings?

Seeing Vorkol smiling at me made me want to scream.

"Can I at least get a wand?" I called out to the Greater demon. "Harry Potter was allowed a wand when he was dueling."

Vorkol stared at me like I was nuts. Hey, I had to try.

No wand. No weapon. No rings. Now what?

A lump of dread dropped in my belly as a wicked, contriving smile spread over Vorkol's face. "What seems to be the problem? Aren't you a powerful witch, Samantha Beaumont?" she said as she crossed her legs. "You killed a Greater demon. The igumo should be nothing to you."

I stared at the igumo's fangs, sharp as razors. Fear settled into me, debilitating. Panicked, I rummaged through my mind for clues on how I could kill it but came up with nothing. My mind was as empty as a blank sheet of paper. I was so screwed.

I licked my lips. "What about a weapon?" I doubted she'd give me anything, but it was worth a shot.

Vorkol never lost her smile. "You can use anything you find *in* the arena."

Your head? Jaw gritted, I glanced around the arena. The first row of seats was too high for me to reach, so borrowing any kind of magic was out of the question.

Movement caught my attention, and I turned to find something flat and dark gray spinning toward me in the air. It landed in the sand with a light thud.

Blinking, I stared at a small dagger, half buried in the sand five feet away from me.

I looked up in time to see Faris lowering himself in his seat. From Vorkol's dark expression, she'd seen him throw it.

I waited to see if she'd object. After five more seconds, I reached down and picked up the small dagger, seeing as Vorkol hadn't said a word. It was obvious she was pissed, but she'd said it herself. I could use anything I found in the arena.

I glanced down a the small pocket knife. Why did Faris throw me something so small? What would it do against a gargantuan-sized spider? The chorus of laughter and whistles that followed sent my face flaming.

I glared at Faris. "A sword would have been better."

The mid-demon said nothing as he leaned back in his seat, a satisfied though worried expression marring his face. He almost looked relieved that I had this puny knife while facing a giant opponent. Was he mad? Maybe he wanted me to die.

He watched me with the same content expression, as though that tiny weapon was my salvation and the answer to my gigantic spider problem. Like I was supposed to know what to do with the knife.

I grasped the tiny knife firmly in my hand. It was better than nothing. Maybe I could poke one of its eyes out, not that it would change anything.

"What are the rules?" I cried out, hating that my voice shook, but there was nothing I could do about it now. Every demon in this godforsaken arena could see and probably smell my fear. I was the witch who had exorcised some of them, and now they were getting payback.

The Greater demon smiled without teeth. "No rules. Except there can only be one winner. The one who survives the duel is the winner."

"And if I win," I said, my voice hoarse. "What happens then? Will you let me go home? Back to my world?" It was a long shot, but it was worth the try, especially with all the demon witnesses.

Vorkol's smile was surreal, hard and cold like a mannequin. "If you win the duel, you may return to your home world," she answered, her expression blank except for the strange smile that never left.

I'd take that. "So, anything goes? No rules, right?"

Vorkol lifted her arms in a gesture of acquiescence. "This is the Netherworld. And anything goes."

Okay, then. I swallowed hard, my head pounding from the hours of the acidic air poisoning my lungs and body.

I knew Faris was watching me. But I couldn't look at him now. The fear that showed on his face would probably ruin any hope I had of surviving this. Maybe I wasn't meant to survive. Maybe this was how I'd die.

The silence around the arena was thick, frighteningly profound, and my breath quickened.

Vorkol clapped her hands once.

And then the igumo charged.

CHAPTER
19

Have you ever had a giant spider chase you? Me neither.

And what's the first thing you do when you do have a giant spider chase you? You run. Well, you scream first—and then you run like hell.

Legs pumping with sweet adrenaline, I ran as fast as they would take me with lack of food and water, which wasn't fast. It was more the equivalent of a heavy smoker trying to run a block while coughing up his lungs. Yeah. I was a spectacle to watch.

Why did Faris toss me a puny knife?

I was glad I had an audience to see me like this. The roar of laughter reached me, but soon all I heard was the thrashing of my heart in my chest. There was only me, that gargantuan killer spider, and a puny knife.

Why had Faris looked at me like he'd just solved all my problems? Like I should know what to do with the knife?

Thank the cauldron the igumo wasn't a great sprinter. I'd run around the arena once now, and the demon spider was still behind me. But I wasn't an idiot, I couldn't run around like this for much longer. If the spider was smart, all it had to do was wait for my energy to run out. Then I was its meal

But I couldn't stop now. Stopping meant death. I didn't want to imagine what it would feel like to have its hairy, disgusting legs touch me or its fangs sinking into my skin. I might vomit.

If I was allowed anything at all, why would Faris toss me such a small thing?

Small knives were good for cutting and slicing.

And then it hit me.

The knife wasn't for the spider. It was for me. He intended for me to use it *on* me.

I spun around. Seeing that the igumo was halfway across from me, I pulled off my left glove, pocketed it, and gripped the knife in my right hand. I slashed it across my left palm, and dark red blood pooled in my palm, lots of it. I needed lots.

Gasps and cries of outrage slammed into the silence, but I didn't dare look at any of them. Especially not Vorkol.

I had power in my blood. Blood was power. All witches had it, some more than others. Blood magic was complicated, and I had never really gotten into it. It was messy. All that blood. Also I could never truly swallow the killing and sacrificing of small animals—

sometimes humans, but they were *bad* humans. I didn't want to go that route with my magic. Having demons do my bidding was easier, and I didn't have to kill a squirrel or a rat for it.

Still, I was in the Netherworld. The balance of magic and all things supernatural was different here. And yet Faris had tossed me a knife. That meant he knew my blood magic would work. I had to believe it. I had to trust him. He'd just risked exposing himself now. Vorkol had seen him. Things would be different for Faris now.

I fell to my knees, my focus clear, which was surprising under the giant-killer-spider demon circumstances.

The igumo halted about a hundred feet from me and cocked it head, seemingly catching a whiff of my blood. It was still for a moment, and then its body shook. A horrible wailing sound erupted from it—a sound a normal spider shouldn't make. This was no ordinary spider.

And then its fur changed from black to red—blood red, as though it were mimicking my blood and anticipating tasting it. Yikes.

I knew I had seconds before the spider attacked. *Here goes nothing.*

Squeezing my left hand, I drew a triangle-shaped sigil using my own blood in the sand before me. Moving quickly, I squeezed more blood out of my hand and added a circle next to the triangle. I wrote the name Sabnock in Latin in the center of the circle.

I looked up to find Faris's dark eyes locked on mine. He gave a small nod of encouragement. He knew exactly what I was doing. It had to work. It had to.

Then came the part where I had no idea if it was going to work.

By the cauldron, let me be right.

Taking a deep breath of acidic air, instead of stepping inside the circle, I stepped into the triangle.

Blood trickled down my left hand. I'd cut myself deeply, but that was the least of my problems.

The igumo screeched, and then it was on the move again.

Shit. Shit. Shit.

Gathering up my courage, I stood with fisted hands and willed my mind to focus as I channeled the magic from the blood summoning circle and triangle.

A wind rose around me, lifting my hair and carrying the scent of sulfur and rotten meat. My skin pricked as energy flowed in and around me. The air shifted, and a cold wave of energy cascaded over me.

It was working.

The igumo demon was only fifty feet away from me and coming fast.

The energy was unfamiliar, and yet I didn't stop. Channeling the blood magic, I recited the incantation as fast as my lips would move, all without pause. I cried, "I conjure you, Sabnock, demon of the Netherworld, to be subject to the will of my soul. I bind you with unbreakable adamantine fetters, and I deliver you into the black chaos in perdition. I invoke you, Sabnock, in the space in front of me!"

Energy rushed through me, cold, dark, and powerful, and I nearly fell backward. I steadied myself as the energy screamed and surged through my core, burning the inside of my body as though my blood were liquid fire.

Damn.

I gasped as the blood circle and triangle at my feet shimmered and sparked into life with yellow and orange flames. The air sizzled with magic, and I watched, amazed, as the energy churned and burned as it flowed around them.

The igumo demon halted at the sight of the fire, seemingly afraid or maybe even curious.

And then the real pain hit.

I reared back as searing pain screamed through my body. The full effect of the blood magic hit me, and it burned, vicious and endless. My body shook in agony. I couldn't breathe.

Blood magic hurt like a bitch. No wonder most witches stayed the hell away from it. But I would take the pain, all of it, if it meant a chance to get back home.

Heat rushed from me, leaving a sick, cold feeling in my stomach—the usual when conjuring demons.

And there, inside my circle, was a lizard demon the size of a rhinoceros.

"Holy shit," I breathed. "It worked."

Chapter

20

Who do you call when a giant spider is out to get you?

A kimono dragon on steroids, that's who.

Sabnock was huge, ugly, and by the roundness of his yellow eyes—pissed as hell. His skin was midnight blue with silver stripes along his back, all the way to his tail, tipped with three sharp spikes. His body was hard and rippling with muscles. Thick forelimbs with slightly higher hind limbs ended in clawed feet that could rip your head clean off with one strike. He opened his mouth and hissed, revealing rows of wickedly sharp teeth the size of kitchen knives. Excellent.

He was magnificent and deadly and mine, for the time being. Part of me wished he'd come in a smaller size. Was he good on a leash?

I shook with excitement, pride, fear, and satisfaction. Even in the Netherworld I could summon its own monsters. I was a true dark witch.

I felt pretty damn good about myself right about now even though I was in the Netherworld about to be eaten by a giant spider as the night's entertainment.

I smiled. I wasn't dead yet.

There was an immediate uproar from the demons, a sudden chorus of shouts and protest as outrage and anger filled the arena. It was music to my ears and filled me with valor. They weren't laughing anymore, and I wasn't just a puny little witch.

I met Faris's gaze, and the demon was smiling proudly at me. He winked and gave a nod of his head. I had no idea how he knew my blood magic would work, but now I owed him big time. Something occurred to me. If he'd known my blood magic would work, perhaps Faris really could get me out of here. The mid-demon was full of surprises.

But the real ticket was Vorkol's expression. Her red eyes focused on me, and her face twisted with rage. With her lips pressed tightly, the anger simmering behind her red eyes was almost palpable. Ooooh. She really hated me now. It made me all giddy inside. I almost did a cartwheel right there and then.

I waited for a moment, expecting her to call me out. But she remained seated, her face a mask of pure hatred and a little surprise. She hadn't expected that. I was going to beat her at her own game.

One for me, and nada for the queen bitch.

Feeling a little rebellious, I gave her a smile and then a tiny wave. Yes, it was overkill, but if I was going to die tonight, I might as well have a little fun.

And there was no time like the present.

"Sabnock," I called, and the lizard demon's huge jaws snapped in rage. "Kill the spider demon!" I commanded the demon, careful not to move from my triangle. If the rules applied here as well, the triangle was my only protection from the demon I'd just summoned until I was finished with him. "And protect me!" I added quickly, just to be sure he wouldn't let the igumo rip me apart.

Sabnock hissed again, and a black forked tongue flicked from his mouth. He shook his body, like a dog shaking the water from his fur, but he didn't move.

Crap. It didn't work. Fear chilled me. He was going to eat me.

But then Sabnock turned and charged head-on at the spider demon.

The igumo's set of yellow eyes flared with a sudden luminance, and it lunged.

With three giant bounds, they hit. The ground shook on impact, the sound like two raging bulls hitting one another followed by the sharp motions of a tiger ripping flesh from its prey.

The sound of flesh hitting flesh and bone snapping crammed the air, drowning the sounds of protests from the demon audience.

It was going to work!

Sabnock's jaws found the igumo's chest with a crunching impact. Bits of broken carapace and red and black flesh fell from the demon's mouth. The spider demon twisted and screeched as it tried to break free from the giant lizard's maw.

And then a spidery leg wound up and hit Sabnock in the eye.

Sabnock howled, a sound disturbingly doglike. He opened his maw, and the igumo broke free, jumping to the side.

Black and green liquid oozed from Sabnock's injured eye, and I held my breath. The damn spider had blinded him in one eye.

Jaws gaping, the igumo let out a screaming screech and leaped at Sabnock. With a powerful thrust, it sank its fangs into the muscles of Sabnock's back.

I had a moment of panic. I knew the igumo's venom was poisonous to mortals, but I had no idea how it would react toward another demon. It was too late to do anything about that now. All I could do was watch and hope.

Damn it. This was not going according to plan.

Sabnock roared in pain. Then he grabbed the igumo by the leg and ripped it off his back with a powerful heave, sending the igumo across the arena and tearing off its leg in the process. Black blood sprayed the sand in ugly sheets, the toxic smell making my eyes water. God, those beasts were nasty.

But igumos were resilient, and the bastard did have another seven legs.

Sabnock shook his body in a violent show of anger. And then the demon hurled himself at the giant spider with a thunderous bellow, rearing up on its hind legs.

Fear hit. How long until the venom started to show? How long until Sabnock was paralyzed and left me unguarded and visible, like a piece of meat dangling before the igumo's eight eyes.

I watched transfixed as the two massive demons fought. It was horrific, and exciting, and I couldn't look away.

Sabnock stirred and then snapped his jaws to one side, closing on one of the spider's back legs and tearing it right off with another spray of black blood and gobs of flesh.

The igumo screeched in pain and heaved itself away from Sabnock. One clawed foot came up toward the lizard demon's other eye, but the lizard was faster.

With a burst of speed, Sabnock's jaws clamped over the igumo's neck. Its exoskeleton broke with audible snaps, and the spider demon squealed in pain, its arms and legs shuddering in spasms.

There was a final snap, and the igumo's head fell from its body and landed with a soft thud on the ground.

Sabnock tossed the spider's body. Then, for good measure, the lizard demon leaped onto its hind legs and came down hard on the spider's chest with such force it simply perforated through the demon's body to the sand beneath it.

I raised a brow. "You're very thorough," I praised him. "Good boy."

I thought about releasing him at that moment, but then I thought better of it. He might just turn on me. It was my fault he'd lost an eye. He'd be furious with me, and demons held grudges. I made a mental note to never summon him ever again, if I got out of this place alive.

But then I knew the longer I had control over him, the angrier he'd be.

Resolute, I dragged my foot across the blood-drawn circle and said, "I release you," breaking the contract and the binding.

A flash of energy spilled through me from the blood circle and triangle. It spun inside me for a moment, and then I let go of the energy.

At the same time, the lizard demon looked up, watched me for a second, and then went back to stomping on the dead igumo.

Well, that's that.

Turning from the lizard demon, I checked my left palm. Crap. The wound was deep, red, and ugly. Worse, my entire hand was already swollen with infection. Great. That's all I needed right now, gangrene or the flesh-eating disease. I liked my hands. I didn't want to amputate one. But if I stayed here, that's exactly what would happen.

I'd have to make a bandage for it later. Cringing, I pulled my left glove over my hand. I was going to need stitches, if nothing else. I pushed Faris's knife into my front pocket.

When I looked up, back to the balcony, I couldn't help the smile that spread all over my face. I'd done it. I'd won. And I was going home.

My heart gave a little whoop of excitement. I met Vorkol's blank expression, which for some reason was more terrifying to me than if she'd been scowling at me.

"I won. Fair and square," I said, my voice steady, though not as loud as I wanted it to be. I couldn't seem to get enough air into my lungs. "I'm ready to leave this shithole," I added, my smile widening at Duvali's scowl. His jaw clenched harder, the muscles in his face bulging. It was lovely.

"Oh, really?" Vorkol said, leaning forward, her red eyes focused on me.

Dizzy, I shifted my weight to hide the fact that my knees wobbled. I was tired, and a fever was festering. "Yeah. Really. A deal's a deal. Unless you demons don't honor your words."

A gasp rippled through the assembled demons. My pulse thrashed, faster and harder.

For a moment, I thought I'd gone too far. She was going to fry my ass. But Vorkol simply tipped back her head and laughed, high pitched and horrid, like the wail of hundreds of dying women. Creepy.

The Greater demon straightened with her bulbous red lips pulled back in a wicked smile. "Well. You certainly were *very* entertaining."

"I aim to please." The sound of crunching reached me, and I turned around to see the lizard demon munching with one of the spider's legs sticking out of his mouth. Nice.

"You said I could go home," I told Vorkol. "Now would be a great time to honor that." I caught a glimpse of Faris. He was shaking his head *no* to me.

Vorkol clicked her tongue. "You would have perished without that miserable-looking blade," she said and turned her head in Faris's direction. The mid-demon was looking at his shoes. "My igumo would have made a meal of your witch flesh."

"Possibly," I said. "But now we'll never know. Will we?" I let out a sigh. Damn. Everything was spinning again. "But I still won. I want to leave now. The game is over."

Vorkol's eyes sparked. "You haven't won, little bird."

I frowned at her. "Excuse me?" Was she for real? My blood pounded in my veins, but I kept my chin high as I said, "I won." I glanced around the arena and spoke in a voice loud enough for every demon to hear. "Every demon here saw it. You saw it."

A round of angry whispers and hushed comments went through the crowd of demons. A series of snickering laughter accompanied some of the quiet mumbles.

"You haven't won until I say you've won," Vorkol mused.

My insides twisted, and I required a concentrated effort not to scream. "What's that supposed to mean?" *You lying, red-eyed bitch.* Faris had gone very, very still.

"It means exactly what I want it to mean." Vorkol smiled without any teeth. "You mortal witches are usually so uncreative, so predictable. But you. No. You're different. Special." She hesitated. "You surprised me."

"You're welcome."

Vorkol raised her perfect brows, but a smile haunted her mouth. "Things have been awfully boring of late. Killing you now, little bird, would be dull."

Duvali's eyes flashed with an impatient look, and his smile turned into a gritting of teeth, like he wanted to taste my flesh.

She let out a long, exaggerated sigh. "This isn't the end of the entertainment. I haven't finished playing with you, little bird. This is too good to pass up, too much fun." She waved a hand in my general direction. "You are going to be very... useful." A murmur of laughter from the seats echoed around me, hitting me like a fist in the gut.

I clamped my jaw. "Screw you." Fury flared inside me. I was furious at her but more at myself for letting myself believe she'd let me go. I was an idiot.

She'd never let me go, not until she got what she wanted, which meant until there was no more me to play with.

Vorkol leaned back in her chair and crossed her legs. "All of this could have been avoided if only you told me how you did it."

Here it comes.

Her expression darkened as she angled her head. "Tell me how you did it. Tell me how you killed Vargal, and you can go home."

Right. Like I was going to believe her now. But I wanted to live. "We fought. I won. That's it. There's nothing to tell." I wished I'd never crossed paths with the Greater demon Vargal.

Vorkol let out another laugh. "Little bird, that's not even a halfway decent lie."

"It's what happened." I swallowed back a wave of nausea. "You saw what I can do. I'm nothing special. Maybe I got lucky."

I could never tell her the truth. Someone like her should never have power like mine. She would slaughter the humans by the masses along with all the half-breeds she could find. I couldn't let that happen, even if it meant my death. I wouldn't be responsible for all that death. I couldn't live with myself.

I looked back over my shoulder, but the lizard demon was gone. So was any trace of the spider's entrails.

Duvali bent down and whispered in Vorkol's ear. The Greater demon smiled as he straightened and said, "I'll ask you one more time. Tell me how you killed Vargal, and all this goes away. You'll be back in your world doing whatever it is that witches do. What is it exactly that you witches do?"

"Work their cauldrons," said Duvali. "That's all they can do. They don't have real power."

Another wave of laughter rolled through the arena, and my anger surged through me, cutting into my fever. God, I hated demons.

If I don't have power, how did I kill your mate, eh?

Vorkol smiled, but I could see through her eyes that she knew I was holding back. She wouldn't stop until she discovered what it was.

"You've decided your fate, little bird," said Vorkol, leaning forward in her chair. "Until you tell me what I want to know, you will never leave this place. And the show must go on."

Warning bells pealed in my mind.

Vorkol settled back in her chair and shouted, "Bring in the mouth breather."

Mouth breather? Horror coiled in my gut.

The steel doors burst open again, and Andromalius strode into the arena. At first, I couldn't see past the big minotaur's shoulders and bulky body. A thick metal chain hung in his hand, and he gave a yank at something behind him.

My eyes went to the crowd and found Faris. His normally olive complexion was ashen. His expression was startled, and his mouth was open in shock.

When Andromalius got closer to me, I gave out a little moan.

Dragging behind the minotaur, with a chain clasped around his neck, was Logan.

CHAPTER
21

Logan.

No. This couldn't be happening. The handsome angel-born, who'd kissed me and who I'd been fantasizing about naked shouldn't be here, but he was shuffling behind the minotaur as they made their way toward me.

This was not how I'd pictured our next encounter—me naked, him naked and preferably on top of me.

A chill slithered down my spine. This was all kinds of wrong. I didn't want to be here. And I especially didn't want Logan here.

He was wearing blue jeans and a gray T-shirt. I recognized them as the same clothes I'd seen on him when he'd showed up at my place yesterday. But now they were stained with sweat and blood, his hair hanging lank and dirty. Purple and red bruises marred his face, and dried blood caked around his nose and the corners of his mouth. He looked like he'd put up a good fight.

His T-shirt was torn just above his right hip, and I could see a perfect, straight, three-inch cut, with dark, spidery veins standing out sharply against it— the mark of a death blade. So the higher demons had cut him to drag him here too.

I felt a surge of dizziness and swayed on my feet. Damn it. I was going to be sick.

Logan was here because of me. They had tortured him because of me. And now, he would die because of me.

I tried to make eye contact, but Logan stared at the ground, his expression set in stone.

Nice going, Sam. He'll never ask you out now.

Andromalius stopped when he reached me and unlocked the shackle around Logan's neck. The minotaur grabbed the chain with one hand. Then with the other, he shoved Logan down into the sand at my feet. Seemingly satisfied, the minotaur turned and moved to stand a few feet away.

Now, this was awkward. What do you say to the guy you have the hots for, who's been beat up and dragged to hell because of you? I had nothing. My mind was blank.

Logan rose to his feet, his features set in wrath.

I swallowed. "Logan, I'm so so—"

The expression of pure hatred he gave me was like a slap in the face, and I felt myself take a step back.

My stomach caved in on itself, and I managed to find my voice again. "I'm going to get you out of here. I swear it. I'm going to make this right."

He shook his head, over and over again. His jaw was clenched, the muscles in his face bulging, and his expression promised murder. Not good.

"Logan?" I searched his face. Dark circles stained under his eyes, and he looked sick. He probably was, just as I was. Mortals couldn't live in the Netherworld indefinitely, just like the demons couldn't live in ours. But he wouldn't look at me. His eyes were on the sand at his feet.

"Logan?" I tried again. Nothing.

His refusal to answer was worse than if he had slapped me across the face. I wish he had. Anything was better than the silent treatment right now. And when he moved away from me, well, that just about made me fall to my knees.

My heart dropped to the sand at my feet. Shame. Regret. Stupidity. All were rushing through my mind and body. It was almost too much.

But then I remembered *she* had done this. Not me. Vorkol wanted to hurt me in any way she could to get what she wanted. I didn't know how she knew about Logan, but the demon bitch was good.

Angry tears threatened to spill down my cheeks as I looked up and met Vorkol's happy expression.

"What the hell is this?" I growled, my voice shaking with rage and sorrow.

She raised a perfect brow, her smile growing to reveal her white teeth. "Consider this a favor," she purred, but I could barely hear her above the blood pounding in my ears.

"Favor?" I let out a short laugh. "You should stop smoking that demon crack." Blood pounded in my temples. "How is this a favor?" *Why don't you come closer so I can slice your throat?* I told her with my eyes.

"To help loosen your tongue, little bird," said Vorkol, seemingly pleased. Duvali gave a little laugh. "I can keep torturing you until you break, or I can keep torturing him until you break. It's your choice. See, you do have choices here, little bird. But you have to make up your mind at some point."

"You psychotic bitch," I cried, my body shaking and my nails digging into the leather of my gloves. "Let him go. He has nothing to do with this."

"Of course he does," she said, her red eyes widening. "I'm giving you a way out. He's not a witch, but I hear the angel-born are warriors. I'm giving him to you."

My lips trembled. "You can't give people away like pets."

Vorkol lifted her hand and pointed. "The angel-born will fight alongside you. He will bleed alongside you. And he will die alongside you. And if you're smart enough," she continued, "you'll give me what I want, and you both can go free."

At that, Logan's head snapped up, and I could feel his eyes on me. I couldn't look at him. If I did, I would lose it. I wouldn't be able to think logically, and I needed to focus. I had to be smart. Stupid and emotional would get me killed. Would get us *both* killed.

"How do I know you're not lying?" I said, breathing hard, my throat burning with every gulp of that foul air. "You told me before if I won the duel I could go home. I killed your damn spider. But I'm still here."

Irritation flickered on Vorkol's face. "You cheated. Interference doesn't count. Meddling is not winning."

I pursed my lips. "If that were true, why did you let me finish? Why didn't you stop the fight?"

Vorkol clicked her tongue and smiled. "I was entertained. You entertain me. Because the entertainment is over when I say it's over." She shrugged and added, "And it's *not* over."

Logan appeared next to me a heartbeat later. "Samantha," he said, and I turned to look at him at the sound of urgency in his voice. "If you know something that can help us get out of here... tell her."

Damn, he was pretty. His disheveled state and the anger rippling on his face made him all the more sexy. My mouth opened, but I closed it again. How could I explain this to him?

"You don't know what you're asking," I told him.

His brown eyes were fierce. "I'm asking you to help us get home. Tell her what she wants. I don't want to think about the alternative." When I didn't answer, he leaned closer until his breath was hot on my neck. "We'll die if we stay here."

I frowned. Like I didn't know that.

"Sam?" he pressed, his breath sending delicious tingles all along my skin. "Tell her. Whatever it is. Just do it."

He really loved giving me orders. I stepped away. His nearness was making it harder to think. My eyes met Vorkol's and I said, "And if I tell you what you want, you'll let us go?" I asked. My eyes moved to Faris, his face tensed and twisted in worry. I swallowed hard. "Both of us?" My eyes were back on the Greater demon.

Vorkol gave me a small, horrible smile. "Yes. Both of you."

"And alive?"

"And alive," agreed Vorkol. "Do we have a deal, little bird?"

Logan's posture eased a little. He thought I was going to tell her. He didn't understand.

I closed my eyes and took a breath, not a deep one. I tried to get a handle on my anger and focus. It wouldn't profit me anything to lose control.

Turning her words over, I looked for loopholes in her phrasing, but I knew I was just fooling myself. I'd been at this a long time. Demons were master tricksters, liars, schemers, and award-winning actors. Vorkol was the most talented of them all.

If I told her how I managed to kill Vargal—about my gift—we were dead. She'd never let us walk out alive, not after she'd taken my blood and my power. She might even kill everyone in this entire arena, just to keep it a secret, to keep it hers. She probably would. That's what I'd do if I were her.

Either way, we were going to die. But if she let us live tonight, I had one more night to figure out how to escape. And escape was my only option.

I opened my eyes and braced myself for what I was about to say, and for Logan's reaction.

"No deal," I said, my voice carrying over the silence for a mere second before the arena burst into a chorus of excitement. The pricks wanted more fighting, but their mistress didn't.

Vorkol's expression became almost grotesque, and she rubbed her fingers across the armrest of her chair. "If you fail the next challenge, there won't be anything left of you for me to play with."

"I'll take my chances," I answered, seeing her eyes narrowing at my answer. That was not what she thought I'd say.

"Are you crazy?" shouted Logan as he whirled at me. "Tell her. Or I'll make you tell her."

I frowned, my anger bubbling to the surface again. "Really? I'd like to see you try."

Logan clenched his jaw, reining in his anger. "You want to die here? Is that what you want?"

"No."

"So tell her how you killed him," said Logan, his voice final, but there was a bit of regret there as well.

219

I shook my head. "There's nothing to tell. We fought. I defeated Vargal." I dared a glance at Faris. His brown eyes were rounder than I remembered.

Logan laughed bitterly. "Do you know what you just did," hissed the angel-born. "You just killed us both. You killed us."

"I know how this looks. But trust me on this."

"Trust you?" Logan's face was twisted in disgust, and I pulled my eyes away from him before I fell apart. *Keep it together, Sam.*

Vorkol's expression turned dark. "You've made your choice. Take the bird back to her cage. And take the other one with her," she said sharply. "We'll see how long you can hold on to your secrets."

The minotaur yanked out his sword. "Move," he ordered as he came around me and hit me hard in the back with the pommel of his sword.

I stumbled forward and nearly lost my balance. White-hot pain laced through my spine, but I wouldn't cry out. I wouldn't show her my pain. I wouldn't show her she was winning.

Logan was silent, his expression dark and especially not friendly as we trudged forward toward the exit.

The last thing I saw before stepping through the door was Vorkol's deep scowl, her gaze locked on Faris.

CHAPTER
22

Sharing a small six-by-six metal cage was not my idea of a great first date or first time alone with Logan.

Yes, the angel-born was hot and sweaty, and so very close. But the sweat wasn't the after-sex sweat and glow, but more of flush from the toxic acidic air on his cheeks and a feverish glow from the death blade's poison. Yeah. Not so great.

I would have much preferred to be home on the couch, watching a movie or a series while Logan poured me some wine.

Well, we couldn't always get what we wanted. Even if he were just sitting across from me. Even if I could just reach out and grab him.

A part of me felt sick. Another part felt angry. I wasn't sure which one was winning.

"This is your fault," Logan said. It was the first time he'd spoken to me since we'd been thrown in the cage three hours ago. His voice was different—cold and terrible and hard. I'd never heard him speak that way before.

Ouch. "I know," I answered. What was I supposed to say?

Logan rubbed his jaw. "You should have told her. Why didn't you tell her? You like it here or something?"

I frowned at the tone of exasperation in his voice. "It's not that simple."

"Really?" His eyes flashed incredulously. "What the hell is wrong with you?"

"Where do I start."

"This isn't funny," he growled, his face a shade darker. "You think this is a joke? My life is a joke to you?"

I sighed. "Of course not. Relax, will you? You're giving me a headache."

Logan's expression was hard. "Fine. We'll just call the minotaur demon and tell him you want to talk to her. Tell her you've changed your mind. Just tell her how you killed the bastard so we can go home."

"Go home?" I took an irritated breath. "You do realize that was never her intention, right? She's never going to let us go home. Unless we can escape, we're never getting out of here."

Logan's face went tight. "I am." He crossed his arms over his chest, a determined look playing on his face. "If you had told her, I wouldn't even be here. I don't get it. I don't get why you're doing this. Why can't you just tell her?"

"Because."

"Because what?" he shouted, making my blood boil, and I imagined slapping his pretty face. And then one more time, just because I felt like it.

I stifled my temper before I started a shouting match. The last thing I needed was for the minotaur to come back with his very large sword. "Because if I told her," I said, "thousands would die. I'm saving lives by not telling her. Don't you get it?"

Logan frowned and rubbed his eyes. "I don't understand you," he said, laughing in impatience.

"No you don't."

Eyebrows high, Logan made a soft sound in his throat. His jaw clenched before he said, "Then explain it to me. It's not like I'm going anywhere. Not for a little while."

I met his gaze. Brown eyes blinking, an intent look came into Logan's eyes, calculating and skeptical.

"Well?" he questioned finally. "I'm all ears."

I watched him, wondering if I could trust him. Then, before I knew what I was doing, my mouth opened, and the words came pouring out.

I told him about how my father had tried to kill me because of what I was and how my grandfather had saved me from the flames. I spoke about how I discovered what I could do, about my special gift, and why I'd kept it a secret all this time. And finally, I recounted the events leading to my fight with Vargal and how I used my gift with Poe to kill him. Since

223

he'd been unconscious at the time, I'd never been sure if he had seen me use my gift, seen all those versions of me.

My heart was pounding when I was finished, but his worried expression melted into one of his famous smiles. I wondered if I had made the right choice about telling him, or if I had damned myself instead. Only time would tell, I supposed.

"If the witches found out I can borrow magic without having to make bargains with demons," I said, "they'd kill me for it. Like my father tried to do. They'd bleed me, wanting it for themselves, or simply just kill me and not allow me to have it." I let out a sigh. "You can imagine what Vorkol will do with that kind of power. I can never let her have it." Logan just sat there facing me. He squinted his eyes, his gaze distant. I had no idea what was transpiring behind those brown eyes. I barely knew the guy. Nervous, I felt the beginnings of regret about telling him. My adrenaline surged. Shit. What had I done?

"I'd been wondering about that," said Logan, a curious glint in his eye. "So all those replicas of you... those were real? I just thought I'd hit my head a little too hard."

My throat contracted as I swallowed. "I'm sorry this happened to you, Logan. But you can't tell her. You can't tell anyone. Promise me." I waited as my fear redoubled. "Promise me," I said again, my voice high with a mix of regret and fear.

Logan looked up, his gaze lingering on me, and I held my breath. "I promise."

I believed him, strangely enough. I let out a shaky breath, not enjoying the fact he'd seen me like this, though my relief was a warm wash through me.

"Your father's a dick," said Logan after a long silence.

"Among other things," I agreed. My insides twisted. In my mind's eye, I could see a malicious smile reflected on my father's face, the evil gleam in his eyes, right before he tossed me into the fire. Some kids block out traumatic events to protect themselves. Me, well, the memory was absolutely crystalline, like it happened just yesterday. The man was a true monster.

Logan's handsome features creased in worry. "It must have been hard growing up with that. I mean, having your own father blaming you for your mother's death and then trying to kill you. That would seriously mess up a little kid."

I shook my head. "Not really." I shifted my weight, trying to find a spot that wasn't so hard on my butt. "I had my grandfather and my great aunt watching over me. It was enough."

"Do you know what happened to him?"

"Who?"

Logan's gaze fixed on me. "Your father."

I looked away. "He disappeared the night of the fire. I never heard from him again." And that was a good thing.

"And if he shows up?"

"I'll kill him." I was shocked at how easily it came out and how true it was. If I survived his place, and my father showed up, I *would* kill him. In fact, I'd

225

been waiting for that day, for that chance. No witch who burns little children alive should live.

"Is that why you wear gloves?" ventured Logan, his gaze going to my hands. "Because of the scars?"

I nodded, a little embarrassed now that he knew my secret. It was either that, or enduring the endless pestering from him.

Silence. Not really complete silence, if you counted the relentless moaning and screeches from the other hundreds of cages, nor the constant scratching sound coming from my scrawny neighbor. He'd been silent since I gave him some food. Now he spent his days rubbing the metal bars of his cage with the water bottle cap.

"So, I hear you're a big hotshot in the angel-born community," I said, wanting to change the subject. Plus his silence was starting to freak me out a little. "I'm not that familiar with your angel-born chain of command, but I'm pretty sure the Head of House Michael is a pretty big deal."

A smile quirked the corners of Logan's mouth, changing his face from handsome to spectacular. "It's all right."

My brows lifted. I knew he was being modest. "You like it?" I asked, not knowing whether he'd wanted the title or if it had been forced on him. I couldn't help but be curious. Having more information was always a good thing.

"It's an honor to be chosen," he said, his tanned hands clasped on his lap. "I try to do right by my people. But it's not always the case. It's not always that easy. You can't please everyone."

"Drama, eh?"

"The nuclear kind," he added. His eyes met mine, his smile stretching to show his white teeth. "It's part of my life now. Of who I am, as an angel-born. I don't get time off."

"You can think of this as a vacation, then," I said and gestured with my hands. "The views are spectacular, but the food sucks."

Logan laughed. The man thought I was funny. Damn, that was seriously dangerous. That last male who thought I was funny ended up naked and in my bed.

"Parents?" I added quickly, my face flushing as my eyes rolled over his two-day-old stubble that gave his flawless features a more rugged look and automatically reached the top of my sexy-meter.

"Still married," he said. "Still happy."

I couldn't picture my life with happy parents. It's not that I was envious. My family life felt complete with my grandfather, aunt, and Poe, and I wouldn't change a thing.

The thought of Poe had worry striking through me. The last I'd seen him he'd gone after a meal. I just prayed the higher demons hadn't hurt him. He was probably sick with worry by now. And if he was worried, it meant that my grandfather and aunt were too. They were probably trying to figure out what had happened to me. It felt as though I'd been in the Netherworld for only a few days, but who knew with the Netherworld. I could have been locked up in this cage for years.

"You're bleeding," he said, his voice gentler than it had been.

I looked up to find him staring at my left hand. I pulled it up. Yup. My blood had managed to soak through my glove and had dripped down my fingers.

"Damn it," Carefully, I pulled off my glove. Blood oozed from my cut, and the wound hadn't even started to cauterize yet.

The cage rattled and swung as Logan shifted around and came to sit next to me. O-o-o-kay.

"Let me take a look," he said, surprising me. But I was more surprised when his thigh brushed mine.

Gently, he held up my hand. "You're going to need stitches," he said, and let it go.

"No shit."

With his hands, he ripped the bottom part of his T-shirt into a long strip and wrapped it around my hand with expert precision.

"I see you've done this before," I said, marveling at how his big hands could be so gentle.

Logan gave me a tight smile. "I have." He made a knot next to my wrist. "It should hold until we can get you some stitches when we get out of here."

"When we get out of here," I repeated, hearing the certainty in my own voice. We had to get out. There was no other way. Not if we wanted to live.

"So," said Logan as he leaned next to me, our shoulders brushing. I could smell his musky scent over the sulfur in the air. It was nice. "Any bright ideas on how to get out of this place?"

I pulled the glove over my left hand. "The only way out I see is the same way we got in."

"You mean through a Rift?"

"Exactly."

"And you know where to find one?"

I looked around at the metal bars. "If I can get out of this cage I might."

Logan made a sound in his throat. "Even if we find one, you think it'll work?"

"If I'm right," I said, a bit of excitement fluttering in my stomach. "We both were stabbed by death blades, which allowed us passage. Right? So, it makes sense to think we can use that same logic to go through them again to go home."

Logan's shoulders tensed. "Maybe. I just hope we can survive the trip. It wasn't exactly a fun ride."

There was that. Our health was diminishing rapidly, and a trip through a Rift was a risk. Logan was right. We might not even make it out alive.

"And where do you suppose we find one of these Rifts?" he asked.

A thought occurred to me. "Faris is going to help." I perked up. "He said he would. He's going to help us find a way home." Knowing I had at least one friend in this hellhole gave me a new sense of hope.

"Maybe." Logan shifted his body, and his shoulder brushed up against mine, sending tiny tingles over my skin. He was so close I could feel his hot breath on my face. He didn't move away. Neither did I.

"But maybe Vorkol killed him," he added.

I jerked and hit my head on the bars. "Why would you say that?" I asked, rubbing my head.

Logan raised his brows. "He helped you by giving you that dagger. I don't think Vorkol's going to let that slide. He screwed himself."

"By helping me." My throat tightened, and I leaned forward to get a better look at his face. "I've killed him too."

"Not necessarily," said Logan. "He's very resourceful. If any demon can get out of this sticky situation, Faris can. Don't worry. He'll be fine."

I peered at the angel-born, curious. "I thought you didn't like him."

Logan shrugged. "I don't. I just don't think he deserves to die. Not after he helped you."

I leaned against the bars, realizing at that moment how much I liked talking with Logan. He was an angel-born and I was a witch. Yet it felt natural, right, and I didn't want it to end.

I met his eyes again and was shocked to find him grinning at me, more than a hint of attraction in his dark gaze.

My heart did five summersaults, two jumping jacks, and a backflip for the finale. Damn, those were some fine eyes... and those lips...

Logan exhaled. "You're the craziest witch I've ever met."

"How sweet of you to say."

"And I also think you're pretty amazing."

My mouth fell open. "You just gave me a compliment. Do you realize you just gave me a compliment? You, an angel-born, complimenting a dark witch?"

Logan laughed, and the sound sent my heart battering in my chest. "I guess I did."

"You did." A smile crept along my face.

"We might die tonight," said Logan, shifting his body and causing his thigh to rub against mine again. Those were some nice, tight, muscled thighs. I couldn't help but picture him naked again. I was a seriously demented witch.

"We might," I agreed, the truth of his words hitting me hard. His face was so very close to mine...

So, what does one do when staring death in the face?

Something stupid, of course.

I grabbed his face between my hands and crushed my lips against his.

Logan flinched in surprise, his eyes wide in a shocked expression, but then he grabbed the back of my head and pulled me closer, kissing me back—slow at first and then harder. A quick hint of his tongue sent a spike of desire to my core.

Damn, he was a good kisser. Even better than I'd remembered.

My breath left me in a moan as I eased against him, one arm wrapped around his neck and the other in his hair, feeling his muscles tighten. His grip on my shoulders was firm with desire, and it was all I could do to keep from ripping off his clothes.

Pulse fast, I pulled away, sucking on his bottom lip one last time.

"What was that for?" asked Logan. His eyes flashed, and his lips were red from my abuse.

I shrugged. "You said we might die." *And I wanted to kiss you one last time, you fool. To see if I was still into you. Hell yeah.*

A wicked grin spread over Logan's face. Desire flashed in his eyes, which had my pulse rising again. "We might die," he said again, eyebrows high, expectant.

I smiled. Naughty boy.

I couldn't look away from his eyes as I grabbed his face again and crushed my lips onto his. Yup, I was a dirty little witch.

His lips pushed aggressively against mine, tasting of salt. Logan shifted his weight, pressing me into him as he pulled me onto his lap. His hands moved under my shirt, and the roughness of his calluses sent my skin riddling in goose bumps. Sensing my desire, his touch became aggressive, and hot ribbons of anticipation spiraled through my core.

We couldn't do this. It was too much. I wasn't thinking clearly. It was too damn good.

I pulled away again before things got out of hand and we were both naked, our bodies clunking in the cage. Yes, I wanted it to happen, just not here. I didn't want to have sex with Logan in a damn cage in the Netherworld.

"We can't do this now," I panted, still sitting on his lap and facing him.

"I know," he answered, his hands around my waist. "But it was nice—"

The sound of wrenching metal pierced the air, and our cage started shuddering. I whipped around and my heart sank.

Andromalius stood on the platform, his thick hand on a lever.

Damn. I'd never even heard the minotaur enter the cave.

Then our cage shifted and fell.

CHAPTER
23

"How did you kill Vargal?" Vorkol's voice echoed up through the arena. Her tone was demanding and expectant, the voice of a queen. "Tell me now, and you and your... *friend* can go home." There was an evil delight to her voice, cementing my anger. She was really enjoying this.

She'd tossed her red pantsuit for a light silver one. Straight black hair hung from her head to her shoulders with straight bangs cut in the Cleopatra style. Probably another wig.

"What will it be, little bird?" Vorkol said, testing the words on her tongue. "You promised me an answer."

"I didn't," I answered, making sure my voice rang out for everyone to hear and glad it was even. The fever in me ran higher every minute, and I didn't

234

know how much longer I could withstand the poisonous air. We needed to get out of here, and soon.

Vorkol sighed and ran her hand over the arm of her chair. "I would have thought you would have learned your lesson by now."

"School was never my thing."

Logan snorted next to me, too low for anyone else but me to hear. Having him with me, fighting alongside one another, gave me a new sense of courage, but it also doubled my sense of urgency. I was responsible for him. He was here because of me, and I needed to get him out.

The plan was to fight off whatever she'd throw at us, keep her entertained, stay alive one more day, and hope Faris could help us find a Rift—and get the hell out of this place.

Yeah. It wasn't the best plan, but it was the only one we had. We needed to stay alive for as long as we could.

"What happened to your rings?" asked Logan, his eyes on my hands. The question heightened his expression, having only just noticed them missing.

My gaze flicked back to the Greater demon. Duvali was whispering something in her ear. "She destroyed them." My jaw clenched in sudden hatred. I could always make new ones, but I happened to really like that pair.

Logan hesitated. "Can you do your blood magic again?"

I looked down at my left hand. "I better," I said, and pulled off my left glove. "Because it's all I have."

Now that I knew I could use my blood magic, I could use some of my spells, though I didn't know how effective they would be, never having used them with blood magic before.

"Give it here," said Logan. He took my glove and slipped it in his jeans pocket.

I quickly undid Logan's makeshift bandage and squeezed my palm. Dark blood pooled out freely. Next, I dipped my right index finger in my blood and drew the fire sigil on my left arm. Just below that, I drew the sigil for wind.

I wasn't even sure they would work in the Netherworld, but I was about to find out.

I yanked Faris's dagger out of my pocket. "Here, take it," I said. "You probably know how to use it better than I do." The fact that the minotaur had let us keep it wasn't a good sign.

Logan grabbed the dagger in his right hand. "Thanks."

Adrenaline stabbed through me as my gaze swept across the arena and the crowds of assembled demons, wondering if these were the same demons as before. It was impossible to tell. Everyone was clad in rich, colorful clothing, made of fine silk and embroidered with golds and silvers and reds. Dispersed among them were lesser demons, but not many. The demons burst into a sudden noise of conversation. Two male demons sitting in Vorkol's balcony were arguing vehemently.

My eyes scanned over the crowd of demons for Faris, but I didn't find him.

My chest tightened, and I swallowed the lump in my throat.

"You look awful, little bird," said Vorkol. "I can keep doing this, day after day, night after night," she purred. "But soon, your bodies will diminish. Soon, you'll be nothing more than ash."

I believed her, but I wasn't planning on staying much longer.

Vorkol leaned forward. "But it doesn't have to be this way. Tell me what I want, and it all goes away."

I stood my ground. "I've already told you. We fought. I won."

Her eyes settled on Logan, and I didn't like what I saw there. "You know," Vorkol mused, leaning against an arm of her throne-like chair. "Maybe I'll let you fight in the pit and take him instead." She ran an eye over Logan. Her smile widened at what she saw on my face. "Yes. Perhaps I'll have different plans for him. He is... quite lovely to look at. Isn't he? I can tell, just by looking into his eyes. I know he's a passionate lover. Isn't he?"

Oh, hell no. This was not happening.

"I'm not for sale," growled Logan, pulling the words right out of my mouth.

Vorkol's smile was feline with lots of teeth. "Everything's for sale."

I'd had enough. "It hurts, doesn't it?"

The Greater demon lifted her brows. "What does?"

"To be rejected." Now it was my turn to smile. "You can't have everything. And it's killing you."

Vorkol's face contorted with pride and anger. "You are mistaken. I have everything I want. Everything I desire."

"You don't," I said flatly. "You don't know how I killed Vargal." I watched the twitch of her smile, the furrowing of her delicate brows. "And it's killing you. Isn't it? Because you knew he was keeping secrets from you. You knew something was up with him, but you didn't know what. He didn't want you to know. Isn't that right?"

Vorkol forced a laugh, her expression one of warning. "You are clearly delusional."

"Sam, what are you doing?" cautioned Logan.

But once the words were flowing, I couldn't stop. "Did you know he was trying to raise a god? Oh. Look at your face. Damn. You didn't know. Did you? Well, he was. All so the god would give him power."

Vorkol's face twisted in disbelief as she bared her teeth and said, "You'll say anything to save your soul, you pathetic little witch."

"It's the truth," I said, my voice rising at her visible discomfort. "And you had no idea what he was doing behind your back. That's freaking priceless. If I were to guess, I'd say he was tired of living in your shadow. Vargal wanted power of his own. He wanted *more* than yours. And knowing him a little—since we shared a few battles—I would also go ahead and say that if he had succeeded, he would have *killed* you."

"That's just great, Sam," grumbled Logan, but I barely heard him.

Vorkol's features twisted into a scowl. The realization of my words hitting her showed in the stiffness of her posture and the tension along her expression. She believed me.

It was a small victory, but I enjoyed every moment of it.

Suck it, Cleopatra.

Vorkol leaned back in her chair and crossed her legs at the knee. "If you're inclined to play games, little bird, I suppose I must oblige."

She snapped her fingers. The steel doors across from us burst open, and through them charged a horde of shuffling, twitching humans of every shape and size—at least a dozen of them.

But when they neared, I could see their empty eyes staring in hollow, dead faces.

Zombies.

"Fuck me," I grumbled.

"Right back at ya," echoed Logan.

Great. I had as much love for zombies as I did a tick. And if you'd imagined zombies as in the Hollywood versions, you'd be right. They nailed it.

Zombies were nothing more than soulless human meat suits, risen from the dead by powerful demonic magic or necromancy magic and forced to obey their master, or whomever created them. Vorkol would get my vote. They existed to kill and to eat flesh, any flesh, to maintain their decomposing bodies.

I hated zombies.

A collective cheer went up from the assembled demons, and then they began applauding enthusiastically. Seemed like the demons loved them. No surprise there.

The zombies advanced, chanting and moaning mindless gibberish, for very few of them had functioning mouths. Their decayed legs thrust forward in a steady, slow rhythm that had bile rising in the back of my throat. The grisly sound of bone on bone and the rustle of decomposed flesh replaced the assembled demons' chatter.

"Here we go," said Logan, Faris's small pocket knife gripped firmly in his hand.

I pulled the energy from my blood sigils. "Have you ever killed a zombie?"

Logan flashed me a smile that would have gotten me into trouble if we weren't in the Netherworld about to fight a horde of zombies. "Only in video games." He crouched down in an attack stance, the dagger brandished before him.

"Get the brain," I told him. Yeah. Hollywood had that right too. You could burn them too, but a shot to the brain usually did it.

However, the zombie virus was all Hollywood. You didn't turn into a zombie if you were bitten, but they did have a mean bite, equipped with everlasting strength. They could rip you apart, and start to munch on your flesh while you were still alive. Yeah. I hated zombies.

The frenzied gurgle-moaning rose in volume. The stench of carrion followed, so intense my eyes watered and I could hardly breathe. I shook off the feeling and focused.

I shuddered as the first wave of zombies hit. Damn, they were nasty.

The nearest zombie, a black female, with its lower jaw and parts of its forehead missing, saw me and charged. Feet planted, I channeled my magic, but Logan got there first.

With a burst of speed, he twisted around the zombie, got behind it, and sank his knife right into the top of the zombie's head. He pushed the knife down into its brain with a soft thud. The zombie twitched once but then was still. Grimacing, Logan yanked the blade from its head, sending a spatter of dark blood onto his face. The zombie collapsed to the ground in a pile of rotten flesh and cloth.

I had to admit, the angel-born had moves. But I wasn't here to stand and watch his handsome dance of death. I had some killing to do.

A flicker of movement appeared in my line of sight.

My turn.

A male zombie came at me, its arms flailing wildly and striking blindly with heavy sweeps of its arms. Its eyes flashed with hunger.

Channeling the blood sigils, and praying they would work, I let the energy wake in me and shouted, "Feurantis!"

A pulse of energy lit through me, burning, as the fire sigil on my arm flashed with an orange light. My blood kindled the spell fully. My teeth clenched at the

241

scorching pain as the blood magic soared through my veins.

A ball of fire rose from my palm, and then I flung it at the oncoming zombie. It hit it right in the chest. The zombie screamed and fell to its knees, writhing madly. With a final screech, it stopped thrashing and was still.

My ears rang and I staggered, feeling drained. My vision blurred, and I blinked as I strained to see clearly, the pain of using my blood magic hitting hard. My limbs were stiff, and I felt as though I'd been hit by a bus. This was not good.

It had worked. But it also hurt like hell and had cost me dearly.

My vision cleared just as another zombie shambled toward me, a thrashing stick-figure with ribbons of rotten flesh. Naked, it was an angry-looking monster. Its mouth was open, sporting two rows of jagged, brown-coated teeth.

Why do I always get the naked ones?

I willed my blood magic to come, lifted my left arm and shouted, "Feurantis!"

As I stifled the pain, another ball of fire soared in the air and hit the zombie in the head. The fire exploded on impact, covering the wailing undead in sheets of yellow and orange flames. It hit the ground—

"Son of a bitch!" I cried out as my right shoulder flamed with pain. The overwhelming scent of carrion hit me, just as the weight of another body pulled me down from behind. Strong hands pinned my arms to my sides. I nearly vomited at the feel of its teeth sinking into my flesh, its rotten tongue tasting my blood. Panic overwhelmed my concentration, and breaking my left arm free, I reached over and jabbed the zombie in the eye with my thumb. The tightness in my shoulder released. I whirled and grabbed its arm as I spun and pulled it off of me.

The trouble was, the arm came right off with a sickening suction noise.

Now I nearly vomited.

That was one of the problems with zombies. They never stayed in one piece.

I stared at the arm, which was mostly just bone with strings of rotten flesh that hung in my hand. "Oh. That's just wrong."

The one-armed zombie howled, most likely pissed that I'd taken its arm without asking, and came at me again in a shuffle of oozing, peeling skin and tattered clothes.

What does one do with a zombie arm? Use it a weapon.

The zombie neared, and I hit it right across the head with its detached arm. The force took its head right off, like I'd hit a ball with a baseball bat. The zombie fell like a dead tree.

I stood for a moment, shocked and a little impressed at my zombie-killing skills.

The amount of blood that spilled down from my shoulder to my chest sobered me right up.

"Look out!" came Logan's cry.

Moving on instinct, I spun around, clutching the zombie arm, and swung it as hard as I could.

I felt a sudden jolt as the arm hit something solid, followed by a thud. Then came the sound of tearing flesh as the arm-weapon decapitated another zombie's head, sending showers of blood and rotten flesh everywhere.

And a forearm. Oops.

I looked down at what was left of my zombie-arm weapon. The bone was shattered and had severed at the elbow.

I tossed it and turned in time to see Logan moving around a cluster of zombies in an unreal grace, slicing and dicing as he spun around them. Zombies landed at his feet. Even with a small knife, he was beating them. I hated that he looked better than me at this, even showered in zombie blood and guts. Some people had it all.

Behind me, the sound of a deep growl neared. I whirled my head around in time to see an enormous wolf running toward me. No, not a wolf, a *zombie-wolf*.

The giant zombie-wolf had fangs the size of Faris's dagger and white, shark-like eyes. Totally creepy. Totally not fair. Demons never played by the rules.

My bowels turned watery. Crap. *Why do I always get stuck with the big ones?*

White bones protruded from rotten flesh. I could see part of its rib cage and the meat that bounced around inside. One ear was torn off, and half its nose was missing. The wolf was practically hairless, except for a few tuffs of gray hair. Its lips were pulled back, and it looked angry as hell. I would be too if I was brought back from the dead.

I felt eyes on me and looked up at the balcony to find a triumphant smile on Vorkol's pale face, but her red eyes were full of hatred. Hatred for me. I had a feeling the zombie-wolf was payback for what I'd said about Vargal. The mutt was overkill but proof I was right.

Still, I should have kept my big mouth shut.

The zombie-wolf slammed into two zombies, its white eyes never leaving me as it galloped forward in great bounds. Bones snapped as the zombies were crushed into the sand by the zombie-wolf's sheer weight, their heads squished like beaten cherry pies.

"Good doggie," I said, pulling on the energy of my blood sigils and pushing down the sick feeling in my gut at the same time.

The zombie-wolf growled and leaped.

Mouth dry, I channeled the magic from my blood sigils, flung out my hand and shouted, "Feurantis!"

A ball of fire shot from my outstretched hand and hit the zombie-wolf in the chest. Howling, it pitched to the side, rolling on the sand, over and over, until the fire was extinguished.

"Bad dog," I expressed, amazed and scared at the same time. "Very bad dog." A smart zombie-wolf? Vorkol was playing hardball.

I winced as waves of pain washed through me, the blood magic settling and taking payment. I took a breath and steadied myself, wrinkling my nose at the stench of wet dog and burnt hair.

I moved my eyes around at the remaining human zombies. They were giving us a wide berth. I was grateful for it, but it also meant Logan would soon be faced with all of them.

My eyes found him through the wall of zombies that stood between us. He was still fighting well, but he was also only fighting off two zombies. Ice licked up my spine. The other four remaining were making their way toward him. He would never be able to fight them all off alone. They were going to kill him. They were going to eat him alive because that's what zombies did.

Damn it. I needed to get to him!

"Screw this." I made to move toward Logan.

The zombie-wolf stood in my way. Its skin still sizzled and popped like an overcooked chicken, black smoke coiling from its rotten corpse.

"And you need to be put on a leash," I declared.

The zombie-wolf snarled, its sharp teeth riddled in decay, with strips of flesh from its last victim still stuck in between its teeth. Nice.

The rotting wolf let out a vicious, spitting growl and then leaped.

Heart racing, I willed my blood magic to come, and it sputtered and spat, the energy not fully rising to the surface. It was like trying to start an old car. The energy rose—then fell.

Oh. Shit.

The zombie-wolf flew at me.

I threw myself down, sliding and rolling over the sand while getting some in my mouth and eyes. I pushed myself up—

The zombie-wolf clamped its jaw over my leg. I cried out as its teeth sank into my flesh, dragging me back. I nearly passed out as surges of pain soared through me, all the way up to my skull. But I took a breath, pushing the pain away before I succumbed to it.

A guttural sound escaped me—a mix of pain and determination. I wouldn't die like this. I wouldn't let this undead thing rip me apart for all the demons to see because I was sure they'd enjoy it. Vorkol most of all.

Adrenaline surged painfully, and I kicked out as hard as I could.

My boot came into contact with its head. There was a snap, and the wolf let go.

My breath came in a ragged gasp as I whirled around and pushed myself up, gritting my teeth as agony sang through me. My left leg throbbed where it had bitten, and every nerve ending pulsed into a burn. The zombie-wolf licked its lips, fresh blood staining them as it lowered itself in an attack crouch.

I limped to a standing pose, a growing sense of fear and desperation giving my legs a Jell-O-like feeling.

Laughter went through the arena, and I looked back to see the demons, their heads falling back with laughter at my pain, at me. Vorkol's mouth spread into a slow, vicious smile, which in turn became a high, rolling laugh. And then Duvali joined in with her.

I felt my face burn. Not with embarrassment but with pure, hot, delicious fury.

And then I lost it.

The zombie-wolf ran toward me.

But I was ready.

Teeth bared, I tapped into my will, pulling the magic from the blood sigils on my arm and molding it to my will. The pulse of magic hit, sending me staggering as it answered.

The zombie-wolf let out a horrible, deep howl—the cry of a beast about to make a kill—and lunged.

Blood magic throbbed through me like adrenaline, only a thousand times stronger. I planted my feet and really let loose as I shouted, "Vento!" at the top of my lungs.

I unleashed everything I had into it. A blast of energy shot through me, and I staggered.

An unseen force hit the zombie-wolf, lifted it from its feet and sent it back with a violent burst of wind. The zombie-wolf soared backward high across the arena in a blur of limbs and dead flesh. Its limbs thrashed as it came down fast.

And impaled on a flag's metal post.

The dead thing slid down to the bottom, the post perforating through its mouth like a skewered pig and leaving a trail of dark blood on the metal.

Heart pounding, my body shook from the spent magic, and I let the agony of the blood magic roll through me. I stood, staring at the wolf for a moment and wondering if it was truly dead. Or would it simply cough up the metal post and spring back on its legs? Stranger things had happened.

But the wolf did not move again.

Only then did I notice the laughter had died. The arena was quiet. Too quiet.

Until I heard Logan's cry from behind me, a scream of utter terror and pain.

CHAPTER
24

My heart stopped. And then a new fear settled in my gut.

Panicked, I spun and saw Logan on the ground, two zombies on top of him. The other four lay in crumpled piles of dead bones and flesh on the ground, dark blood seeping from their skulls.

"Logan!"

My own pain forgotten, I ran as fast as my injured leg could take me without tripping. The sand pulled at my boots with each step, making it harder and slowing the process. It was like running through quicksand.

The harsh sound of Logan screaming continued, and then it just stopped.

No!

My eyes focused on Logan. From where I was, the two zombies obscured my view of him. I couldn't see his face, only a scrap of his jeans showing from under the pile of zombies. I couldn't see if he was still alive.

Bastards.

I growled in rage, arms pumping and spindling the blood magic in me until I burned with fever, and all I saw was red and death and destruction.

The two zombies looked up at the sound of my approach, their jaws open with driblets of blood spilling from their mouths. Logan's blood.

The feeling of fury burned, feeding my blood magic with the added power of emotions and giving my magic a mega boost. Pain pulled me, and I felt like I was going to be split in two. Blood magic sucked. But it was all I had.

The adrenaline rushed through me, wild and mindless. I wanted to kill them.

My blood magic soared to the surface, and power rushed out of my palms.

"Vento!" I howled and flung out my hands.

A rush of invisible force caught the zombies and propelled them back. Their limbs thrashed wildly and frantically as they flew in the air.

Trembling with rage, and the need to destroy them, I shouted, "Feurantis!"

Twin fireballs shot out of my outstretched hands and caught the two zombies midair. An explosion of yellow and orange light was followed by howls of agony as the undead ignited in flames as though they'd been doused in gasoline.

I watched as the two smoldering zombies flew like flaming cannonballs and hit the far wall of the arena with a horrible crunch. They slid to the ground in heaps of jumbled limbs and charred flesh.

And then I was moving again.

My knees shook, and I let myself fall next to Logan. My lips parted and a moan escaped me.

He was a mess of blood.

His jeans were torn and soaked in blood from ankle to thigh. Teeth marks stabbed his right collarbone, where the zombies had bitten him but had not managed to take away chunks of flesh. His shirt was ripped, revealing a series of long wounds that ran the width of his stomach, just above his belly button, as though the claws from a werewolf had sliced him. My stomach churned, and I looked away. The sand beneath him was scarlet.

Damn. His face was pale and pasty with a large red bruise just above his left eyebrow. His jaw shook as he tried to hide the pain from his face, but it was there.

He was alive, but he was going to bleed out if I couldn't get him to an angel-born hospital, or any damn human hospital, soon.

His eyes met mine, and a smile twitched on his lips. "You should see the other guy," he said, his voice forced and laced with pain. His right hand was still clutched around the small knife.

I swallowed hard, trying to keep it together. "Damn it, Logan. You should have called for help."

His features twisted, and he showed me a weary smile for a moment. "While you were fighting that zombie dog? No way," he said, his tone quiet and rough.

"You need a doctor."

Logan blinked up at me. "That bad, huh?"

"Yeah, that bad." I let out a breath and raised my hand toward his face. Then I thought better of it and instead let it fall in my lap. "We're going home. We've won. We're going to get you fixed up."

Vorkol had better let us go, or I was going to kill her next.

Sure enough, when I looked up, the Greater demon was watching me, her red eyes laced with a pure hatred that matched my own. So we had something in common after all. Good.

"Game over," I said, my voice loud over the enraged mumblings of the assembled demons. "We've won. We've killed your zombies. It's time for you to live up to your end of the deal."

I knew it was a long shot—part of me had always known she'd lied—but I had to try. For Logan's sake. I had to get him out of here. He wasn't going to make it.

"Deal?" mocked Vorkol, her delicate brows rising in question. "I don't make deals with little birds," she said, and Duvali laughed behind her on cue like a good dog.

Heat rose from my neck to my face. "You gave me your word!" I shouted, my body shaking with the spent adrenaline and blood magic.

Vorkol gave me a liquid smile, her expression condescending. "I lied," she said, and an echo of laughter from the demons ran along the arena, amplifying her words. "No demon or mortal ever goes free, silly bird." She bared her teeth and said, "Put the bird back in her cage. Let her rot to the end of her days. I've no more use for her."

With a bored expression, she turned back to Duvali, and the other demons assembled on the balcony. And just like that, I was forgotten. She'd gotten all the fun she'd wanted from me, and now I was discarded like one of her old costumes.

Then I understood. Vorkol had seemingly dropped all matters pertaining to Vargal. She didn't want anyone talking about it anymore. She knew the truth now. Perhaps she was a little embarrassed. Perhaps she didn't care. The name Vargal meant nothing to her anymore, just like I held no more interest in her eyes.

The sound of scrambling feet jerked my attention, and I looked up as some demons started to get up and leave.

The show was over.

My insides dropped to my feet. No. It couldn't be. This wasn't how it was supposed to go. I had to get out of here. I had to get Logan to a hospital.

"He needs a doctor," I shouted, my anger flaming. "Hey! He needs a doctor, damn it! I'm

254

talking to you!" I waited to get Vorkol's attention, but she was deep in conversation with a female demon sporting a shaved head in a white kimono-looking dress.

I knew she heard me. And yet she couldn't be bothered with me anymore.

There was only one thing left for me to do, only one thing I'd sworn never to do, never to tell. It was the only thing that could save Logan. She'd listen to me, then.

My lips parted—

"Don't," wheezed Logan, and my eyes dropped to him. "Don't tell her."

I frowned at his perceptiveness. "Damn it, Logan," I hissed, and feeling nauseated, I added, "I don't care anymore. If I don't tell her, you'll die. I need to get you to a hospital. It's the only way."

His face twisted in pain, and he tried to smile. "I was dead anyway." He swallowed and added, "You were right. She was never going to let us go. You can't tell her."

"Shut up." His words rang true, but I refused to accept them. "Come on. I'm getting us out."

With whatever remaining strength I had, I managed to pull Logan up and wrapped his left arm around my shoulder. Supporting most of his weight, I stood and dragged him with me. My legs shook under his weight, but with his help, we managed to stay in a vertical position. I took the knife from his hand and slipped it into my back pocket.

"Are we going to walk out?" came Logan's voice next to my ear. The laughter in his voice almost made me smile.

"Something like that." Why not. No one was paying any attention.

My plan worked for about three seconds, and then the minotaur appeared in my line of sight.

Andromalius approached us, his muscular shoulders swaying. "What of the male?" he called out, when he reached us, his sword pointed at Logan. He looked over his shoulder to his mistress.

I frowned. "His name is Logan," I said darkly. Not that it mattered.

The minotaur demon flared his nostrils at me, and a guttural growl rumbled from his throat, a sound of pure hostility and death that would have terrified me a few days ago. Now, I was just too tired.

Andromalius stood calmly and steadily, his sword's tip in the sand with his hands folded over the weighted pommel, awaiting her instruction.

"I have no more use for the mortal if he can't fight," Vorkol said finally, a quick glance in our general direction before returning her attention to the demon in the white kimono. She snapped her fingers again. "Give him to the hounds. Mortal flesh is always best when it's still warm."

My lips parted, and real fear hit hard. I couldn't get any of that damned, acidic air into my lungs. My knees wobbled, and I cried out as Logan's weight crushed me. I strained to keep from falling over.

Andromalius's feet moved toward us.

Shit. Shit. Shit.

Cold terror rose, sudden and complete, and I braced myself as my body trembled in panic.

This was it. I'd failed. We were both going to die—

"Wait!" came a shout from the crowd.

Heart racing, I turned my head toward the voice.

Faris stood near the lowest row of seats, right above the wall of concrete that separated us and the sand. Dressed all in black, his eyes met mine for a moment before he looked at Vorkol.

"You were banned from the games, Farissael," said Duvali as he left the balcony and made his way forward toward Faris with a murderous look in his eye.

Faris flashed his perfect white teeth. "When did *banning* ever stop me," said the mid-demon, his voice loud and clear, and the demons around him laughed.

"What's he doing?" asked Logan, his breath on my cheek and his voice low with pain.

Keeping my eyes on Faris, I answered, voice trembling, "No idea. But I don't have a good feeling about this." Faris was reckless. *Faris, what are you doing?*

"Duvali," commanded Vorkol, and her demon servant halted a few seats before Faris, looking like he wanted nothing more than to rip into him. "What do you want, Farissael?" asked Vorkol. The threat in her voice was palpable. It wasn't the usual villainous emphasis one would expect, but she said it in a calm, almost bored tone, as though she were commenting on his clothes.

Faris turned and our gazes met. I could see the muscles in his jaw tense, even from a distance, but his face was expressionless. Only his eyes held traces of a hidden meaning as they focused on me. He was trying to tell me something. But what?

He gave me a tight smile and said, "Him." The mid-demon pointed to Logan. "Let me have the mortal," said Faris.

My heart stopped. And then started up again

The demons in the arena laughed, thinking this was another one of Faris's many pranks. But Vorkol's face was stiff, which meant she wasn't buying it.

"And *why* do you want *this* mortal?" asked Vorkol, regarding him with a casual mistrust as she leaned back against her thronelike chair.

Faris shrugged like he didn't have a care in the world. It was Oscar-worthy. "You obviously don't have use for him anymore." He gestured with his hands. "Look at him. He's leaking. Why not just give him to me? Let me take him off your hands. He's nothing to you. It'll save you the hassle, not to mention the slippery mess the hounds leave after a meal. Think of it as a favor," he added, and I could almost see a twinkle in his eye.

"Why, Farissael?" pressed the Greater demon, her hands gripping the arms of her chair. "And no more lies. Lie to me again, and I will let you join him."

"Because," said Faris, his voice loud. He straightened, looked Vorkol straight in the eyes and said, "He's my lover."

I choked on my spit.

Then there was an abrupt and profound silence in the arena. Demons stood stock still and stared at Faris.

I exhaled slowly and watched Faris's face, amazed at how genuinely frank that had come out. Hell, if I didn't know him, I would have *believed* him. Even his eyes carried that devoted emotion you'd expect from lovers.

Okay. He was good. But would Vorkol buy it?

The Greater demon gave Faris a considering smile. "Fine," she said, dismissing the thing like it was nothing to her, as though discussing Logan's life was as unimportant as the life of a flea on one of her hounds. She picked at her nail and said, "You can have him."

Giving Vorkol a brilliant smile, Faris bowed at the waist. "You are too kind, Vorkol."

"Sam," began Logan, panic rising in his voice. His body trembled.

I shifted his weight on my shoulder. "Shhh. It's fine. Faris will take care of you."

My heart swelled. My eyes burned in gratitude, and it was hard work to keep the tears from spilling down my face and ruining Faris's Oscar-worthy performance.

The mid-demon was already striding across the sand toward us when I looked back. His face was grim and worried, which only added to the overall effect. If I ever got out of this alive, I would give him free rein in the mortal world whenever he wished.

"I'll take it from here, witch," said Faris, loudly enough for the minotaur to hear, his voice laced with contempt. "I think you've done enough." Faris moved to Logan's right side and wrapped the angel-born's arm over his shoulder.

"Can you get him out?" I whispered as we exchanged Logan's weight.

Faris kept his face blank. "Yes," he answered back. "I'll be back for you."

I swallowed hard. "Just get him out. And hurry. He's lost a lot of blood."

With a small nod of his head, Faris held Logan up. "Come on, sweetheart. Let's go," he purred, and led Logan across the sandpit.

I watched them go in silence until they went out the steel doors and melted with the dark shadows beyond. They were gone.

The noise level in the arena had risen again. Vorkol and Duvali were gone, and so were their entire balcony company.

I stood in the arena, tired and shaking from fever and the overuse of blood magic that I knew I would pay for later.

What will happen to me now?

By the time I heard something large and heavy coming my way, it was already too late.

The blow connected, and I choked down a cry as I fell, seeing Andromalius's meaty fist before my eyes.

And blackness fell.

260

CHAPTER
25

My stomach let out a loud, rumbling growl that lasted about five seconds. If I didn't know any better, it sounded like I had a gremlin living inside my rib cage. Apparently, it wanted out. So did I.

I'd grown accustomed to the sounds of my stomach, the sounds of the demon lamentations around me, and the metal bars of my cage.

Little bird...

If only I had wings, I could fly away from this hell.

An aching, lonely hurt welled inside me. I missed my family terribly—my grandfather, my eccentric aunt, and especially Poe. He was probably beside himself with worry. Now I might never see them again.

My life had not turned out how I'd planned it. I had not planned on spending the rest of my days rotting in a cage in the depths of the demon realm.

Logan was safe. I had to believe Faris had managed to get him out of the Netherworld. That had been two days ago, if my calculations were correct.

Faris hadn't come back for me yet, but I knew he would. He wouldn't let me die down here alone, not after what he'd sacrificed to get Logan out.

No. Faris was coming for me. I just had to sit tight and wait, yet I couldn't help an icy feeling that had settled deep inside my gut, leaving me quivering.

The steel doors burst open, and the minotaur demon marched into the cave.

There was a chorus of growls and hisses filled with rage around me from the neighboring cages, mixed in with whimpers and cries for help.

I sat up, watching him make his way over to my cage. I should have felt fear—a rational person would have—but I only felt rage. A hot, delicious rage spilled into my body. I was going insane. I hated these demons, but I hated what they'd done to me most of all.

Andromalius closed the distance between us and stood below my cage. He looked up. "Mistress Vorkol wishes me to convey a message to you."

I frowned. I didn't like the sound of that. "She does, does she?"

Andromalius folded his muscular arms over his large chest. "Yes."

I squinted at the demon. "I know you're not the most talkative demon, but are you just going to stand there, batting your eyelashes at me? Or are you going to tell me?"

The minotaur flared his nostrils, looking pissed. "She wishes to tell you Farissael won't be coming to rescue you."

Oh. Shit.

I gave a small laugh. "Who says he was?" Damn. Damn. Damn.

"He did," answered Andromalius with a sneer in his voice.

Crap.

I swallowed hard, trying to keep my shaking to a minimum. "He told you that?" I asked, my voice high and panicky. Did Faris really betray me? I felt ill. What about Logan? Oh, God, Logan!

The minotaur let out a breath. "He did not. But he was caught trying to make a deal with Krampus—one of our Rift experts—for your return to your world," said the minotaur, his words twisted and snarling. "Stupid bastard. He's awaiting his trial."

"His trial?" My insides twisted into a hard knot. Faris hadn't betrayed me, but it didn't sound like a victory. "What happens if he's found guilty?"

"Death."

Anxiously, I wrapped my hands around the bars, trying to keep them from shaking. The cold, familiar feeling of dread settled in me, and my gut clenched.

I opened my mouth and asked the question I most feared. "What happened to Logan?" I barely knew the guy, but it had been my fault he'd been stuck in here with me. The thought of him escaping had given me a small sense of relief. Now, I felt only dread and hollowness.

Andromalius leaned back. "Who?"

I rolled my eyes. "His lover. The angel-born?" Hadn't he been paying attention? Yeah, not the sharpest sword in the Netherworld armory.

The minotaur waved a hand in dismissal, his expression irate. "I don't know anything about that."

Oh God. It was worse than I thought.

"It is not the first time Farissael got himself mixed up with a witch," said Andromalius, feeling chatty all of a sudden. "It seems he's developed a taste for mortals over the years."

"What are you talking about?" I didn't think the big demon bull would answer, but it was worth a shot.

"I do not know all the details," said Andromalius. "But I do know the idiot had wed some witch, long before your time and long before there were automobiles and radios."

Faris was married to a witch? The damned demon was full of surprises. Why hadn't he told me? Being married to a witch must have been a big deal. I looked at the satisfied gleam in the demon's yellow eyes. "What happened to her?"

The minotaur smiled, revealing his twin rows of sharp teeth. "Tortured and killed, obviously. Her soul devoured. As it should be."

"You sick bastards," I spat, wishing I could fry his ugly cow ass right now. I was dying for a cheeseburger.

"Mortals breed like a cancer. And we've been dealing with relations between humans and demons for centuries. Our laws are very clear on the matter. No demons are allowed to mate with mortals." He gave me a look of pure disgust. "Look what happened when we did. A weak race of half-breeds emerged. It is forbidden."

This news was nothing new. I'd grown up hearing the stories of how the pure demons despised our half-breed races. It wasn't that we were weak. It was because we were strong and could walk in the sun and live in our world when they could not. And they all hated us for it.

But it explained why Vorkol hadn't seemed very concerned about Faris's declaration of love for Logan. Two males couldn't procreate. It was why he'd chosen Logan and not me.

I let go of the bars and slumped back. The thought of a child from Faris's marriage came to my mind. But I wouldn't risk voicing it. What if there *had* been a child? If I said anything now, Vorkol was vindictive enough to go after the entirety of Faris's living descendants and kill them all. The demon bitch was cold.

"One more thing," said Andromalius.

"You're just full of sunshine and rainbows today," I grumbled.

The minotaur's yellow eyes flashed. "Mistress Vorkol wishes you a nice and happy, long, long life."

Anger flared. "Can you give her a message as well? Tell her to kiss my witch ass. I bet she'd like that very much. Thank you," I added cheerfully.

But the effect was wasted as the minotaur laughed. At least that's what the strange, guttural gargling I heard coming from his throat, as he marched away and disappeared through the steel door, sounded like.

The door slammed shut with a boom that reverberated in the large cave. It felt final somehow.

Fear was a festering wound in my gut. In the right situations, a small, insignificant fear could suddenly grow, swelling up to monstrous proportions. That would happen right now if I didn't put a stop to it.

Without Faris's help, I was doomed.

I wrapped my arms over my middle, a sickly little feeling of dread rolling through me. I sat there for a moment, gathering my wits and my thoughts.

Damn it. This wasn't me. I wasn't going to let this be my end. Hell no. I was going to get out of here.

"I'm a dark witch," I told myself. "I have magic. Blood magic. And I'm going to get my ass home," I added, my voice loud and filled with a heated determination. "Even if I have to break through this damn cage with my bare hands."

"Home!" exclaimed my scrawny neighbor, and I turned to look at him. With a closer inspection, he almost appeared healthier. His blue eyes were clear and didn't bulge out as much. His face was fuller, and there was more meat on his bones, more muscle. I could even spot some rosy tint in his skin. It was almost as though those cold cuts and water I'd given him had filled him with a new healthy body.

He hadn't uttered a single word to me for two days. He'd been too busy scraping the bars on his cage. Looking at them now, not a single spot on his cage's bars wasn't scratched. Weird.

"That's right," I told him. I let out a sigh as I looked around my own cage. "There's got to be a way out of this cage," I said, peering through the bars. "If only I could reach the lever somehow..." But how could I? I was too big to pass through the bars.

A thought occurred to me. "Hey, buddy," I said, and crab-walked over to the other side so I was staring directly at him. "Do you want to go home?" I asked. Seeing how tiny the demon was, there was a real a chance it would work.

"Home!" exclaimed the demon, eyes wide, and he clapped his hands together.

"Yes, home," I said, and I waited for him to settle down. "Listen carefully. I need you to squeeze through the bars of your cage and jump down. Can you do that?" It was about a ten-foot drop. It might be too high for him to jump. His body might shatter on impact.

The demon's face creased in concern, and he looked at me like it was the first time he'd ever laid eyes on me. Then he gawked at the bars of his cage, eyes wide.

"Home," said the tiny demon, formulating the word as though trying to remember the language.

I took that as a yes. "Good. That's good. Really good." By the cauldron, this was going to work! Excitement pounded through my chest. "Okay. When you get to the ground, you need to go to the platform with all those levers and pull mine down. It's the third row—the last one on the left. Can you do that?"

The demon eyed me, his features scrunched up in a small frown.

"See. If you do that," I encouraged, "then we can both go home. You want to go home, don't you?"

The demon met my eyes and then moved to the front of his cage, facing me. He pressed his body against the bars and then slipped his right arm easily through them.

I stared at his outstretched hand. "Ah... okay. Maybe you didn't understand me the first time." I pointed to him. "All of you." Then I pointed down. "Down to the ground. Get it?"

The demon beckoned with his hand. "Hand," he said again, wiggling his fingers.

My shoulders slumped. "Hell. You don't get it, do you? And here I thought we were making progress."

Reluctantly, I stared at his thin, gangly, and dirty fingers, knowing he wanted me to take it. But why? Maybe he just wanted to thank me for the food.

"You don't have to thank me for the food," I said, and a real smile formed on my face. "It wasn't that much. Just a snack, really."

"Hand," pressed the demon, his long fingers wiggling as he waved his hand impatiently.

I shrugged. "What? You want us to hold hands and sing Kumbaya? Not sure that's going to help us escape."

He gestured with his hand again.

"Ah—what the hell. If it'll make you happy." What's the worst that could happen? "Fine. I'll shake your hand." Feeling like a fool, I slipped my arm through the bars, stretched it as far as it would go, and clasped the demon's hand.

I flinched at his touch. His skin was cold but surprisingly soft.

"Okay. This is really awkward." I said, and I shook his hand. "You're welcome." I didn't know what else to say. When I tried to pull my hand away, his hand locked onto mine with the strength of a bear.

"Hey. What are you doing?" I said, panic filling me. Shit. Faris was right. He wanted to kill me. Possibly eat me.

I pulled and pulled as hard as I could, but it was like trying to pull a car with my pinky. I barely had any strength left as it was.

Fear slid through me, paralyzing and cold. "Let go of me," I cried. "Let go!" What had I done?

"Friend," said the little demon, and I looked up to find his face cracking into a smile. His three teeth

269

were chipped and stained, and big fat tears slipped down his face.

My lips parted. "What?" I asked stupidly. My eyes widened as I felt the hum of power, of magic running from his hand to mine, like static electricity. A shiver took me. It wasn't the normal cold demonic energy. It was warm. My fingertips pulsed with magic, and then it spread to my arm, to my chest, all the way to my toes. I was prickling with magic.

Another strong pulse of magic hit, and my breath was pushed out of my lungs. I stared, openmouthed, at the tiny demon, his eyes sparkling with a golden glow. A shot of energy raced from my hand to my core, to my soul. Heat exploded in my chest, and then white light exploded all around, growing until white light flooded my eyes, and I was forced to shut them.

The breath was pushed out of my lungs again, and I felt myself falling, falling fast.

Holy crap!

Another prickling washed through me, and my lungs rebounded, filling with cool, sweet air. I gasped as my boots slammed into the hard ground. My jaw snapped closed, and I bit my tongue.

Dizzy, I stood for a moment, confused. I opened my eyes.

I stood in the middle of a dark street and heard the sounds of cars off in the distance. I looked around and realized I knew this place. It was Mystic Quarter. I was... home.

Only then did I realize I was still holding on to the little demon.

I looked down at him. "You brought me home? How? How is this possible?" *And why didn't you bring me home sooner*, I wanted to shout, though that sounded a little too ungrateful. *Be nice to the little demon*, I told myself, *cause he might send your ass back.*

I stared at him with my mouth open. I'd never heard of a demon capable of jumping realities, jumping through worlds as though he could create his own Rifts. He created his own portal somehow, with his magic, and took me home. That, ladies and gents, is some *serious* magic.

"That was truly impressive," I said, a huge smile on my face, wondering if the food I'd given him was the reason his magic had resurfaced. I inspected him the way I might inspect a new spell. "You're not a demon, are you?"

The tiny man's blue eyes glittered brightly as his face crinkled in a smile.

"I'm going to take that as a no," I told him. "I don't even know your name. But I thank you. Thank you for bringing me home." *The wards*, I realized. He'd scratched them all off.

The little man slipped his hand from mine and said, "You're welcome."

And with a pop, the tiny man vanished.

CHAPTER
26

There's nothing in the world more glorious than waking up in one's own bed—except perhaps, sleeping in one's own bed. Especially after having spent days sleeping in a cold metal cage in a world where the air was toxic. I felt like I was sleeping on puffy white clouds, and I never wanted to get up. But I had to.

The first thing I did when I got home was hug my grandfather, whose face was drawn with worry. I gave Poe a big kiss on his head, thankful he was safe, and then jumped into a steaming-hot shower. A half hour later, as soon as my head hit my pillow, I went to dreamland.

I stretched, feeling better, but not completely healed, and refreshed. The Netherworld had taken a lot from me, including my health and a part of my soul. Granted, I didn't feel any different, but that didn't mean I was whole again. I had no idea what the effect would be to me later on.

Last night, before my shower, Poe informed me that Logan had come by earlier that day. He'd been in an angel-born hospital recovering and had told my grandfather and Poe everything. Logan told them he was working on a plan to get me back, that he'd been in contact with Kyllian, and they were trying to work out a deal with the Angel Legion.

Faris had been true to his word. My insides squirmed. It didn't seem right or fair that I was back home safely whereas Faris was awaiting trial. It felt as though I had failed him.

But I wouldn't let him rot in the Netherworld.

I rolled over and grabbed my alarm clock from my nightstand. Seven p.m. Crap. I'd slept the whole day away, and there was still so much to be done.

I swung my legs off the bed and went to my dresser. After pulling on a pair of jeans, a black T-shirt, and a pair of flat boots, my eyes drifted back to my nightstand. Faris's small dagger lay next to my alarm clock. I picked it up, now that I wasn't facing imminent death, and took my time to inspect it.

It was heavy for such a small blade, as long as my hand. Forged with some dark gray metal, sharp as a shard of glass, demonic sigils and runes were carved along the blade. The hilt was molded with the face of a wailing, horned demon.

"Creepy." I slipped the blade into my back pocket and stepped into the hallway. The house was unusually dark and silent. I stopped over the staircase and listened. Only the constant hum of the refrigerator answered back.

"Poe?" I called. "Gramps?" Nothing.

Then I perked up at the sound of muffled voices. I turned around. It came from my grandfather's room.

I let out a sigh. "What are you up to, old man?" With a small smile I went across the hall to my grandfather's room and pushed open the door.

"Hey, Grandpa. Can I borrow your phone—"

There, in his bed, was my grandfather and a female witch.

Which would have been fine if they'd been wearing clothes. As it was, they were both on top of the sheets—butt naked.

"Oh. My. God!" I covered my eyes with my hands. But it was too late. The image of two, saggy, wrinkled, and very naked bodies was imprinted on the backs of my eyelids.

"Oh, hi, Samantha," said my grandfather, his voice bright and cheery like he was commenting on a new batch of his gin. "I'd like you to meet, Charlotte. Charlotte—this is my granddaughter, Samantha."

"Hello," came Charlotte's happy voice. "Your grandfather's told me so much about you. I feel like we're friends already."

"Hang on while I go wash out my eyes with bleach," I said, my hands still covering my eyes, but the images of their naked bodies kept flashing in my mind's eye. "You do realize you've scarred me for life. There's no going back from this."

"Nonsense," chirped my grandfather. "This is all very natural. There is no shame in being undressed. Why are people so uptight about being naked? We should embrace our bodies not be ashamed of them."

"Why are you naked?" I howled.

My grandfather chuckled. "Well, it would be rather difficult to have sex with our clothes on—"

"Stop!" I shouted. I was the idiot for asking that. I swallowed and said, "Why didn't you tell me you had company?"

"My dear girl," said my grandfather, his tone amused. "I don't need your permission to have sex—"

"Stop saying that word!" I cried, my hands slipping from my eyes. Crap. I looked again. Moaning, I covered my eyes again. "I'm never going to be the same again."

"You are overreacting, Samantha," soothed my grandfather. "Besides, we were finished. Unless... Charlotte... you'd like to go for another round?"

The bed squeaked, and then I heard the sound of bodies moving. There was a slap on skin. "Why, you naughty witch," squealed Charlotte.

Shoot me now. "I should have stayed in the Netherworld."

A flutter of wings appeared behind me. "What's all the shouting about—Oh. Boy."

275

"I have to get out of here." I spun, ran out the room, and headed for the staircase, the sound of Charlotte's laugh trailing behind me.

I took the stairs up to the third floor and hurried over to my worktable.

Poe landed on a cleared spot on the table. "What are you doing?"

As I rummaged through the stack of papers, books, and candles, a white chalk peered from under my *Wicca for the Modern Witch* book. I grabbed it, "I'm getting Faris out of the Netherworld," I said as I headed to the spot on the wood floor where I could make out the faint traces of the summoning triangle and circle I'd used before.

"Right," said the raven. "About that. Listen, while you were napping, there was another murder."

I halted, tension spiking through me. I knew exactly what he meant by murder. "Are you sure?"

The raven nodded his head. "Another young witch that fits your description. But if what you told me was true, why is Vorkol still having this vampire working to kill you? I thought she grew bored of you?"

Heart thumping, I dropped to my knees and began to trace the Circle of Solomon. "Maybe he doesn't know. I don't think she cared enough to tell him."

Poe walked over to the edge of the table. "So, what are we going to do about it?"

I sighed, trying to focus. "First, we get Faris back. Then, we go find that bloodsucker."

"How? He could be anywhere."

"Then we'll look everywhere," I snapped, regretting it immediately. I took a calming breath and said, "I don't care. But this has to stop. I don't want to think about all those dead witches."

I quickly finished tracing the Goetia triangle, wrote Farissael in the center followed by his unique sigil, and stood, heart pounding with excitement and fear. I hoped I wasn't too late. Maybe I should have summoned him last night.

"Where are your gloves?" questioned the raven. "You never go anywhere without them."

I glanced at my hands and the scars that marred them. I flipped them over, palms facing up, and I could see a faint, darkened line of scar tissue along my left palm where I'd cut myself. I thought I would need stitches, but my grandfather had sealed up the would expertly with a healing spell last night.

"I forgot to put them on," I said, surprised that it had totally slipped my mind. Now, *that* was a first.

Though I only had the one glove. Logan had kept the other one.

"And your rings?"

I clenched my jaw. "Vorkol destroyed them. There's no time to make new ones. But as my great aunt would say, 'A wise dark witch must always have backups.' I have an extra one somewhere around here. It's not as powerful, but it will do just fine to fry an old vampire."

I shook my body, trying to rid it of the sudden tension and focused as I drew the energy from the circle and triangle.

Please be alive...

"I conjure you, Farissael, demon of the Netherworld to be subject to the will of my soul. I bind you with unbreakable adamantine fetters," I continued, channeling the magic, and letting the power spill into me, "and I deliver you into the black chaos in perdition. I invoke you, Farissael, in the space in front of me!"

I held my breath. Magic pulsed through me in waves, mixed with my adrenaline.

Please be alive...

There was a sudden burst of wind.

And then Faris materialized in the triangle.

My knees shook with relief. He was alive. But as my eyes rolled over him, I cringed at what I saw.

His lip was split and swollen, and bruises and dried blood stained his face. His open shirt revealed a nasty band of bruised skin that ran from his left shoulder to his chest. I'd never seen him look so disheveled. He looked like he'd been banged up by a demon heavyweight.

"Took you long enough," said the mid-demon, as he tried to gather what little self-respect he had left. He brushed the hair from his eyes. "I was beginning to think you didn't love me anymore, Sammy," he added, his voice a little higher than usual.

I let out a breath. "I see they roughed you up a little."

"Yes, well." Faris gave me a tight smile. "Nothing I wouldn't do to them."

Demons were a strange bunch. "Okay, then." I dragged my foot over the chalk-drawn triangle. "I release you," I said, and let go of the energy from the circle and triangle.

There was a sudden influx of power, and then it was gone.

"You'll be safe here until I can figure out a spell that'll keep you on our side of the world for a little longer," I said, stepping out of my circle. If there was one, I would find it. I owed him that much.

"I need a shower," said the mid-demon. "Can you get decent water pressure in this primordial establishment? I can't have soap residue in my hair. I'll look like a peasant." I felt a pang of guilt when he ran his shaking hand through his hair again in a recognizable sign of stress.

If I did hugs, I might have attempted one on him right now. "Down one floor to the left." I dropped the chalk on the table next to Poe. "You'll find towels and just poke around for anything else you might need."

"Thank you." Faris walked away. I couldn't help but wonder at his past, his wife, and how hard that must have been for him. I'd never understand demons. But then again, they weren't much different from us.

"Where did they find the last murdered witch?" I asked Poe, thinking that if we went looking at the area of his last victim, we might get lucky.

"In Queens," answered the raven.

"Queens?" I shot the raven a look. "You sure?"

"Yup."

What was the vampire doing in Queens? My frustration rose. I had to do something, his being out of range or not.

A hand clasped around my heart and squeezed it. "It has to stop. We have to find him. Tonight." Now that the higher demons were off my back, I had more wiggle room, but I still didn't know *where he was* or *when* he was going to strike next.

"What's that *demon* doing in my bathroom!" My grandfather stormed in, his blue bathrobe swaying and a glass of what I guessed was gin in his hand. "I'm not *sharing* my water with a *demon*."

I raised a brow. "I don't think he'd like it if you went in there with him either," I added with a smile.

My grandfather's face darkened. "Are you out of your witching mind! Why on earth would I want to do that?"

I sighed through my nose. This was going to be a long night. "Grandpa. Faris is going to be staying with us for a while. And I need you to be nice to him." He opened his mouth to protest and I added quickly, "He saved Logan's life *and* mine in the fighting pit. I wouldn't be here if it weren't for him. Demon or not, he's my friend." I was surprised at how natural the word friend came out, especially referring to a demon. But I knew it to be true.

My grandfather bit back a snort and mumbled something under his breath. He took a swig of his drink. "Friends with demons. That's like asking a cat to be friends with a mouse." He made a face. "What's this world coming to?"

"A better one." Tension had me wire tight. I had less than nine hours to find the vampire *and* figure out a spell that could keep Faris on this side of the world before the sun came up.

I looked at my grandfather. "Do you know of a spell that could keep a demon on this side of the planes?" I asked, seeing and ignoring the sudden alarm in his eyes. "For a little while." When he said nothing, I added, "Remember, he saved my life. If he goes back before sunrise, they'll kill him."

He took another gulp of his gin and smacked his lips.

I arched a brow. "Fine. I'll just ask Aunt Evanora—"

"I might know of a spell," he answered quickly, knowing how much it would kill him if I went to her instead of him. These two had been rivals ever since I could remember. Epic in scale and worse than two kids refusing to share their toys on the playground.

Poe gave a snort, and I crossed my arms over my chest. "Go on."

The old witch looked up from his gin. "It's a *very* complex spell. Only a handful of witches can pull it off. Me, being one. It'll take days of preparation."

"You've got nine hours."

My grandfather scowled. "That should be fine."

I felt a tinge of relief that he was going to help me with Faris, even if a bit grudgingly. I knew I could count on him. "How does the spell work exactly?" I found it curious that I had never heard of it before.

"It's a binding spell, more or less," he answered. "It works to tie the demon to this world. To secure the demon and to break the Netherworld's hold on him. It's how witches came to have familiars. It took some serious spell work, but over the years, the bond between the two was strong and fed off the witch's own energy. That helped perpetuate the demon's resistance to this world, enabling them to stay indefinitely. This spell will work the same way."

"Sounds great," I said, my voice rising with excitement. "Whatever it takes to keep Faris here with us." Now that he was going to help me with Faris, I could concentrate on finding the old vampire.

I watched as my grandfather tipped his glass to his lips and finished the last of his gin. I realized something was missing. "What happened to your friend Charlotte?"

"The damnedest thing," said my grandfather, staring at his empty glass as though he couldn't explain where all the alcohol had gone. "Her daughter called. Apparently, her granddaughter's gone missing. She went out to get cream from the local bodega," he said, and made a gesture with his free hand, "and she never came back."

A deep chill shook the core of my being. I shared a sidelong look with Poe, ice rolling up and down my spine and making me shiver.

"Is her granddaughter a witch?" I had to ask. Not all witches mated with other witches. It was rare, but some witches married outside the witch community and got hitched with humans.

My grandfather frowned. "Of course she's a witch."

Alarm hit me. "How long ago was this?"

He shrugged. "A few minutes before I came upstairs. Why? Charlotte went to see if she could help find her granddaughter and calm her daughter. I'm sure it's nothing."

"Oh, it's something, all right," I told him, my pulse fast. If this just happened, I still had time. "Where does Charlotte's granddaughter live?"

"In Queens with her mother."

"You know the address?"

"One Ninety-Fifth Street on the corner of 73rd Avenue." He watched me for a moment, shifting his feet. He gave me a hard look. "I know that face. What are you not telling me, Sam?"

My heart thumped in my chest. "The vampire's got her."

"What?" cried my grandfather, incredulous, his thick white brows lowering. "Don't be ridiculous. She probably just went out to see some friends."

"Sure," I said. "Which is why her mother's having a fit. No. The vampire's got her." My lips curled into a wicked smile. "And now *I've* got him."

CHAPTER
27

This was it. This was how I was going to get the murderous vampire and kill him.

You're mine, you bastard.

Excitement, hope, and anticipation rose high. The vampire was in for a nasty surprise.

"Uh—Samantha," said Poe as he slammed his beak on a tiny spider that had been crawling along my worktable. "I hate to break this to you, but"—he paused as he gulped down the spider—"you'll never make it in time. Even with the fastest car, traffic's a bitch in New York City. Getting from here to Queens will most likely take you over an hour. She'll be dead by then."

"Right," I said, my mind swirling with possibilities. "Then I need to hurry, don't I?"

Heart thudding, I ran to my bookshelf at the far wall and pulled out an old, green leather-bound book, rushing it back to my table. With one hand, I cleared off some space in the middle, and then I dropped the large book with a heavy plop.

The title of the book had been worn off over the years, but I didn't need a title to know what it was.

I flipped it open, the smell of musk hitting me, and I sneezed at the sudden puffs of dust. My fingers, shaking with excitement and adrenaline, never stopped fiddling through the thick, yellowed pages.

"I know what book that is," grumbled my grandfather, appearing over my shoulder. He took a breath. "What are you doing, Sam? This is a *very* dangerous book."

"I know."

"This is *not* an Ars Goetia," he proclaimed, his tone high, and I felt him fidget next to me. "The demons in here cannot be controlled."

I looked up at him. "I can control them." God, I hoped so. Otherwise, I was a very dead witch.

His eyes narrowed, and he grimaced. "This is your aunt's doing. Isn't it? She gave you that damn book."

I pressed my lips together. I wasn't about to get my aunt into trouble, not after I begged her to lend me the book.

My grandfather frowned. "Stop doing that."

"What?"

"That brain of yours is working again," he added dryly. "Stop it. You just got back. You should be resting."

"Can't," I answered as I flipped another page.

"What are you looking for?" questioned Poe as he walked over to get a better look at the book.

"There," I said and pointed my finger to the top right of the page next to a faded, black and white illustration. "*He's going to take* me to Queens."

Poe whistled. He looked at the page and then up at me. "Pegasus? The horse demon?"

"The *flying* horse demon," I added proudly, seeing Poe's nod of agreement. "Just look at him. Isn't he glorious? Look at those wings. Those are some badass wings. And it says here he can fly up to a hundred miles per hour. He's the Concorde of flying horses."

My grandfather slammed his empty glass on my table, making me jerk. "He's wild. A feral beast. There's a reason he's not part of the Goetia demons. He's reckless. He's a loose cannon. Only a fool would risk her life like this."

I leaned back and pressed my hands against my hips. "If Harry Potter can ride a thestral, *I* can ride Pegasus," I added smugly. Hell yes.

My grandfather smacked his forehead in disbelief. "You can't fly across town riding a flying demon horse," he argued. "It's a demon horse!"

"Yes, I heard you the first time."

"The humans will see you."

"No they won't. I have the perfect glamour for that," I added proudly. "Don't worry. The humans will never see us."

"That's it," said my grandfather darkly. "She's lost her witch mind."

Someone cleared their throat behind me, and I turned to see Faris with a drink in his hand. His face was blood free and clean. I could even smell the shea butter soap from where he stood. "Have you ever ridden a horse before?"

"No." Crap. Was that important?

Faris smiled and settled into an empty chair. "That should be very interesting. You might want to bring a parachute. You know... in case you fall off."

I scowled. "I won't fall off."

"Whatever you say, Sammy," said the mid-demon and crossed his legs at the knee. He stared into his drink, his focus far away.

My grandfather crossed his arms over his chest, clearly upset. "Well, you're not summoning that thing in here. It's too big. It'll destroy my house."

"*Our* house," I corrected, seeing as I was now paying the bills, not to mention putting the food on the table.

"Have you seen the size of horse droppings?" he added, irritation crossing his face.

I gave him a sidelong glance. "I'm going out back to do it." My eyes moved to the mid-demon. "Faris. My grandfather is going to stay here with you."

"I don't need a babysitter," said Faris as he lifted his eyes from his drink.

"Yeah, you do. He's going to help us with the spell to keep you here for a while. Right, Gordon?" I said, sweeping my attention back to my grandfather.

My grandfather made a face, moved toward his worktable, grabbed a brown leather-bound book and began rummaging through it.

"Please try and be civil to each other while I'm gone," I told them. "I don't want to come back here and find you both dead."

Faris blew out a breath. "For that—I'm going to need a lot more alcohol."

My eyebrows rose and I shook my head. I didn't have time to stay here and babysit both of them. I had to go.

I turned my attention back to the book. After I'd memorized Pegasus's name in Latin and his unique sigil, I pulled open the top drawer from my worktable, grabbed my spare golden sigil ring, and slipped it on my finger.

I reached out and grabbed the chalk. "Come on, Poe. Let's go," I said and crossed the room.

"Yes, ma'am." The clatter of wings rose, and then the raven zipped past me and flew down the stairs.

Excitement rushed through my body as I ran down after him. I hit the bottom, ran across the kitchen, and moved out through the back door to the small paver patio area. I held the door open for Poe, and he flew past me and into our backyard.

Our backyard was the size of a large living room. But it was large enough to fit a horse.

Yellow light spilled from Vera's windows, but if the witch had heard me, she would have been out here by now. Still, I had to hurry.

Moving fast, I knelt on the gray paver stone patio and quickly drew my summoning circle and triangle with Pegasus's name in the center along with his sigil.

"What happens if he eats you?" said the raven as he settled on the patio next to me.

I stood up. "Horses don't eat meat."

"Demon horses do."

Yikes. I tried not to think about it as I pulled on the energy from the circle and triangle, channeled the magic, and recited the summoning spell in one breath.

"I conjure you, Pegasus, demon of the Netherworld to be subject to the will of my soul. I bind you with unbreakable adamantine fetters, and I deliver you into the black chaos in perdition. I invoke you, Pegasus, in the space in front of me!"

It happened a lot faster than I'd expected.

There, standing on my backyard patio was Pegasus.

My mouth fell open.

This was not the cutesy white horse with angelic wings. This was hell's version.

He had a broad chest and four heavy hooves, and he was covered with a glistening black coat as sleek as silk. Large, black feathered wings were folded against his sides. A generous mane fell over his neck and a tail of long, black tresses swooped the ground. He was huge. His back was taller than me. He was a giant, kingly horse and looked more like a Clydesdale than a thinner, more refined thoroughbred.

He pricked his ears forward, yellow, intelligent eyes watching me. Pegasus was both terrifying and glorious. Hot damn. I was all giddy inside. I almost applauded.

Pegasus neighed, and his lips pulled back, revealing two rows of sharp teeth. Now I got the meat part.

If I'd been human, I would have run away screaming. As it was, I was a dark witch, so, of course, I was grinning at this scary beast. He was spectacular. Hell's steed. But I didn't have time to drool over this magnificent creature. I needed a ride.

"Pegasus," I said, in way of greeting, meeting his eyes. "I need you to take me to 195th Street, corner of 73rd Avenue, in Queens," I ordered, my heart pounding in my throat. And then I added, "Please."

Pegasus raised his right leg and pawed at the ground. He lifted his head, his ears swiveling.

I looked down at Poe. "What's he saying?"

"How the hell should I know?" said the raven. "I don't speak horse."

I gritted my teeth. I'd done the summoning properly. Pegasus couldn't hurt me. If he could, he would have done it by now.

"I'm going to climb on your back now. Okay?" I said, shifting nervously. "So, please don't eat me."

My breath came fast and I took a careful step toward the horse. My head came to the middle of its stomach. "I think I'm going to need a ladder."

Poe let out a cawing laugh. "There's no saddle either. Faris was right, you should have brought a parachute."

"Don't start," I said, annoyed.

But then Pegasus shifted and lowered himself down on his knees, low enough for me to climb up onto his back.

"This is going to be fun." Or this was going to be the death of me. With my hands gripped firmly around a mass of his mane, I swung my right leg over his back and pulled myself up. The scent of sulfur was strong, but so was the scent of earth and oil.

Pegasus shifted his body and then stood.

"Don't let me fall," I said. I tightened my grip around his mane, twisting my fingers along locks of his black hair, and squeezed my thighs around his muscular sides.

The horse neighed and thrashed his powerful head back and forth. He spread his giant wings on either side, possessing a wingspan of about twenty feet.

And then with a powerful thrust of his wings, he leaped into the air—and me with him.

My head fell back, and I screamed at the top of my lungs like a bloody banshee.

If Vera hadn't heard me before, that would do it.

"Holy crap!" I shrilled as I hung on for dear life. Pegasus climbed higher and higher, the beating of his wings like giant drums, sending my hair in my eyes and mouth. I felt like I was on a roller coaster, rolling up to the highest peak without the protection of a seat belt. I felt both fear and excitement all at once, adrenaline pounding through me.

This had to be the stupidest thing I'd ever done.

"Uh—Samantha?" came Poe's voice as he flew next to me. "Shouldn't you do the glamour spell? Unless you want to be splattered all over social media tomorrow morning."

Right. I'd forgotten.

"Ut occultatum!" I breathed as I pulled on the magic from my sigil ring. A wash of energy rippled through me and out toward Pegasus. I felt the energy pull out and then settle, and I knew the glamour had snapped into place. The only indication that it was working was the constant tingling over my skin. If the horse demon felt anything, it didn't show.

Pegasus flapped his wings and banked hard, the world tilting and then shooting behind. He navigated expertly in the night sky, flying hard and fast. He let out a fierce, exuberant cry that reverberated over every bone in my body. I smiled. The demon horse was having fun.

Flying on a winged horse made me feel a little reckless, a little wild. It made me do stupid things like howl and laugh out hysterically. The only thing left for me to do was look down.

New York City's lights blurred up at me, bright, alive. Wow, Pegasus was fast. I couldn't recognize anything as I squinted, eyes watering at the wind tearing at my eyes. A chill wind brushed my face, clogging my nose.

"Can you tell the beast to slow down," shouted Poe, flapping wildly beside us. "I'm just a little bird!"

I let out a hysterical laugh. "Maybe you should hitch a ride if you can't keep up." I laughed harder at the scowl on the raven's face.

Pegasus tucked in his wings, and we fell, my heart lurching to my throat as we dropped. I closed my eyes to keep from throwing up because I knew I would.

The horse pulled back, and my stomach bounced as we settled in a horizontal position. I opened my eyes. We were low enough now that I could clearly make out buildings and streets as we flew two hundred feet above ground, give or take.

The sign for 195th Street came into view. We were near. Houses and shops lined the streets. My eyes locked on to the nearest bodega. I scanned the dark alleys next to it, my eyes squinting in the wind. I should have brought goggles.

And then I saw him.

"There!" I shouted, pointing at the barely visible shape of a person looming over another in a dark alley. "Take me down right next to that alley behind that apartment building. But not too close. I don't want to ruin the surprise." *I've got you now, you sonofabitch.*

Pegasus did as I commanded, tucking his wings and diving for that alley. He landed in an expert canter, folded his wings and knelt. I slid off his back and fell to the ground. Yeah, not exactly the graceful landing I'd envisioned, but after squeezing my thighs like that for so long, I couldn't feel my legs.

Ignoring Poe's laugh, I pushed myself to my feet. "You have until sunrise to return to the Netherworld," I told the horse, rubbing my thighs to try and get the circulation back. "Unless you want me to send you back now?"

Pegasus shook his head, gave a neigh that sounded a lot like a thank you, and then, with a great beat of his wings, he soared into the air like a giant black eagle and disappeared into the night sky.

Pretty horse. I was definitely going to use him again.

I whirled around and started running, pulling on my sigil ring as I shot toward the alley.

"Gotcha, you filthy bloodsucker," I cried, as I turned the corner and stumbled into the alley.

The vampire was leaning over what I assumed was Charlotte's granddaughter's body. The pull of his dark magic was strong, and the air grew cooler the closer I got to him.

I slowed my run to a walk. "It's over, you sonofabitch," I panted.

The vampire turned around.

I froze.

Trouble was, he wasn't a vampire at all. He was a witch.

CHAPTER
28

"You!" I cried, shocked and pissed all at the same time. "No. It can't be." My mouth fell open, torn between fury and shock, and my face went cold.

Darius stood very slowly and turned to face me. "Yes, it's me," said the elderly male witch as he straightened. His black robe swished around him, and his bald head was covered with a cowl.

I frowned. His face looked different, smoother and younger somehow. His beard was dark and marked with silver, and he was taller than I remembered. Gone was the old, crippled man bent with age, and in his place stood a younger, stronger version of the head of the dark witch court.

There was only one way he could have regenerated his body like that. He was consuming the witches' magic and life force.

Somehow he had figured out how to suck the life force out of the witches, just like a demon.

My body shook as the realization dawned on me. "You twisted bastard. What have you done?" I raged. The flutter of wings sounded as Poe settled himself on a nearby post. I stared at the witch. Her face was pale, but smooth with fleshy cheeks. She was still alive. He hadn't drained her yet.

"What I must," answered Darius, like that was supposed to mean something to me.

A snarl escaped me. "I don't know how you figured it out, but you must have made quite a deal with a powerful demon if they told you how to drain the life force of a witch. That's some serious twisted shit. And probably *really* forbidden."

Darius smiled like I'd just given him a compliment. "Our numbers are failing. But demons are on the rise. They're coming for us. Don't you understand? Soon they will break free from their world and destroy us all," he said, a feverish gleam in his eyes. A bestial grunt jerked from his throat. "I won't let them. They will not control *our* magic, and I will not be tethered to them. I will not be their slave." He reached up and touched the scar on his face. "Never again." He lowered his hand, his eyes meeting mine. "Once I had the spell, I took what was rightfully mine."

"I don't care what happened to you in the past," I growled, my head throbbing with rage. "Their lives were not for you to take." Disgust and adrenaline sparked through me. "You killed them. You evil

296

sonofabitch. And for what? So you wouldn't have to summon up some demon for more power? How demented is that? These witches had families who cared about them. They were daughters. Mothers. Wives. You had no right to take away their lives."

Darius smiled. It was an odd thing having a younger face but still the stained and worn teeth of an old man. "Yes. That is exactly right. I took their lives." He blinked and then stared at me with yellow, glowing eyes—the eyes of a demon.

Bile rose in the back of my throat. "You're a sick, sick, little witch, and a fucking coward," I said, and Poe cawed in approval. "It's why you didn't want the vampire court involved, isn't it?" I said. "Because they would have found you out. And they would have killed you."

I felt a cold pulse of magic rippling in the air, dark and powerful as it wove around us. He was trying to intimidate me with his magic. It wasn't working.

I took a step forward, challenging him while spindling my own magic from my ring. "Since we're having this lovely chat. Tell me. Why didn't you kill me when you had the chance?"

He watched me, and his smile became wider, more impish and demon-like.

"Why only female witches?" I pressed. "Why not the males?"

"Because the young female witches are so easily persuaded to help"—he bent down, imitating his older self—"poor old Darius." He straightened, a dark laugh rumbling in his chest. "Naïve. But that's in your nature. The females always are."

I cocked a brow. "It's in my nature to kill your ass."

Darius gave me a wicked smile, his dark magic pulsing around us and coming toward me.

My eyes darted to a metal garbage bin to my left. "Rebis Tollunt!" I shouted and flung out my hand, sending the heavy metal bin straight for the old witch like a missile.

With a simple flick of his wrist, Darius sent the bin crashing into the wall of the neighboring building. Impressive for a witch. But I was just getting started.

Heart thrashing, I pulled on the magic of my sigil ring and cried, "Hasta Feuro!" A yellow-orange, spear-like fire shot from my extended hand.

The old witch clapped his hands together, and my spear exploded into tiny sparks.

Darius snarled, the whites of his eyes showing as dark magic dripped from his hands.

"Oh. Shit."

He flung his hands at me.

"Sphaeras!" I shouted, and a sphere-shaped shield of golden energy expanded over me just as his tendril of darkness hit. My sphere shook, and then it fell.

"This isn't going so well," I said as fear pounded through me. The bastard was very powerful.

The raven cawed above me, and Poe dove for Darius, a black arrow of death. As fast as a bullet, in a blur of black, Poe went for the witch's eye.

Darius mumbled a word, and Poe was swatted to the side by an invisible force like a giant flyswatter. He hit the side of a parked car with a dull thud, slid down, and was gone.

Fear gripped my throat. I whipped my head around. "You bastard!"

Darius stood, his fingers dancing merrily in a dark spell. He gave me the briefest flicker of a look, viciously amused.

Standing legs apart, I went deep into my core, shaking with power and rage and letting it leak over my soul. Spindling a wad of it in me, I shouted, "Fulgur chordis!"

Ribbons of blue electricity shot from my palms and hit the witch. He didn't even move as the blue electricity coiled around his body, licking his skin and even his insides. He should have been screaming in pain, but he wasn't. In fact, he just smiled.

Oh. Crap.

With a burst of speed, I saw a blur of black, and then his hands were wrapped around my neck, cutting off my air.

We crashed to the ground, his weight adding to the crushing of his hands around my throat.

Darius smiled down at me. "And that's only a taste," he sneered, spit flying into my face. "You think you can beat me with your tiny witch magic?" He laughed and squeezed harder until I thought he was going to break my neck. "You're nothing but a broodmare—a worthless female. Powerless. How does it feel knowing that your life ends tonight?"

I clamped my hands around his, trying to pry them open, but my fingers kept slipping, and my vision blurred as darkness crept in. Despite all my preparations, I was helpless. He was too strong. It was like fighting off a dozen witches at once. I wasn't strong enough. My magic didn't compare to his. I couldn't fight him.

"And you," he seethed, the cold expression on his face making him all the more demon. "You surprise me, Samantha. I never expected you to find me out. You were meant to keep the court entertained with this idea of a killer vampire. That's the only reason I didn't kill you in that alley all those days ago. You see, *I* picked you because you were *supposed* to *fail*. Such a sad little witch. You were never meant to amount to anything."

The darkness was stronger now. My head felt like it was exploding. I was dying.

"You are a meddling, insufferable witch, Samantha Beaumont. But I will take your magic as well."

You were supposed to fail...

But I hadn't failed.

He squeezed harder.

I let go of his hands and slipped my right hand under me to my pocket and gripped the small dagger.

And with all the strength I could muster, with the last of my will, I slammed it into his left ear, shoving it into his brain.

Darius's mouth opened in a silent scream, and the bastard let go of my neck and rolled off of me.

Coughing, I took deep buckets of air into my lungs, backpedaling as far as I could.

My neck throbbed, and I watched as the witch made horrible hacking sounds while he convulsed on the ground. His hands tore at the skin on his face, his legs flailing, writhing. He thrashed around for a moment, his face and the skin on his hands blackening. The skin cracked and peeled, shriveling, flaking, and adding the scent of burnt hair to the air.

And then he burst into a cloud of gray ash.

Just like a demon.

CHAPTER
29

I couldn't sleep. I was so wired after defeating Darius and having to explain to the other members of the dark witch court what the pile of ashes was and why it was there. Sleep was the last thing on my mind.

And with Ruby's—Charlotte's granddaughter's—eyewitness account to the dark witch court, by the time I'd got home, it was almost eight in the morning.

So, what does one do when they can't sleep? They eat.

I flipped my blueberry pancake over in my frying pan. "You can take off those sunglasses." I glanced over to the mid-demon, sitting at the kitchen table, facing the assortment of breakfast condiments—raspberry jam, bananas, a bowl of blueberries, a loaf of brown bread, orange juice, a milk carton, and some organic sugar. I hadn't asked my grandfather yet how the spell had gone, but with having Faris here still at sunup, I didn't think it really mattered.

Faris looked at me from under the rim of his glasses. "They're called sunglasses for a reason." He pointed to the window. "There's the sun. The glasses stay."

"Fine." I had a feeling the glasses were some sort of comfort mechanism. I had no idea how long or if he'd ever been in the sun. I moved over to him and plopped the hot pancake onto his plate. "Help yourself to the maple syrup and butter over there."

"Thanks," said Faris as he took a sip of his coffee, which smelled strongly of whiskey.

"Keep still, you damn bird!" yelled my grandfather, sitting across from Faris, as he attempted to apply some ointment on Poe's wing. "I'm trying to help you. You ungrateful, flying house cat!"

The raven moved back, cradling his injured wing against his body. "How do I know if that's even true?" accused the raven. "Not a few hours ago, a witch tried to kill me. An *old* witch. Like you."

"Shut your beak," growled my grandfather. He reached out and tugged a little too forcefully on the bird's wing. "Or I'll break the other one."

"Go ahead, you old broom," threatened Poe. "And I'll tell Charlotte about Terresa and Anne."

My grandfather's hand froze in the ointment jar, fear making his wrinkles deepen around his eyes.

I set the frying pan on the stove and faced my grandfather. "Who're Terresa and Anne?" I let out an exasperated breath of air. "My grandpa's a manwhore."

"And I'll tell Samantha," warned my grandfather, "why you've been stealing all those watches and rings."

Poe's eyes narrowed, and for a second, I thought he was going to jump in my grandfather's face.

"Poe?" I questioned. "What's he talking about?"

"Nothing," said the bird dryly, "The witch is senile."

Faris let out a snort, and I turned to see a smile on his face. It was the first time I'd seen him smile all morning. It looked good on him.

Who knew? This new living arrangement might actually work.

I turned to grab the pancake mix.

The doorbell rang.

"I'll get it," I ordered, pointing a finger at my grandfather and Poe. Wiping some excess flour on my jeans, I crossed the hallway and pulled open my front door.

Logan stood on my doorstep.

Two things happened at once. First, my heart exploded against my rib cage, and second, I took an involuntary step forward. I couldn't help it. The damned angel-born had bewitched me.

I rolled my eyes over the pretty angel-born. A few faded bruises marred his jaw and upper brow, but his eyes were alight with a healthy glow. A tight shirt showed off his fit chest under a black leather motorcycle jacket. He stood all molded to perfection in those faded jeans.

Yum. Yum. Yum.

Damn, he looked good. He'd probably look even better with nothing on. Yes, I was a naughty witch.

"You look terrible," I told him, hoping to mask the flush on my face and my dangerous thoughts.

The angel-born grinned. "Thought you might want your glove back." He held out my bloodstained glove.

I took it. "Thanks. But I don't think I'll be needing them anymore." I shoved the glove in my pocket and glanced down at my hands, at the scars that marred my skin. Somehow I didn't feel ashamed about them anymore. Instead, I felt a sense of pride and joy mixing with a sense of relief.

Logan gave me another of his drool-worthy smiles. If he didn't stop that, I might have to do something about it.

"Want to come in? I'm making pancakes."

Logan beamed, and a wicked part of me wanted to grab his face and kiss the hell out of him.

"Yeah. Pancakes sound great," he answered as he stepped inside and walked past me.

I smiled. There he was, alive. We were both alive.

And then I closed the door behind me.

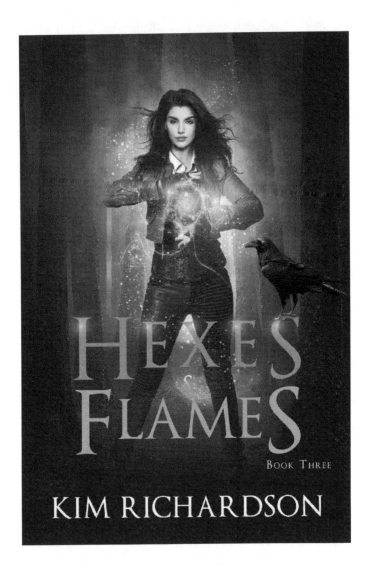

Don't miss the next book in The Dark Files series!
Coming Winter 2020

ABOUT THE AUTHOR

KIM RICHARDSON is the award-winning author of the bestselling SOUL GUARDIANS series. She lives in the eastern part of Canada with her husband, two dogs and a very old cat. She is the author of the SOUL GUARDIANS series, the MYSTICS series, and the DIVIDED REALMS series. Kim's books are available in print editions, and translations are available in over seven languages.

To learn more about the author, please visit:

www.kimrichardsonbooks.com

Made in the USA
San Bernardino, CA
14 January 2020

63167391R00192